THE ICE MASK

Richard Woodman titles available from Severn House Large Print

Dead Man Talking
The East Indiaman
The Privateersman

THE ICE MASK

Richard Woodman

Severn House Large Print
London & New York

SPITSBERGEN
(SVALBARD)

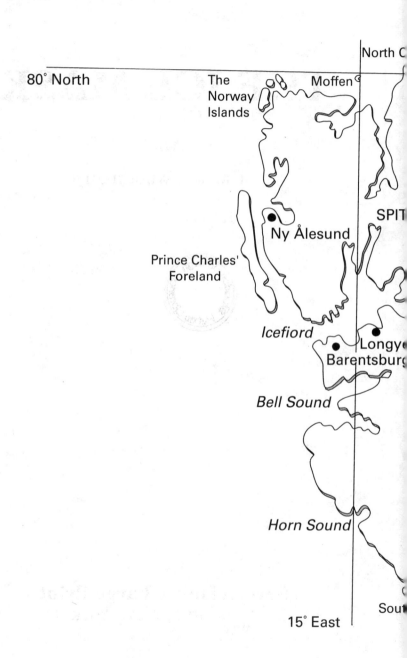

80° North   The Norway Islands   Moffen   North C

SPIT

Ny Ålesund

Prince Charles' Foreland

Icefiord   Longy

Barentsburg

Bell Sound

Horn Sound

15° East   Sou

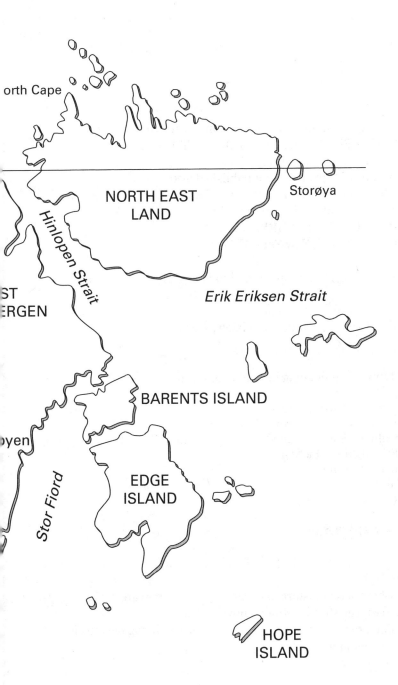

orth Cape

NORTH EAST
LAND

Storøya

Hinlopen Strait

Erik Eriksen Strait

ST
ERGEN

BARENTS ISLAND

øyen

Stor Fiord

EDGE
ISLAND

HOPE
ISLAND

ape

This first large print edition published in Great Britain 2004 by
SEVERN HOUSE LARGE PRINT BOOKS LTD of
9-15 High Street, Sutton, Surrey, SM1 1DF.
First world regular print edition published 2003 by
Severn House Publishers, London and New York.
This first large print edition published in the USA 2004 by
SEVERN HOUSE PUBLISHERS INC., of
595 Madison Avenue, New York, NY 10022.

British Library Cataloguing in Publication Data

Woodman, Richard, 1944 -
    The ice mask - Large print ed.
    1. Sailing, Single-handed - Arctic Ocean - Fiction
    2. Friendship - Fiction
    3. Large type books
    I. Title
    823.9'14 [F]

    ISBN 0-7278-7383-0

Printed and bound in Great Britain by
MPG Books Ltd, Bodmin, Cornwall.

The First Part

He was a changed man when he came back from the Spitsbergen voyage.

It was not surprising, of course; even today, when all sorts of people sail yachts to the remotest places, getting to Spitsbergen, or Svalbard as I suppose I should properly call it, is no small achievement. In fact I had anticipated his changing, but not in the way he did and not with such disastrous consequences. I had expected more confidence, the sense of accomplishment lending a bullishness to an already fulsome character. God knows, we had been friends for long enough. At least, that is what I thought at the time.

What returned was a diminished character, the shadow of a man who had been damaged by the experience. It was all quite contrary to what we all expected and a terrible, destructive surprise. For years he had dreamed of the voyage and for months he had planned it – meticulously, as he always did everything he was really interested in. And we had all helped in one way or another, keen to help him fulfil this really quite modest ambition. But afterwards, we all made excuses for him:

he was exhausted; he had had a tough time of it – and even when he became reclusive we believed the excuse he made: that he was preoccupied working on his book about the trip.

'It's harder work than sailing in the Arctic,' he would say, making a joke out of it; but he fooled no one looking into his newly haunted eyes. Needless to say, the typescript never progressed beyond a pile of typed, scribbled-over sheets of paper which gathered dust on his desk beside his computer.

'Something happened to him up there,' Karen said, her voice catching and her own eyes bright with tears, and the expression 'up there' stuck as a kind of tacit reference between us all – Karen, Susan, Jack and myself – to the fact that Guy had been somewhere not merely geographically remote, but spiritually beyond the experience of the rest of us who plodded through our tediously ordinary lives.

Karen had been with him for about fifteen years, I had gathered, ever since Guy had left the army. We simply accepted her as Guy's partner and I assumed Karen was the reason Guy's marriage had come to grief in his very private past. They never married and their lives together were intermittently interrupted by absences, though this was not surprising, given that after leaving the army Guy had become a travel writer visiting odd spots round the world, while Karen was a producer for BBC Radio. But they made a handsome pair at a dinner party and I grew fond of them, and not a little in awe of their completeness as a couple. My own disastrous relationship left me with a lingering envy of such contentment that entertained no jealousy, only a kind of wonder at the good fortune of others and the presumption that romantic love did, in fact, appear possible for some people.

But when he came back from Spitsbergen he seemed to have rejected her with a kind of indefinable finality. I sensed that they had ceased being lovers, at least in the technical sense, though her concern for him remained nothing if not loving.

Susan took a more detached view, but then she was the remotest of us from Guy, part of our circle, if that is the right word, because she had married Jack – as his second wife, of course.

'Guy's getting on, you know,' Susan said in her forthright manner; 'this trip's knocked the stuffing out of him. Maybe he cracked up a bit and has had to come to terms with himself. You know what a macho bastard he was. It can't have been easy. Poor old Karen.' I noticed the use of the past tense and the shift of subject, and she emphasized this by flaring up in her characteristic way. 'Why can't you men grow old gracefully?' she demanded, and put period to the statement with a fierce, glowing draw on her ubiquitous cigarette.

Susan thought Guy showed self-indulgence by planning the voyage in the first place and

I think I half-agreed with her. But that *was*, on my part at least, a form of jealousy. Susan and I had one thing in common: we came from vastly less privileged backgrounds than Guy, or Karen for that matter. I admired Guy and it irritated me in a mild but permanent way that he had had opportunities denied to others – me especially. I had really envied him his voyage to Spitsbergen for, as a seafaring man, I should have liked to do something similar myself had I had the time and the money. Such resources, alas, were beyond my means and even these were to a degree dependent upon Guy's largesse, as I shall explain. But I acknowledged my own manifold inadequacies by agreeing with Susan and thinking Guy self-indulgent. He was one of the lucky people: good family, old money, Winchester, Sandhurst and a commission in a hussar regiment. It combined with stocky, sandy good looks and a gold medal in 1960 at the Rome Olympics as a *sabreur*.

We first met when I was still at sea as chief officer of a large box-boat, before the shipping company I worked for put their fleet under a flag of convenience and threw their British officers on the beach. Guy had come aboard in Southampton to collect a package we had brought over from the States *per favour of the master*, as it used to be quaintly expressed. I wonder what HM Government does now there are few British merchant ships left to carry these discreet little packages for them? Anyway, the Old Man was

10

ashore and Guy had left the parcel with me, to pass on to the captain when he returned. I liked Guy on sight and, as he seemed to be in no hurry, we discovered over a beer in my cabin that we were almost neighbours in rural Essex.

'The county that dare not breathe its name,' Guy joked. 'You must come and have dinner when you are on leave,' was his parting shot. I demurred, but he insisted. It seemed an unlikely invitation, but he seemed genuine when in due course I telephoned. I had second thoughts when I drove up to his house, a Jacobean hall of modest proportions, I am told, but rambling and impressive to a lad raised in a suburban London semi.

Anyway, that is how I met Guy and Karen, whom I took then for a married couple, so secure did they seem together. As an alternative to the dole queue I spent the next three months helping him to fit out his ketch. Actually I did most of the work myself, Guy taking a trip to the Karakoram halfway through our labours. I refused any offer of money, since I had a little put by, but when he was there he insisted he paid for my lunches in the local pub and he used to give me twenty-pound notes – rarities then – for my petrol. Later, as the ketch neared completion and he returned from his mountains with expressions of appreciation at the progress that had been made, he put me in touch with Jack Codrington, who was looking for a sales manager for his small but expanding

11

computer software firm, which he ran from Colchester. Both Jack and Guy had been in the army together and I never really understood why they let me into the post-military *brüderbond*. Perhaps it was because the only thing I did accept was Guy's dinner invitations; I had once served on passenger liners and could be companionably jolly, making myself pleasant with a certain amount of practised ease. That is probably why my presence became rather a regular feature at the hall; I accepted because I liked Guy very much, and I was already under Karen's spell. Besides, acceptance in such grand surroundings somehow compensated a little for the loss of my chosen profession.

Compared with some of my former shipmates, I fell on my feet.

My own marriage had crashed six years earlier and when that happens it knocks, as Susan would say, the stuffing out of a man. It was not Claire's fault, though I had some pretty hard things to say about her at the time. The truth was that my absences at sea removed me from her life. I was not in attendance and she found someone who could be. He took over my wife, my home and my son Adam. Did a very complete and competent job of it too, and while I have never been shipwrecked, I have certainly been cast adrift.

So, from my fortuitous meeting with Guy, grew my involvement with his boat, his lovely mistress Karen, Jack and Susan and my new life as a sales manager. Within two years Jack and I were business partners and Susan was doing her best to find me a bed partner. I think she thought it rather dubious for the firm to have a single male, forty-something, knocking about the office. The term 'confirmed bachelor' has rather gone out of fashion in these sex-obsessed days; consequently I dined in the company of a succession of divorcees, separated women and two widows, and while a trio of these developed into relationships of a kind, none proved durable. They were, however, sufficient to reassure Susan of my sexual orientation, something which seemed to bother her, with her fussy, well-meaning but unsubtle nosiness and her silly presumption that seamen were, by definition, gay.

'Well, Nicholas my dear, I've done my best,' she would say in her archly despairing tone as she learned of the termination of my latest short-lived liaison. Then she sighed, swept the stiff linen napkin from her lap and lit a cigarette.

'He's perfectly all right on his own,' said her husband with a hint of exasperation. Jack had his own views on libido and selling, being a brilliant man in his own field – the mumbo-jumbo of the digitized alternative to reality. As a salesman he was quite useless and my predecessors had not done the firm any real good. 'Nick doesn't have to come running home every night,' he said, giving me an approving nod.

It was true, of course: my tiny cottage, bought out of the residue of my settlement with Claire, was fine for leaving between voyages and as a place to doss as I made myself a new life. Moreover, to my astonishment, I discovered a flair for selling and an interest in Jack's products. There were enough electronic gismos on an advanced merchant ship such as my last container-carrier had been, to have given me a good grounding in the whole culture. Besides, I had it easy: it was a seller's market in those halcyon days. I also gained something of a name in the writing of the technical manuals accompanying Jack's wondrous wizardry. This started as a mere sideline but, in due course and along with my salesmanship, earned me a place of my own on the board. Writing comprehensible instructions seemed a simple enough matter to me, but it was, and is, a universal deficiency in the industry, and our lucidity added to our reputation in the marketplace.

So, that is how I acquired my new friends, or rather how they acquired me: Jack and Susan, Guy and Karen. They never reproached me for my lack of a partner after Susan's well-meant but failed initiatives. After my success as Jack's sales manager and my elevation to the board as marketing director, my chief value to Guy and Karen was as crew on the ketch. Karen loved sailing, but her work often prevented her from joining Guy, and his bouts of restlessness could be extreme, assuaged only by a brisk thrash across the North Sea, usually to Breskens, where he loved the bustle of the Dutch fishing port, contrasting it dolefully with the shrivelling industry on our own side of the North Sea.

'Don't know what the bloody government are doing to you fellows at sea,' he would say, shaking his head with a deep and genuine concern. 'They've sold you out, all of you, damn them.'

I did not have to agree; as a seafarer I was part of the refuse in one corner of the global marketplace, whatever my success in another.

Altogether we seemed to fit together rather well, enjoying a contentment that retrospect reveals as real happiness. I think Susan was the first to realize I had fallen in love with Karen.

Personally, I had old-fashioned notions about such things. When a man has had his wife and son poached, he is not necessarily out to revenge himself on a chap who has given him a new life. At least I was not. I liked Guy, and his having Karen was somehow part of what made him luckier than me. I am, after all, an Englishman, and I carried my class burden very competently.

Besides, and more practically, I had grown to like my self-sufficient life; I was unwilling to commit myself to anything approaching the responsibilities, agonies and introversions of a new relationship. As a seaman I was quite capable of looking after myself and I was very

15

busy selling software and writing paragraphs on how best to use Jack's more robust products, as busy as Karen with her radio programmes and Guy with his writing, travelling and his ketch. What leisure I had I spent eagerly dickering around with the yacht, which was called *Rolissa*. She was a handsome, thirty-eight-foot boat designed and built to the specification of Guy's father. Her name was a corruption of Roliça, a Peninsular battle in which a distant forbear of Guy's had taken part and after which this military ancestor had named a charger. Guy's family had owned bloodstock of that name ever since, though he himself took no interest in the stud his sister ran near Newmarket. The ketch and the stud were, like the hall, a little heady to someone who had been at sea since he was sixteen.

Anyway, Karen never looked at me – well not in a way that suggested anything other than friendship, despite the fact that we were occasionally thrown together aboard *Rolissa* in circumstances that elsewhere would have approached the lasciviously intimate. Besides, we all got on so very well. Frankly, I valued their friendship far too much to squander it on a silly attempt to make a play for a lovely woman whom I knew would be horrified at any approach. Such a folly would only end in humiliating rejection. The game was simply not worth the candle.

A fly on the wall observing us at that dinner Karen cooked for us all shortly before Guy left for the Arctic would have judged us as comfortably off, middle-aged people with successful careers and more than our fair share of this world's riches. In fact we were unremarkable in our good fortune at that time and in that corner of rural Essex, even to the extent of Guy's imminent departure north.

'Lots of people do this kind of thing,' Guy said dismissively.

'He's right,' I added, 'I've seen the silly blighters dismasted in mid-Atlantic!'

'Oh don't!' protested Karen, but they all laughed and Guy made a pretty speech about how he had found true friends in Jack and Susan, not least for the navigational package Jack had wired into *Rolissa*, and in me for my assistance in preparing his charts, my advice and my help in fitting out the ketch.

'As for Karen,' he said, taking her hand and turning to her so that I had to look away and Susan's too-sharp eyes caught mine for the necessary microsecond to confirm all her suspicions, 'you all know what I owe to her.' Guy gallantly raised Karen's hand to his lips.

'You don't have to go to prove anything,' she said in her low voice, looking down so that her straight, short hair fell forward.

'I prove nothing so much as my desire to do it!' Guy said fiercely, letting her hand go. 'And doing it will be the fulfilment of my will.' Seizing his glass he glared defiantly round at us. We all recalled the earlier discussions about motivation and the row that had almost disturbed our tranquillity when Karen had proposed I accompanied him. Jack had snorted indignantly at the effect of my absence on the company, which was flattering in a way, though something inside me lurched with a half-fearful, half-eager expectation. Guy had defused the moment with a dismissive affirmation that the voyage was to be solo. I sensed his present defiance sprang from the recollection.

'God knows if I'll succeed, but, hell and damnation, I'm going to have a bloody good try!'

He was the perfect hussar, straight out of the Brigadier Gerard stories of Conan Doyle with his slight air of boastfulness and a confidence that was overweening but, experience suggested, rarely misplaced. We all raised our glasses, tapped our acclamation on the table with our free hands until the cutlery rang and, having swallowed the claret, cheered him with unequivocal enthusiasm.

I am sure there were lots of other encouraging things we said before the evening ended, and although I personally drove Guy over to Pin Mill and took him off in the tender the morning he left, that is how I remember him before he sailed for Spitsbergen: confident, defiant, a little drunk, but courageous and determined at heart. Moreover, in my own mind he was quite heroic. You see, to one trained to the sea life and big ships, anyone who could take on the sea in a small yacht *was* heroic, and I knew Guy well enough to know he knew the odds.

There was one significant moment in that early-dawn departure which I rather wiped from my memory in favour of Guy bibulous and boastful, for it touched a nerve and both hurt and excited me.

I had just got him aboard from the little clinker-built motor tender that was itself a relic of an earlier, more genteel age. He hauled the last of his personal gear after him, refusing any offer of help and would not even allow me on board, saying it would be bad luck. From his own moment of embarkation it was to be a solo effort. He leaned over the rail and we shook hands with real affection, our last farewells half-shouted over the sputtering of the idling one-and-a-half horse-power Stuart-Turner inboard engine.

'Good luck,' I said, shoving off as we had agreed.

'Bye, Nick. Thanks for all your help.' He dropped the painter in the bow.

Taking the tiller and thrusting the engine into gear with my right hand, I nodded, an unmanly lump in my throat. He dropped back into the cockpit, suddenly looking small, his disembodied head poking above the dodger, his fine sandy hair tousling in the westerly breeze that blew down the hill from Chelmondiston and through the rustling trees of the hanging woods above Pin Mill.

'I rely upon you to keep an eye on Karen...' he called out as the tide began to carry me gently astern. I think I nodded again; I know

I did not say anything. 'I'm bloody glad I met you and I trust you,' he added. Then he disappeared and I swung the tender round, heading back through the moorings for Pin Mill, cocooned by the racket made by the Stuart-Turner and feeling the burden of the obligation he had laid upon me. I wished he had not made that last remark, not because by not making it he would have given me any sort of licence – I have already explained I was touchy on the subject – but somehow I felt the difference between us again. I took it badly – almost as though he had given me an order.

The confession does me little credit, but a normal English reticence simply will not do any more if I am to recount events as I truly saw them, because it was this reticence that was designed to mute me – to keep me, as it were, in my place. It was class, of course; it always bloody well is. On the surface it was just a nasty resentment and a sudden irritated jealousy of Guy as one of the golden ones. He went off to enjoy himself confident in the knowledge that a trusted inferior would keep his loyal eyes on things. Guy would return a hero and regard it not merely as a measure of his achievement, but as his birthright, an affirmation of his privilege. He would deny this, of course, but I knew it to be true, just as my deference to him was true – deference to his superior and privileged position, the old money, the hall and the choices which freedom from scrabbling for his daily bread

20

gave him. That is why I felt the trip was an indulgence, despite my admiration for his attempting it – admiration which, as far as it went, was no less genuine.

Of course it was this ambivalence that kept me in thrall – this inner contradiction, this appealing to my innate (or was it implanted?) sense of fairness. I was a superficially reasonable person: had I been in Guy's position, I would have behaved as Guy behaved. Instead I merely aspired to be like Guy, knowing emulation was impossible, and this feeling of unworthiness further compounded my confusion.

By the time I headed the tender in towards the hard and felt it ground on the gravel, I had worked through my silent rage and thoroughly despised myself. By the time I had dragged the little clinker boat above high water, Guy had slipped the mooring and *Rolissa* was already sliding down the River Orwell under her jib. He was a tiny red figure in his oilskins, hoisting the mainsail.

I remember I stood there for a long time, letting my silly, rather childish anger ebb away with the falling tide. It was still early and birdsong floated down from the trees beyond the Butt and Oyster. Someone stirred on one of the houseboats as they grounded again; Guy had the full run of the ebb tide, which would take him out of the River Orwell, through Harwich Harbour, round Landguard Point and north, away towards Orfordness and the grey North Sea beyond.

That half-enviable, half-intimidating prospect of the vastness of the ocean confronted me and made me turn away and tramp up towards the car.

That was the other thing that irked: it was me, *me*, Nicholas Allan, master-bloody-mariner, who should have been at sea. Not a fucking retired lieutenant colonel from the Queen's Own Royal Hussars!

'Bugger him,' I recall muttering, though the recollection appals me now.

It was only when I had begun driving Guy's Jaguar back up the lane towards Chelmondiston that I thought of Karen left behind, as Penelope to Guy's Odysseus. Perhaps subconsciously I had submerged any thought of her beneath my own reaction to Guy's departure; perhaps it was because I was driving Guy's car back to the hall and would have to meet her, that I now considered his remarks about her in relation to myself. I did not want to be in any way responsible for Karen and was damned sure Karen did not want me to be either. I felt the notion to be as patronizing to Karen as it was overbearing to me. Had I then known all the facts about their relationship, I might not have judged Guy so harshly in that rather bleak moment; but I did not know all the facts.

Karen was due in London later that day and had, by common consent with Guy, agreed not to come to Pin Mill to see him off. I supposed their private farewells had been said in bed the previous night. Our valedictory dinner had been on the previous Saturday night. Jack had agreed I could take Monday and Tuesday off to help Guy make the final preparations for his departure and the three of us had enjoyed a drink in the Butt and Oyster on the Monday evening. Guy had taken Wednesday to drive over and see his sister and then spent that night alone with Karen. I had collected him at five that following morning – Thursday – which promised a beautiful June day and it was still only just after nine when I got back to the hall. Karen had the percolator on and was busying herself scooping papers into her briefcase and looking preoccupied with her own day. She smiled and offered me coffee rather off-handedly.

'He went off all right,' I offered, putting the car keys on the big kitchen table that dominated the room around which the life of the hall seemed to revolve. It had probably done so for centuries, though under rather different circumstances; it was still a kitchen, but in addition to the Aga, a personal computer, fax machine and answerphone stood where once the butter churn or some such obscure domestic contrivance had once resided.

'Good,' she said curtly. 'Look, I've a busy day, Nick. I've a train to catch and it will take me at least half an hour to get into Colchester. Lock up for me when you've had coffee.'

Three minutes later her Peugeot scrunched

the gravel drive and she was gone. I lingered over my coffee, thinking of the fun we had had in this room, and of Guy, who would have doubled Landguard Point by now and would be properly at sea. I wondered if he too was wondering about this cosy room and the happiness it seemed to embody. I knew the *tristesse* of departure only too well.

In the event, it seemed an odd, anti-climactic send-off, but perhaps that is how it always is for those left behind. In the past it had been me who departed. I did not have much experience of remaining ashore. I thought of Claire, who had endured several of these abandonments, but the moment of insight vanished and I felt about to be overwhelmed by a second dose of petulant bitterness, so I finished the coffee, put the Jag into the garage as Guy had asked, and locked up. I had volunteered my own car, but Guy had insisted we ran over to Pin Mill in the Jag.

'Call it ju-ju,' he had said dismissively, and I had concurred. It had then still been twilight and I had still been half-dopey with sleep.

Now, as I suppose, I thought too of Karen and the fact that she would be left alone in the hall, but subsequent events have clouded my memory. Getting into my car, I swung away from the broad, warm brick facade upon which the morning sun fell, thinking how well the fine old house looked, how it seemed part of the land itself. Its right to exist seemed unassailable, sweeping aside my own parvenu ambitions.

'Upstart,' it seemed to whisper to me, maintaining this sibilant dismissal as it receded in my rear-view mirror while I drove down the drive in my company-owned Vauxhall. I do clearly remember wondering how in hell Guy could leave all this.

With Guy's departure we settled into a new, less intimate routine and I realized it had been Guy who had been the catalyst between us. Without him our dinner parties lost their sparkle and regularity, and hence some of their appeal. It had often been Guy himself who had cooked, and while Karen enjoyed being creative in the kitchen, not surprisingly she was not eager to entertain us as a single hostess. Besides, she was then very busy at the BBC, producing a major drama series. She claimed not to be lonely in the hall and in fact she was not entirely on her own there, for a housekeeper lived in and a part-time gardener and odd-job man with a distinctly ex-army air was always pottering about the grounds. She also often stayed overnight in London, in a flat Guy owned in Chelsea, when her commitments at the BBC demanded it. I mention this only to emphasize the fact that Karen was not isolated, not as further evidence of my inferiority complex: I had, after all, been used to the attentions of a ship's stewards myself.

Jack was, as ever, busy with his infernal

electronics and Susan did not cook with the same enthusiasm as Guy and Karen had formerly done. Besides, she was as busy as Jack with a deserved upswing in the business. Once, when for some reason which I forget, the two of us were momentarily alone in the kitchen of her house during one of her rare dinners, Susan asked me, 'Are you taking Karen home?'

'No,' I replied, 'she drove herself here and she's not drinking. Besides...'

'You don't fool me, Nick.' She was a little drunk and lit yet another cigarette, continuing even as she shook the match to extinguish it so that the thing waggled accusingly between her red lips, 'You want her, don't you? It's written all over you.'

'I hope to God it isn't,' I said, horrified. 'I think she's lovely, but I had my own wife stolen when I was at sea and I simply wouldn't do that to Guy – or to Karen come to that. Besides, a cat may look at a queen; it doesn't mean the queen feels any affection for the cat.'

Susan threw back her head and laughed; smoke emerged from her mouth and her nostrils and I had the curious sensation of unreality about the encounter. I can still see her laughing, with a kind of knowing superiority, as though she knew something beyond the fact that I fancied Karen. But Susan always possessed a kind of brittle, insubstantial quality, as though her body was a frail shell for the formidable nervous energy it

26

contained. At work, as company secretary, she was dynamic, handling all the paperwork, the accounts, invoices, VAT, a telephone often at her head, a cigarette always in her mouth. I think she may just have wanted to see me settled; as a single man I was rather a loose cannon in the business. She could be like that: over-motherly to Jack and rather patronizing to the rest of us. It was understandable, because the firm was doing very well.

As for me myself, I too was caught up in this excitement. Some months earlier Jack had hit on the idea of exploiting the navigation package he had originally designed for *Rolissa*. It had been tailored to Guy's special needs for navigation in high latitudes, so by rationalizing it and producing it on a commercial basis Jack was on to a winner. Yachtsmen may not be planning a voyage to the polar regions, but the notion of having the capability of doing so appealed to them in the same way that even a non-swimmer would rather buy a watch capable of being submerged 100 metres than one that is only good for ten. Moreover, I liked to think that, as a professional navigator, I gave him a few tips on data presentation, but the idea had been gestating in Jack's fertile brain for a long time and *Rolissa*'s integrated unit was more or less the first production model, rather than a raw prototype. It would not have been Jack's way to have sent Guy off with an untested rig. My input was minimal really – more to do with the user's attitude than anything else –

and of course I produced the technical documentation which accompanied the thing. It was Jack's genius that made the kit a neat, robust, consolidated, reasonably priced and highly user-friendly gismo. I had no trouble selling it and we had a spate of orders after launching it at the East Coast Boat Show at Burnham that year. In fact it became a world leader.

I suppose in retrospect the launch of the Arctic NavPac, which occurred just after Guy had left, marked the high point in our lives together. Guy had said he would not telephone until he was on his way home, because he believed it an upsetting means of communication, but he sent us a postcard from Bergen and this augured well; we all seemed to be successful, and I had forgotten the corrosion of my class envy and the mild disturbance Guy's parting remark had made upon my self-possession as the demands of day-to-day life reasserted themselves.

Towards the end of June I had a letter from Guy. He was about to leave Hammerfest, heading for Bear Island and Spitsbergen. I threw a dinner party the following Saturday in celebration of his having completed what we had all come to regard as the first phase of his voyage. I had spent some time and money sprucing up the cottage and was quite proud of the outcome. Karen came early to help me cook and I got a meaningful glance from Susan when she and Jack arrived later.

My small place was crowded, and the

intimacy made up for Guy's absence to the extent that Jack felt moved to remark that Guy seemed to be with us in spirit.

'You sagacious old sweetie,' laughed Susan, suddenly leaning towards him in a gesture of at least publicly uncharacteristic tenderness. We all raised our glasses and drank to absent friends, to stout hearts and stout hulls. I shot a look at Karen and saw her eyes full of tears. At that moment I truly believed Guy was a most fortunate man.

But in view of what happened, I am not certain that Jack, the most logical and un-superstitious of men, was not absolutely right.

I suppose it would have all been different if we had had children around. I had a child: my son Adam; but since Claire had won her custody battle with ease – how does a seaman prove he is a competent father? – I was simply expected to cough up money. What a curious world we have made for ourselves! I am ashamed to say that I played no part in Adam's life after our divorce. I had to return to sea: it was my job and the only way I knew of earning a living – at least until my employer considered my services too expensive and threw me ashore. I now also had the obligatory alimony to pay. I mastered the bitterness a long time ago, believing that on balance it was probably better if Adam grew to like and love (though it pains me to say so) the man whom his mother loved. I say I had mastered the bitterness, which is only partly true because I had trained myself to dismiss the matter from my mind. In truth just writing it all down brings back the gall in full measure. Suffice it to say that Adam played no part in these events; nor did the children of Jack's first marriage, who were in their late twenties.

But Guy had a daughter, though only Karen knew of her existence at this time, and I mention her now to divert my mind from Adam. The point is that, had we not been products of our time and the easy social mores of late twentieth-century Britain, it is quite probable that the work-load of domestic preoccupation would have prevented us being so successful, so self-indulgent, and in the end saved us from ourselves. Except Guy, that is; being privileged he had the choices inherent in wealth, but I believe that if Susan had had children and not been caught up in the business, she would not have smoked and probably would not have died when she did.

As it was, she died with astonishing rapidity. The cancer was diagnosed three days before Guy got home in early October, muting our joy at his safe return and, I ungenerously thought at the time, miffing him in this deprivation of triumph. I was not perceptive enough to know then that Guy's strange change owed nothing whatsoever to Susan's illness.

Susan insisted that we held a celebratory dinner for Guy, but it was overshadowed by her diagnosis. It was a measure of her spirit that she insisted upon cooking and acting as hostess and for a while we collectively determined that Guy's success and not Susan's cancer should dominate our world. Inevitably the evening needed a lot of alcohol to sustain this admirable intention but, to be fair to Susan, it was she who continued to divert our attention to the change that had come over Guy after his experiences 'up there' in the Arctic. Perhaps it was the means by which she inculcated that positiveness that she had been assured was a component in the fight against her disease. Certainly her concern for Guy, and for the relationship between him and Karen, was a genuine one. Characteristically too, it was Susan whose nosy interest in her friends first identified the depth and extent of the change in Guy. Jack and I dismissed her opinion as fussily maternal.

'The poor man's exhausted,' Jack said; 'you yourself said that he was no spring chicken.'

'He's endured difficulties before,' Susan said pointedly.

'Maybe he has,' Jack responded with a quick sideways glance at me that hinted at male exasperation with female intransigence, 'but he was considerably younger then.'

Predictably, Susan remained unconvinced by Jack's simplistic explanation. 'No,' she asserted firmly, 'something happened...'

And Jack and I chorused 'Up there!' with a brittle and entirely spurious humour.

'What were his earlier difficulties?' I asked.

'Oh,' said Jack dismissively, 'he spent some time in Northern Ireland.' He leaned over with the bottle of whisky. 'Here,' he said, 'have the other half...'

In fact Jack too was already disintegrating. He knew what Susan's cancer meant, not just for their marriage but for the company and himself. We tried to accommodate her illness and her concomitant absences for treatment; she insisted she could carry on working from home when her therapy interfered with her presence in the office and for a while we managed. I should say *she* managed, with a courage and determination which were humbling to those of us who moaned about the travails of our everyday problems. But it was clear that things were never going to be the same again. In a fiercely competitive market, the firm quickly lost its edge. Jack could not face the fact that, for the good of the enterprise, he had to confront Susan with the fact that she had to hand over her work to someone capable of continuing after her.

Unsurprisingly, no one had the courage to tell her – except the disease, of course. By February, when things had already begun to unravel, Susan had been admitted to a hospice at Colchester. Jack took the day off and I called on him that evening, hoping I could entice him out for a meal. He refused and I left him consuming what was to be the first of many, many bottles of whisky. Poor Susan died one beautiful March afternoon and Jack could barely stand at the crematorium. Soon afterwards he went completely to pieces. I had by then discovered that, without consulting me, he had already accepted a buy-out deal by a large electronics company. In fact, my share of the spoils was generous and I acquiesced without protest – one does not remonstrate with a man prostrated by grief. Besides, with Jack drifting off into a world of alcohol, the company was no longer viable. Its inventive heart had been failing for some time and all I could do was ensure the work-force was preserved and taken over with the company name and its products. Needless to say, all this excepted the marketing director, hence the redundancy package. That and some residual, freelance work as a writer of technical manuals!

Meanwhile, during the early period of Susan's illness in the early winter, Guy had asked me to look after *Rolissa*. She had suffered damage in the Arctic ice and he wanted the repairs put in hand at Frank Halls' yard at Walton-on-the-Naze, where they still knew about wooden boats.

'I've had enough of sailing for the time being,' Guy had said with a sad smile; 'besides I need to concentrate on writing my book while things are still fresh in my mind. Be a good chap and see to it all, will you?'

I welcomed the distraction and agreed, thinking that once again Guy had rescued me from contemplating what was already the prospect of unemployment. I never considered that his reluctance to sail *Rolissa* the short distance from the Orwell over to Walton had any more profound roots than these simple considerations. I sailed the ketch over from Pin Mill, through Harwich Harbour and across the flats single-handed one freezing December day, berthing her alongside Halls' quay on the top of a spring high-water. I recall rejoicing in the few hours of freedom, the inevitable preoccupation, even on so short a voyage of no more than a few miles. Therapeutically, the demands of the boat superseded everything else. There was not a cloud in the sky, but a biting northerly wind reminded me whence she had come. The yard was already crowded with laid-up yachts all covered with tarpaulins, giving the place a thoroughly wintry, closed-up appearance, which was only emphasized by the skeins of dark Brent geese that wheeled in to land and forage on the widening strip of mud that uncovered as the tide fell rapidly. I recalled that they too came from the Arctic, or 'up there'.

Amid the turmoil of the company's take-over I did not really do more than carry out a superficial inspection of *Rolissa*'s hull at the time. Instead I merely noted the most conspicuous damage that she had sustained in the ice. Discussing this with the yard, it was put to me that it would be some time before they hauled the ketch into the shed and started work on her. We could postpone a specification for the work to be undertaken until the new year and I agreed to come back and do a joint survey later. They would let me know, and in the end I contented myself with removing her considerable amount of stores and the queer assortment of gear a cruising yachtsman feels is indispensable to his needs. It took me about a week of to-ing and fro-ing, almost filling the large outhouse attached to the hall which Guy used as a garage, workshop and boat-store. The truth was that, as well as being preoccupied with the take-over and my last dealings with Jack, I was deeply depressed and went about my task with a dilatory air. As I have already said, Guy's mood had long since impinged upon us all and then Susan's death shocked us with its impact. Even though it had been in-evitable, its actual finality hurt, for she had become a close friend. In its wake, Jack's decline also had a curious ineluctability about it. After Susan's death he quickly let it be known that he did not want to see any of us, even Guy. Guy seemed so curiously indif-ferent to what amounted to a snub that I seemed to hear Susan say, 'There, I told you this was more than mere exhaustion!'

As for myself personally, I had again lost a good job, and with it any hope of sustaining my life at its former level. The settlement Jack had obtained for me would keep me for a year or two, if I was frugal, but beyond that I could foresee nothing more than a dwindling number of commissions for technical author-ship, and that was scarcely a prospect that appealed. I was under no illusions: age was against me finding anything else and after I had finished attending to *Rolissa*, Guy thanked me and then said, 'Well, things have changed, haven't they?' Without waiting for a response he added, 'You'll want to sort yourself out now.'

I sensed a dismissal in his tone, an indication that Susan had indeed been correct and the change in him was more profound than I had guessed. I took his outstretched hand as he said, 'Bye, Nick.'

'Any more mad exploits planned?' I asked, still shaking his hand as I prevaricated. He shook his handsome head, his expression oddly indefinable and elusive and yet it seemed within the compass of my experience to recognize it. 'Well,' I went blunderingly on, 'if you want someone to fit *Rolissa* out in the spring...'

'...I know who to call on. Yes, I shan't forget.' Then, after a pause in which, I thought later, something had occurred to him, he added, 'Of course I shan't forget you.'

It seemed a distant promise, as though our parting had already been measured and the gap was widening.

I went home troubled by that strange expression of Guy's. It was singular and untypical of him, yet somewhere, somehow I had seen it before. Then I remembered. It had been a long time ago, when I had been a cadet sharing a cabin with another aspiring officer. We had just berthed in Hamburg and among his personal mail he had received a plain envelope. It contained the news that his blood had reacted positively to a Wassermann reaction. Seeing the expression on his face, I had asked what was the matter and without a word he had handed me the small piece of paper sent from Singapore. He was only seventeen but his expression had been identical with that of Guy – that of a man bearing an insupportable burden.

Ten days after that curious farewell from Guy, about an hour after dark and as a gale lashed the birch trees that stood in my neglected rectangle of overgrown back garden, my telephone rang. It was Karen, and her voice was tense with anguish.

'Please come, Nicholas, please come at once!'

'What's the matter?'

'Guy's shot himself.'

The Second Part

In recollection, the next few weeks pass in something of a blur. I recall driving to the hall hardly thinking what I was doing, such was the impact of the shock. I recall this neglect because I almost hit a small car – a Ford Fiesta I think it was – just as I swung round the bend upon the far side of which the drive up to the hall joined the road. Karen had opened the front door in anticipation of my arrival and inside I found her sitting outside Guy's study, her face numb and drawn. Seeing me, she fell into my arms and broke into sobs, which racked her body and against which I had to brace myself.

The police then arrived. There were two of them, a young constable and a rather hardbitten WPC who seemed at the time to glare at me with ill-concealed resentment.

'Who are you, sir?' she insisted on asking.

'A close family friend.'

'Oh.' The syllable seemed pregnant with unspecified accusation.

After a few moments Karen grew quiet and straightened up, wiping her eyes and withdrawing from my embrace. 'Oh Nick, Nick, it's terrible,' she said at last. 'You must see him,' she insisted, nodding and releasing me. 'You must ... see ... what he has done ... to himself ... to us...' The sobs were dry now as she mastered the first wave of shock.

'Do you think that's a good idea?' the WPC asked, but Karen brushed her aside and, taking my arm, preceded me. The WPC followed, taking out her pocketbook while the young constable seemed reluctant to follow.

'Oh shit,' he murmured behind me as we stood contemplating the mess.

What was left of Guy was horrible. He had been sitting at his desk in an ancient leather-upholstered swivel chair; his body had been thrown backwards with the impact of the bullet. He had put the revolver's muzzle against the roof of his mouth and blown his brains all over the wallpaper behind him. Some of the slimy residue still ran slowly down the ancient wall. I felt a strong desire to throw up as the constable was then doing on the gravel drive outside the open front door. A very pale WPC was calling for assistance from the CID, who seemed to arrive with commendable speed, assaulting Karen and me with a spate of questions.

'Who are you, sir?' they began, and I stammered out my identity and our relationship, and somehow Karen and I got through the next hour of interrogation. I was bemused by their attentions, given that it was so obviously suicide. Our interlocutors were crudely insensitive and it was clear that, if not actually guilty of some vague complicity in Guy's ignoble end, we were assumed to be complicit until we had argued our innocent detachment. Not for the first time I felt a deep ambivalence to the attitude of the police. They seemed to find the lack of a suicide note a complication, as though Guy had reprehensibly failed to follow the correct procedure in taking his own life, and I heard Karen repeating the assertion that he had been away and for many months afterwards had seemed very depressed. After we seemed to have satisfied them, the policewoman took over again. She appeared to have changed her attitude somewhat, and now displayed a degree of solicitude for Karen at least. It was all very professional, of course, even a touch patronizing.

Some time around midnight Guy's body was taken away and an hour or so later I persuaded Karen to go upstairs to bed. I crashed out on a settee about half past three, having cleaned up the mess in the study helped by one of the dogs who slipped into the study and lapped up his late master's brains. I was little better than an animal myself, a shuddering, vomiting mess, sustained only by my training as a merchant navy cadet to undertake the most odious tasks when necessary. Mercifully much of the memory has been wiped, but there is a certain odour I sometimes smell when passing a high-street butcher that will make me blench and gag involuntarily.

After that there was the business of the

40

inquest and the verdict of suicide. It was a foregone conclusion, of course, but the matter was settled and, apart from the delayed funeral, my part in Guy's life was over – or so I thought. I know nothing of the process of probate, though I think Karen was involved.

Jack came to the funeral. Karen had asked him especially and he was faultlessly sober for the occasion, though it was clear that it was all a terrible effort. Karen was as poised and lovely as I had ever seen her and I marvelled, not for the first time, that Guy's depression must have been profound to set aside life with such a person. She knew it was going to be difficult because, of course, Guy's former wife turned up with their daughter, a beautiful young woman in her late teens, along with Guy's sister Catherine and other members of the Edwardes clan. I gathered Guy's estrangement and divorce had separated him from more than his former wife, for I felt the savage ostracism extended to Karen as the family reclaimed their lost property. 'Blood's thicker than water,' Jack muttered, the remark constituting the most profound contribution he could make from the general state to which he had already descended. After the church service and the windy graveside committal, while the congregation held on to their hats and exchanged those oddly cheerful platitudes that seem to follow even the most melancholy of funeral rites, I found him behind a yew tree upending a hip-

41

flask, which he tried to hide with a sheepish smile.

'You're not driving, I hope,' I said, by way of a caution. He just shrugged.

'It's all over, Nick,' he said. 'Best follow him as fast as I can. Wish I had the nerve to do the same.' It was the first public reference I had heard that day to the fact that Guy had taken his own life. The eulogium, given by an unknown male relative, had made no reference to Guy's end, only to his achievements, especially his distinguished military career and his peripatetic authorship.

'It looks as though you've just taken a slower route,' I said as Jack lifted the hip-flask again.

'What the hell...'

'Well go easy on that stuff, at least until we've got Karen home.'

'Home? She'll be damned lucky if she's got a home when that crowd of vultures have finished...'

I dragged him back to where Karen was speaking with the vicar. He, sensible and sensitive man, had kept an eye on her, knowing that it was she whom Guy had loved and lived with for so long. Nevertheless, he seemed pleased to see Jack and me return to our charge, and he went off to pay his ritual respects to Catherine. Somehow we got the horror of the wake over, and by the end of it I had assumed responsibility for Jack as well as Karen. My training again, I suppose. In due course the three of us were all that was left and, as Karen's housekeeper cleared away, Karen asked me to take Jack home.

'Will *you* be all right?' I asked.

She smiled and nodded. 'Yes, of course. I'm quite all right now it's all over.' She kissed me quickly on the cheek, just as she had always done. 'Thanks, Nick. Just see Jack's OK. We'll sort his car out later.'

'I'll give you a ring tomorrow.'

'Yes.'

Jack slumped in my Vauxhall (I had been allowed to keep it as part of my settlement) and as we left the entrance to the drive, I asked him, 'What did you mean about Karen not having a home when the vultures had finished?'

Jack stirred himself and looked blearily at me. 'Well you know they weren't married,' he slurred; 'she's no right to the hall and I'll put money on Catherine getting her claws into it if she can.'

'Surely Guy wouldn't leave Karen destitute?' I remonstrated, appalled at the very notion.

'Oh no, of course not,' Jack said, making an effort to sit up and pull himself together. 'But I doubt that he'll have let the old hall go out of the family's hands. Blokes like Guy simply don't do that sort of thing. Family's the thing ... no doubt about that. Friendship's one thing but family – well, that's another bloody matter altogether. He might...' Jack said, stringing the word out as though it was extremely doubtful ... 'he might have made some provision for her continuing to live there in her lifetime, I suppose, but I doubt it. It all depends upon when he last updated his will. Not being a suicidal type, I have no idea of the mind-set one acquires as one approaches so final and terminal an act.' He paused and then added, 'I rather wish I did.'

'Well,' I added, 'I know he revised his will before he sailed for Spitsbergen.'

'Well in the state he's been in since he got back, he might have done something more, but it'll be the family that benefits. Bloody awful lot, if you ask me.'

It did not seem fair to say that it appeared Jack had adopted some of the insight formerly deployed by Susan.

Then I rather forgot about Karen's future as I tried to wean Jack off his devotion to drink, succeeding to the extent of taking him out to eat what I thought was probably the most balanced meal he had consumed in weeks. He toyed with his food and expatiated on his long friendship with Guy. He had served under Guy in the army and Guy had recognized Jack's skills when the latter had been his squadron communications number. Guy had put money into Jack's early enterprise, as I had long suspected. He was a 'marvellous man, the best commanding officer one could possibly serve under and a true friend.' Jack paused then added, 'Of course Northern Ireland fucked him up. Fucked a lot of good men up.'

'What did he do in Ulster?' I asked curiously.

'Oh, intelligence work,' Jack said obscurely.

'You mean he went under cover?'

'Oh he was in it up to his fetlocks.' Jack paused and I waited for more information, but he was not yet so drunk that he found a trap, even a gentle one, unavoidable. 'Talking of fetlocks, what did you think of sister Catherine? Handsome mare, isn't she?'

'She's certainly got Guy's good looks.'

'She's a vicious bitch,' Jack added. 'She'll do for Karen.'

I never did sort Jack's car out. Karen saw to the matter herself and I took this as a gentle indication that she was intending to operate quite independently of me. Her request for my support on the evening of Guy's suicide had been, so it seemed, a desperate expedient. She needed someone there to help and, I thought ruefully, to clean up the mess. I confess to having been hurt by this show of independence, but I was in no position to question it and I respected Karen's desire for privacy. In short, I dismissed the matter as yet another peevish and unworthy thought, burying myself in my own affairs, which is a rather grand way of saying I tackled my overgrown garden and considered my future. Actually it was the other way round: having considered the latter, the bleakness of the prospect persuaded me that the only field in which I might be active was in laying waste the thistles and nettles that, beyond a rectangle of mown lawn, constituted my garden. In the evenings I tried to formulate a game-plan by eking out my redundancy pay-off on paper for a period of three years, sending off a couple of articles on electronic navigation to *Yachting Monthly* and offering my services to anyone I thought might be vaguely interested in the matter of technical journalism. The articles were accepted for publication, but that was my only triumph; all other appeals fell upon deaf ears. No one wanted a yacht delivered anywhere, nor any marine consultancy carried out. Nevertheless, the money sent by the magazine staved off what I had come to call 'Armageddon' for a month, and I thought that the odd stroke of luck, some casual labouring and even the stacking of supermarket shelves, might pay for the groceries and postpone my descent into hell for a little. Being a seaman, I was conditioned to be optimistic, though there was precious little justification for it. In fact I was still quite well off, but the prospect of depleting my capital frightened me and I knew that I had to find some form of employment.

During these weeks I received a telephone call from Halls' boatyard asking about *Rolissa*. They had tried ringing Colonel Edwardes, they informed me, but there was never anyone there. I supposed that I should have thought of the yacht, but I was trying to cut myself off from any contact with the hall to avoid thoughts of Karen, employing the same mental tactics that I used to avoid unhappy memories and bitter reflections of Claire and Adam. Anyway, I apologized and explained the situation, assuring them that I anticipated the ketch would have to be put up for sale after the settlement of Guy's estate, but that they would be recompensed for the storage charges incurred. The voice at the end of the line seemed resigned.

'I'm sorry,' I said, 'but it isn't in my remit, I'm afraid.' The line went dead. I felt un-accountably embarrassed, and then the notion surfaced that I should sell the cottage, buy *Rolissa* and become a sea-gipsy. I reckoned that I could live cheaply on the boat, returning to the sea at which I had first set my cap when Dame Fortune called me from the schoolroom. It seemed the right thing to do: to reclaim my birthright as a master-mariner, an appropriate recompense for my earlier, if imagined, humiliations. Perhaps, after all, I could trump Guy's class ace! Anyway, there was absolutely no reason for hanging about in my cottage.

Such euphoric dreams kept me awake at night for a while and I teased myself with the notion that by buying *Rolissa* I would do Guy's family a favour. To this end I set aside Jack's assessment of Guy's sister and actually wrote a letter to Catherine offering to pur-chase the boat if she would consider it. I received no reply from her, only a starchy note from a firm of solicitors in Bury St Edmunds telling me that disposal of Guy

Edwardes' estate was in their hands and the yacht *Rolissa* was not for sale. I felt a presumptuous ass and returned to the garden and my lower-middle-class fulminations. The idea was silly and I gave it up, not even considering that there were plenty of other boats for sale.

It can have been no more than ten days after this rebuff when Karen telephoned me. She asked me to accompany her to that same firm of solicitors in Bury. I presumed that the summons was driven by dire necessity – that, as on the night of Guy's death, I was the only one available for the task of what I hear now is called 'being there' for someone. I could understand why she did not want to go alone; if Jack's worst fears were confirmed, things might become unpleasant. Of course, I agreed; after all I had nothing else to do and it would at least ensure that we had lunch together, for her appointment was for eleven o'clock in the morning, and to that I looked forward with true eagerness.

I arrived at the hall in the Vauxhall, but she insisted we took the Jag. She had had Tom Wilkins, the odd-job-man-cum-gardener, get it out and it stood gleaming in the sunshine as she shut the dogs in the house and got in beside me, her legs making a slight and sensuous susurration as she sank into the adjacent seat. She pecked me sociably on the cheek.

'Are you all right?' I asked with unintended brusqueness.

'Perfectly,' she responded coolly. I noticed she wore no make-up. I moved the selector and the wheels scrunched on the drive as we rolled forward. The last time I had driven the big car had been when I took Guy down to *Rolissa* that June dawn. It was less than a year ago, yet it seemed a lifetime.

'Guy always said it was auspicious to go anywhere important in the Jaguar,' she said as we headed for the A12 and the westwards intersection with the A14 just south of Ipswich. It was the first time we had a conversation prefaced by some such expression as 'Guy said...' It was to be the first of many.

'Good ju-ju,' I said, smiling and explaining that I had last driven him down to Pin Mill that June morning when it seemed we all lived in a different world. There seemed to be some magic in the notion because, sitting amid the smell of leather with a bright if intermittently cloudy day all about us, I felt pleased and a little light-headed in Karen's company. She looked cool and lovely, elegant almost to the point of severity in one of the dark suits I had so often seen her wearing as she left for London and her production work at the BBC.

'I'm sorry I haven't been in touch,' she said, lowering the sun visor and applying a little lipstick in the mirror on its reverse.

'That's all right; I've been busy,' I lied.

'I've been away. Work, a lot of location stuff, and then a holiday...'

'On your own?' I asked, looking at her, and

49

she shook her head, staring straight ahead as she replied, 'No, I took off with an old school friend. She was widowed about the same time that Guy killed himself. We hadn't been particularly close, but we'd kept in touch.'

'Was it a success?'

'It wasn't a disaster. We've agreed to have lunch soon.'

'Good.'

We drove for a while in silence and then she said with a catch in her voice, 'I ... er ... I never thanked you for your help on the night ... for clearing up that terrible mess.'

'That's all right.'

'It was good of you. I ought to have mentioned it earlier. It must have been awful.'

'It was,' I replied, not wanting to think about the disgusting chore. I forbore mentioning the part played by the dogs and once again silence fell between us as we retreated into our own individual memories of that ghastly night. After a while I threw off the recollections and thought of the task in hand. 'Forgive me, Karen,' I said, 'it's none of my business, but Jack alerted me to the possibility of your losing your home ... the hall, that is.'

She was silent for so long that I turned to look at her. She met my gaze. 'You're right,' she said coolly, 'it *is* none of your business, but yes, there is such a possibility.'

I felt that, after the fulsome if long-overdue gratitude, I had been slapped in the face and I coloured up, saying, without thinking, 'I'm sorry, I didn't mean to offend, but Guy asked me to keep an eye on you ... to help you if you needed anything...'

'When on earth did he ask you that?' She seemed truly startled, though whether it was because Guy had asked the favour, or because I had voiced it, I was uncertain.

'The morning I put him aboard *Rolissa* before he sailed for the Arctic.'

'Oh, did he? Well that's rather a long time ago,' she said, referring to the *status quo ante*. The Jaguar sailed serenely through the Suffolk countryside as we sat in mute isolation within it. Karen did not speak again until we turned off the A14 and entered Bury St Edmunds, and then it was only to direct me to the small car park tucked in behind the elegant Georgian house that now served Guy's family solicitors – I forget their name; some improbable combination, like Lobscouse and Grabbit.

'I'll stay and wait in the car,' I said as she got out.

She turned and bent to speak to me, a tone of mild surprise in her voice. 'No you won't, Nick. You're wanted inside. I could have driven here myself, you know.'

My feelings of foolishness were compounded, overlaying for a moment my surprise at being 'wanted inside'. I supposed, if I supposed anything, that Guy *might* have left me a few quid – a thousand perhaps, as a token of friendship. As I had told Jack, I knew he had revised his will before his departure for Spitsbergen and the Arctic, for he had told me as much and I had agreed that it was a sensible idea. I also supposed, despite the ambivalence of her attitude, that Karen for her part *might* have wanted me with her as a sort of heavy escort, a kind of physical buffer against the massed forces of the Edwardes clan.

This theory of mine seemed confirmed when the first person that I saw in the waiting room was Catherine: her acknowledgement of our arrival was frigidly polite. She was so extraordinarily like Guy, yet she was as emphatically female as Guy had been male. It is a constant source of wonderment to me that, given the basic building bricks of the human face – two eyes, two ears, a nose and mouth all set in skulls which, stripped of their flesh and gristle, seem to me to be virtually indistinguishable – we should all possess small differences that not only make us individually distinct, but recognizably and memorably so. Of course there are *types* of faces, and one might know several people with a feature or two in common; but when the genetic link is so strong that the cast of each feature is almost identical, as with Guy and his sister, the distinction, even aided by the differences in sex, is perhaps even more remarkably subtle.

With such deliberately distracting thoughts I sought out Guy's daughter, having noted that girls more often look like their fathers than their mothers, and vice versa. She was sitting quietly with her mother. My rule of thumb stood the test in so far as the young woman was concerned, but the resemblance was not so marked as between Catherine and her sibling. As for Guy's first wife, she was a well-built woman, running a little to fat but comely nevertheless, with an attractive, open face that circumstances had overlain with the lines of age, worry and perhaps disappointment. Like Karen beside me, she too wore a formal costume – of dark maroon I think it was – along with a hat, which I recall struck me as modish; not that I knew anything about such matters. After a few minutes these fruitless considerations were swept aside as we were all ushered into a large consulting room and a middle-aged man with a file took the chair at the head of the table. He introduced himself as Mr Lobscouse or something – I forget his name – and made a few prefatory remarks before beginning the reading of Guy's will. I was correct in my assumption that it had been revised, for it was dated the previous May and I am ashamed to confess that thereafter my attention wandered. Mr Lobscouse had a dull delivery and the preamble dealt with matters I felt impertinent listening to. It was only when I suddenly felt my hand grasped by Karen that I was jerked back to reality. Lobscouse had just mentioned Karen's name as Guy's 'long-term partner'.

She was left a substantial sum of money and the tenancy of a small flat in Chelsea, but she had to remove herself from the hall within one month of the reading of the will. The grip on my hand increased as Lobscouse read this chilling provision, and I recalled Jack's warning, looking across at Catherine, who remained motionless. I could feel Karen almost quivering and placed my free hand over hers in a feeble gesture of solidarity. Worse was to come, though not for Karen.

Guy's ex-wife sat pale-faced, almost fainting when she learned the bequest left to her – a mere three thousand pounds. I knew her to have remarried and to be very comfortably off, though it was clear she had expected some sort of legacy. To rub her nose in her humiliation, Guy had left the same sum to Jack and me, 'as a small token of friendship,' the unsolicitous Lobscouse intoned. The daughter, whose name I discovered was Sarah, had already reached her majority and Guy had left her a generous sum of money. I caught the look of delight cross the young woman's face and reflected that she had matured in the Thatcher years, and consequently acquisitiveness was as much a part of her birthright as fresh air. The hall and the residue of the estate, which as far as I knew amounted to a cottage in Wales as well as *Rolissa*, went to Catherine.

When he had finished, Mr Lobscouse lowered the will and the assembled beneficiaries moved uneasily, prior to rising; but the worthy man announced there was a codicil, dated two days before Guy's death which made some modification to the will as he had read it. Everyone froze, as though caught out in some act of improper conduct, and I wondered why the man could not have simply omitted the bequest which was about to change. But he was, apparently, a stickler for proper form. Afterwards I thought the procedure had been stage-managed by Catherine as a cheap means to demonstrate her own material loss amid the mood of disappointed expectation among the females of Guy's own generation. At the time, the faces about me wore varied expressions of apprehension or expectation as the solicitor lifted a single sheet of paper and began to read:

'Notwithstanding any former provision for its disposal, my yacht *Rolissa* is to be given free of any entailment to my friend Nicholas Allan to keep or dispose of as he feels able or sees fit, along with the sum of a further £5,000 to put her in good order.'

'Good God!' I said out loud, such was my astonishment.

The Third Part

I recall the next few days as being a time of personal turmoil. The completely unexpected acquisition of a beautiful yacht was as overwhelming as it was surprising. I was conscious that this was the second time that Guy had helped me in a significant way at a low point in my life, and yet his generous benefaction did not jar with me. I felt no condescension in his wonderful gift, only a tremendous affection for his thoughtfulness and a vast sadness that he had taken his own life when I was content to share in his own love of sailing and his boat. I supposed at the time that he wanted the boat to go to a good home and he knew that I greatly admired *Rolissa*. I also recalled his remark that he would not forget me; with the recollection came the disturbing query of whether, at the time he had made it, he was already contemplating suicide. Of course he left me free to sell the boat if I simply could not keep her, but he knew very well that I would not do so.

On the journey home from Bury St Edmunds I was compelled to submerge my good fortune under Karen's bitterness.

'I had hoped for the hall, at least for the

56

term of my natural life,' she said, controlling herself with difficulty and spurning my invitation to lunch.

'Karen,' I said, 'I'm so sorry...'

'You've done all right,' she snapped, and I turned towards her. She was staring out of the window, biting her right forefinger, and I caught the wet gleam of tears on her cheek. She must have felt my eyes upon her, because she swung towards me with a sniff, brushed aside the tears and said, 'I'm sorry, you really didn't deserve that.'

'Forget it.' I shrugged the matter aside. 'Jack warned me that Catherine might be your nemesis.'

'Yes. She used to come over when I was away and have long sessions with her brother, but I'm still surprised Guy didn't leave more to Sarah.'

'The hall, you mean?'

'Yes. Blood's generally thicker than anything else where these things are concerned. Catherine obviously persuaded him the Edwardes bloodline will run better through her own side of the family. She's got a son.'

'But he won't be an Edwardes,' I said, bloodlines being unfamiliar territory where I was concerned, though I fully understood the ground rules – or thought I did.

'Oh, that's nothing; he won't be the first inheritor to change his surname to his mother's maiden name.'

She relapsed into silence, emerging only to say with a heartfelt sigh, 'I suppose I should

57

be grateful for Chelsea. I'm going to have to get used to it on a permanent basis,' she added, referring to her intermittent use of the pied-à-terre. She said nothing to me until we reached the hall. Getting out of the Jaguar she stared up at the mellow brick facade wrapped in its blue haze of budding wisteria and said, 'Once I was really happy here. Now perhaps it is better that I leave.'

I left her thinking that she had reconciled herself to her future, which looked bright enough to me. I can see her there now: austerely beautiful, her face introspective, the very essence of an educated, late twentieth-century woman, almost iconic in her independence. A pang of desire and longing shot through me like a physical shock.

'Shall I see you...?' I asked tentatively.

She turned from her contemplation of the hall and gave me a quick smile. 'I expect so,' she said, then added ominously, 'from time to time.'

Hurt, I handed her the keys to the Jag and walked over to the Vauxhall, fumbling for my own set. 'I wonder what happens to the Jag,' she was saying. 'I suppose it goes to Catherine as part of the chattels of the hall.'

I thought that would be the last time I saw her.

I was left to contemplate my own changed fortune, and in the days that followed I turned over plans which, kaleidoscopically, seemed to teem in my imagination. Incredibly,

Guy had managed to ensure the materialization of my fantasy! Moreover he had granted me the luxury of deciding what to do with my house. I could let it and live aboard *Rolissa*! The possibilities seemed marvellous and I had not then succumbed to feeling bad about myself, which came later with the realization that Guy had trumped, with his munificence, my inferior peevishness.

The next week I passed in a busy delirium, driving over to Walton-on-the-Naze and the boatyard. I inspected *Rolissa* thoroughly and was fortunate in securing the yard's services without any delay, for the season's launchings were almost over and they were prepared to postpone a large repair job in order to get rid of *Rolissa* and her insistent new owner. The ice damage was limited to some deep scarring of her topsides, mostly along the waterline, and we agreed on a price to scarf in three new planks and to replace four cracked ribs. There was some other superficial repair work which was cosmetic rather than essential and they said it would take them about three weeks, so I made a mental note of allowing them a month and set to myself to tidy her up, both inside and on deck, before embarking upon some restorative painting and varnishing to her upperworks. Guy had kept *Rolissa* generally to such high standards that it was only necessary to make good the ravages of the Spitsbergen voyage, which, apart from the exterior of the hull, were not much. The yard would undercoat and paint her hull and attend to the antifouling below the waterline after finishing the repair work and prior to launching her. If all went well, I could disappear for a cruise by August, perhaps even by late July, after which – well, the world was my oyster.

I was in so euphoric a state that, as I worked on her, chi-iking with the lads from the yard as they cut out the scored strakes, I was lost in a dream of revisiting the blue seas and sandy, palm-covered shores that I had once been to in my early years at sea. There was little doubt that *Rolissa* was not only capable of worldwide voyaging, for she had been to the Caribbean and the Mediterranean as well as the Barents Sea, but ought to be so employed. Moreover, it entered my conceited head, that Nicholas Allan, master-mariner, beached by the economics of late twentieth-century Britain, was the right man to take her. I was so occupied with this romantic nonsense that I scarcely noticed the small things that Guy had left behind as evidence of his own so-recent occupancy of the boat, even as I cleaned them out of *Rolissa*'s neglected lockers. This was partly because I had previously worked aboard the ketch, and as my mind wandered, there were moments that I had to remind myself that I would be alone, that Guy would not be coming with me and that it was his death and generosity that had created my own possession of the little ship. When I reminded myself of the reality of the situation, I found myself shaking my head with a kind of sad surprise, a diminishing echo of my unfeigned and astonished outburst in the solicitors' office in Bury St Edmunds.

Among other things, I came across a pair of brass dividers that had clearly slid across the chart table in some anxious moment of excessive rolling and found their way into the bilge under the port quarter-berth. Among other detritus were a few torn-out pages of the tide tables from the Macmillan Almanac that had somehow detached themselves during bad weather; judging from their wrinkled state the almanac had become sodden and its disintegration was quite readily imagined. As I had stripped the boat, there had seemed to be only these few personal reminders of Guy – one could not call them surprises or even unusual – and I noticed little at the time of anything one might call odd, though I do recall the severed end of braided rope that was secured to a ring-bolt on the foredeck. I had cut it clear and dropped it on to the concrete of the boat-shed, to be swept up later, remarking to Harry that we could do without any of what, by an unkind maritime tradition, were known with political incorrectness as 'Irish pennants'. Harry had been removing a forty-foot mahogany plank at the time and had looked up at me and just grinned. He had to humour yacht owners as part of his job, though every owner respected his unsurpassable skills as a shipwright, especially if theirs was a wooden boat and half her topsides were torn off.

It was at about this stage that Karen got in touch with me. The telephone was ringing one evening as I returned to my cottage tired, grubby but happy with my day's work. As I picked it up, the line went dead and I lowered the receiver and turned to put the kettle on, entirely unconcerned as to the identity of the caller. I was just pouring the boiling water into the teapot when the phone rang again. It was Karen.

'Where have you been?' she asked peremptorily.

'At the boatyard,' I replied. 'Did you ring just now? I picked up but the line went dead.'

'I must see you,' she fired back, her voice urgent and insistent. 'I'm coming over...'

I hurried into the shower, abandoning my tea and had only just put on clean trousers and a T-shirt when I saw Karen's car draw up outside. She was wearing her working outfit and I guessed, correctly as it transpired, she had come directly from Colchester station. I recalled she had a mobile phone, then something of an innovation.

'Look, I'm sorry if this is inconvenient,' she began as she came into the little kitchen, running a hand through her hair. She looked tired, harassed and suddenly, I thought, doubtful about her purpose in calling on me.

'It's OK, Karen. Go and sit down; I won't be a moment. I'll make some fresh tea.' I put the kettle on again and then followed her through into the tiny sitting room. She seemed to have collapsed into rather than on to the untidy sofa, and retreated into a distant abstraction. I smiled and admitted, 'It's good to see you.' And it was; in my preoccupation with the boat I had forgotten how much I missed her. 'The kettle won't be a moment.'

She stirred, resettled herself and looked up at me. 'Thanks; tea would be wonderful.'

I retired to the kitchen again, made the tea and returned with a tray, sat opposite her and poured two mugsful. 'Sorry,' I jested rather feebly as I handed her a mug, 'this is bachelor style.'

She ignored the joke and sipped the tea. It was much too hot for me, so I leaned forward, my elbows on my knees, my own mug in both hands, waiting for the tea to cool a little.

'What are you intending to do with *Rolissa?*' she asked, looking at me properly for the first time since her arrival.

'*Rolissa?*' I queried in surprise but, catching her look went on, 'Well, I've put work in hand and when it's finished I was thinking of going over to The Netherlands on a shake-down cruise...' A sudden happy thought occurred to me. 'Why, d'you want to come? I guess you could do with a break.' Then I thought of something else. 'You've to be out of the hall – what? – next week?'

'Catherine's given me an extra month, largely because ... Well, it doesn't matter. Look, Nick, are we too late to go up there...?'

Thinking of the hall, it took me a second to grasp the question. 'Up there? You mean the Arctic?'

'Yes. Spitsbergen, Svalbard. Or Norway at least.'

'Well, the boat's not ready...' I temporized, thinking that I should have liked to oblige but the Arctic was far away from my notions of palm trees and silver strands, and that it would require an enormous amount of preparation.

'Well, when could it be ready? Guy left in June and it's already June now, but I recall him once saying that the absolute deadline was early July. Could you be ready by early July? You have nothing else to do and you could go north as easily as over to The Netherlands.'

I was taken aback, not only by the direction this catechism was taking, but the assumption that even if I could get *Rolissa* ready, I should be willing to toddle off to the North Pole at Karen's behest. But I was aware of something else too: that Karen was uncommonly intense – flustered even – as though she was being driven by some private demon. I remember this insight so well, probably because it proved to be very accurate. It prompted my next question.

'Hang on a moment, Karen. I think you had better tell me what all this is about. Why on earth do you want to rush off to the Arctic? It won't bring Guy back and may prove personally painful to you...' As it happened, I could not have chosen my words more appropriately, but I knew nothing of all the baggage and, in any case, Karen had been ready for this very obvious line of enquiry and I took her reply, true in so far as it went, at face value as a total expression of her reasons.

'Look, Nicky,' she said, staring directly at me and somehow compelling me to fix her gaze, 'I've had a truly terrible time. Somehow I coped with the bloody man's suicide; somehow I coped with the funeral and the grief and the getting used to him not being around; somehow I kept going at work – but after that dreadful morning in Bury everything changed. I've been left in the hall for a week or two on sufferance, a beneficiary of grace and favour, tolerated but not welcome. I know it's silly,' she added, putting up a hand and ducking her head so that her hair hung forward against some imagined protest on my part, 'but his bloody family...' She bit her lip and broke off her tirade before it was properly under way.

I did actually want to remonstrate, though not in the way she thought. I wanted to say that, knowing he intended to kill himself, Guy had made a generous financial provision for her; but I forbore. I was not conversant with Guy's family and I knew nothing of the extent to which Karen herself had invested time and money in the hall in anticipation of living the rest of her life there. Nor, of course, had I the least idea of her relationship with

65

Catherine, though I again recalled what Jack had said. Anyway, Karen's inner emotions were her own business and she was entitled to feel as she did. Besides, Karen had not finished. She was shaking her head emphatically as she went on.

'I simply cannot live there anyway, I haven't slept properly for weeks; everything's changed since Guy blew his brains all over the wall in his study ... Oh, I'm not fearful about ghosts, but now there's another side to it all.' She looked up at me, her eyes brimful of tears. 'I've lost my bloody job, Nicky.'

'Karen, I'm so sorry, I had no idea...' I put my tea down and made a slight move in her direction, holding out my hands; but again her head dropped forward and the curtain of her hair fell again across her face as she shook it.

'Oh they're farming work out to small production companies, getting rid of a lot of in-house production. People like me are not cost-effective, we're just too bloody good, which means we must go. "Be released," the bastards call it, the bloody euphemism a measure of their moral cowardice. Like everything else in this godforsaken country, the BBC are reducing everything to the absurd and the trivial, as Guy used to say, because the bloody bean-counters say it's all too expensive. If it's too expensive, they'd do better to close it all down...'

'Like the merchant navy...' I interjected with some feeling, now wholly on what I

66

thought was the entire extent of her wave-length.

'Yes, you've been through all this crappy logic...' She suddenly reached for her hand-bag and rummaged in it, taking out a packet of cigarettes.

Impulsively I leaned forward and put my hand over the flip-top, stopping her from withdrawing one. 'Don't start that up,' I said, the allusion to Susan clear between us. She jerked her hand away and removed a cigar-ette, lighting it from a cheap Zippo.

'You're too late, Nicky darling,' she said, recovering some of her independent spirit and blowing the smoke in my face, 'I've been back on the weed for three weeks.'

'Well you're a bloody fool,' I said, settling back in my seat, angered by the smoke and the arrogance of the gesture, adding, 'and if you think I'm going to take a neurotic cigarette smoker in a yacht to the Arctic, you can think again.'

'You bastard,' she said, her expression suddenly pinched as she narrowed her eyes with the intensity of her annoyance.

'I'm serious.'

'So am I,' she said, standing up as if to go. Then it seemed something struck her and she sat down again, her face softening. I was not fooled, but the artifice was effective in its way. 'If I stop smoking, you'll take me?' she asked.

'I didn't say that...'

'But you will consider it?'

'Well yes, I'll consider it, but why do you

want to go north? Why not just come to The Netherlands in August to forget...'

'But I don't want to forget!' Karen said, 'I want to *understand*. For God's sake, Nick, Guy and I were lovers, as close as man and wife, closer perhaps. Something up there changed him, we all know that...'

'But Karen, whatever it was, it isn't going to jump out and bite us on the nose. Whatever happened to Guy happened to him exclusively, privately ... It isn't going to replicate itself just because we turn up in his bloody yacht!'

'You don't know that,' she said with such severity that I knew it was no use arguing. I recalled Claire at such insistent moments. It was the point at which an argument between a man and a woman left the rails of logic, though both believed with increasing fervour that they and they alone were pursuing the rational path. I sidestepped the issue.

'Look,' I said exaggerating to add emphasis to my point, 'I have to tell you that at the moment half of *Rolissa*'s bilge is hanging out all over the boat-shed floor and she isn't going anywhere until the work has been completed.'

She met the softening of my own tone: 'I can help with money...'

'Karen, don't be silly and for heaven's sake don't you adopt the attitude that throwing money at a problem will solve it – it isn't necessary; Guy left me plenty – nor will it speed matters up...' I thought of Harry and his patient but unhurried workmanship.

'It'll help store the boat. You will need a lot of help for that, and since we are birds of a feather, being unemployed, I don't see that you can refuse me.'

Having presented her irrefutable argument, she rose to her feet again and this time made to leave. I stood up, feeling that I had entirely lost control of the argument; she swept past me with an air of triumph.

'Thanks for the tea,' she said.

Such was the extent of my bewilderment that I let her go without further remonstration. Besides, working away within me was an unsettling series of thoughts. Uncorking a bottle of wine that I would willingly have shared with Karen had she stayed, I considered what she proposed.

It would be a hell of an adventure. When Guy had left for his voyage north there had been that strong sense of jealousy on my part. What he could do, I could do if I had the boat and the opportunity. That is what I had always secretly thought, and now he was calling my bluff from beyond the grave. The thought made me laugh, thinking of the dark, gallows humour that we had shared and that came from our common experience of the sea and the world of men without women. Now I had boat and opportunity, and an attractive crew to sweeten the pill, for at the heart of my response lay the seductive prospect of spending weeks in a small boat with a woman whom I had long coveted. All the practical realities of a trip 'up there' were swept aside by my sad desire, and I went to bed half-drunk, to masturbate pathetically over the unrealistic fantasy of Karen expressing her gratitude at my heroic decision to sail north by a sweet and sexual compliance.

I felt shamed by this bibulous stupidity the next morning as I drove over to the boatyard. The whole thing was a nonsense: Karen did not find me attractive, she was only using me in some fantastic search for her own past; she was escaping the humiliation of losing her job and we would fall out in the confinement of a cruising yacht in inhospitable waters. It could turn out to be an unmitigated disaster – indeed it probably would. The whole thing was a dangerous idea and I was being tempted out of foolish pride, lust, jealousy – in fact all the deadly sins seemed to sit alongside the headache of my mild hangover.

I swore thoroughly and comprehensively.

Besides, my mind rolled relentlessly on, *Rolissa* would not be ready in time to get to the Arctic that summer. I would temporize, promise Karen a trip next year and suggest a shake-down together to The Netherlands. That way we could see whether we were compatible on deck and, perhaps, in a bunk.

No, I was going to stick to my plan and I would explain all this to Karen that evening. In fact I would be a nice chap and take her out to dinner: with the boost of Guy's generous legacy I could now afford such an extravagance and it would be well worth the expense. Who knew but that we might cobble our lives together and perhaps jointly fight off the stigmatic demon of unemployment?

As I got out of the car I saw the Jag parked outside the boatyard. I checked the registration, thinking that I was being foolish, but it was Guy's car all right and Karen was in Halls' office chatting them up as she could when she wanted something. She turned as I entered.

'Oh Nick, we've just been discussing *Rolissa* and they can get her finished in a fortnight, if they work some overtime, and I know that you'd like that so I've agreed...'

'Well that's splendid,' I lied, smiling with fake joy, 'but unfortunately I'm not certain...'

'Oh, that's all right, I've agreed the terms.'

I looked from Karen to Mr Halls and his wife, who acted as office manager. They were both smiling. 'What does Harry think?' I asked.

'Oh Harry will do as he is told,' said Mr Halls, swirling the remains of a mug of coffee round.

'I don't want him skimping the work,' I said, and instantly regretted the rudeness.

Halls looked up at me. 'We don't skimp work, Mr Allan. If necessary I'll turn to myself, but don't you worry. Harry'll finish *Rolissa* and she'll be in the water by the twenty-third.'

'Of June?' I asked incredulously.

'Uh-huh,' Halls nodded, and I tasted defeat. It was clear they had discussed all the

71

points and I was unwilling to betray a rift between Karen and myself. As if divining my weakness, Karen said, 'That's what you wanted, Nicky, isn't it?'

By tacking that little question on to the end she invited my complicity. 'Yes, absolutely. That's exactly what I want,' I lied in front of strangers.

'Thank you so much,' said Karen, flashing a winning smile at the Halls as she led me out of the office. I followed, half-angry, half-resigned. A lot could go wrong between now and 23 June and with sailing boats the best laid plans of mice, men and manipulative women oft went very much agley.

Outside, Karen walked swiftly towards the Jag. I caught up with her as she turned the key in the door. 'Karen,' I began, but she smiled at me as she opened the door.

'Come to dinner tonight. Be there at seven. We can discuss it all then...'

'But Karen...'

She got into the car and lowered the window. The smell of warm leather rose along with the scent of her perfume. 'You've got a lot to do, Nicky darling, and you know we're in a hurry. I'm off to order a new life raft. Guy ditched the old one: it was time-expired. See you later.'

I was so exasperated that the mention of the life raft entirely escaped me.

The Fourth Part

Halls were almost as good as their word and *Rolissa* slid into the water at the head of Foundry Creek on 24 June. Ten days later I was hoisting the mainsail, just as I had watched Guy doing a year earlier, as we set out on our curious adventure. But I anticipate; it is necessary to narrate a few of the details of those ten frantic days the culmination of which owed much to Karen's organizational skills and the dynamic energy that the BBC had so wantonly cast aside. Their loss was *Rolissa*'s gain and the immaculate ketch rode daily deeper in the water as we carted aboard all those bits and pieces essential to a cruising voyage. To be honest, my own experience was limited, despite my years at sea, and while I was perfectly capable of organizing such things as the portfolios of charts, tide tables and the preparation of the Arctic NavPac with its satellite navigation receiver (which provided our global navigation system, or GPS), I was distinctly unfamiliar with such matters as planning food for a three-month voyage. And while I was happy mucking about with rigging and sails, and even stowing all the multifarious bits and pieces of kit that Guy had taken with him (for we largely followed his own notes, which we had found among the papers he had assembled for his never-to-be-written book), I was utterly at a loss when it came to the finer points of diesel engine care and maintenance, let alone mastering the intricacies of the electrical system which, in a boat of *Rolissa*'s veteran vintage, was idiosyncratic and had ramified over the years. Even at that moment on 4 July, as I hove on the main halliard while *Rolissa* motored down the Pye Channel with Karen at the helm, I was certain only of the fact that I thought our preparations incomplete.

Of course I had become familiar with Guy's *modus operandi*, for he was a yachtsman of the old, Corinthian school. Not for him the household conveniences to be found in the modern glass-reinforced-plastic production yacht from Jeanneau, Westerly, Bavaria or any of the other manufacturers. There was no fridge, for instance, nor was the galley a cloned fitting from home. Guy had been a believer in self-sufficiency at sea and in an ability to avoid reliance upon the shore, so that bread baked into rusks, stocks of heat-treated milk and tinned butter removed the need to worry about perishables. On deck were lockers containing potatoes and onions, two staples without which Guy refused to cross even the North Sea; in the saloon fruit and vegetables hung in nets swinging from the coach roof, while *Rolissa*'s water tanks were, like her fuel capacity, installed at the expense of the comfort of her crew. Perhaps the most idiosyncratic fitting related to Guy's solution of the lone-sailor problem. A tough and practical man, Guy knew the debilitating effects of long, solitary watches, of the slow weakening of a man unable or unwilling to leave the deck for reasons of weather or heavy shipping traffic, and how often the cooking of a meal was, for one reason or another, an impossibility. Most yachtsmen, even for a short passage of two or three days, prepare high-energy foods. Bars of Kendal mint cake and other commercial preparations have long been spin-offs from the military into the leisure world and Guy, like other yachtsmen and women, carried a large jar of 'scroggin', an easily eaten mixture of nuts, raisins, desiccated coconut, dried fruit, sesame seeds and so on; but his most eccentric means of sustaining himself *in extremis* was the 'chest of drawers'. This was, I think, an invention of his father's and consisted of a series of aluminium trays set like drawers in a locker. When withdrawn, each tray contained a large bread pudding, sectioned into portions and providing a sticky and sweet accompaniment to a mug of tea at any time of the day or night. Karen had long ago mastered the recondite art of such antediluvian cooking (which incorporated a substantial amount of cognac) and had spent one of her busy pre-departure evenings filling up the four trays.

The only place where anything remotely 'modern' or hi-tech appeared was around the chart table in *Rolissa*'s doghouse. There Guy had installed not only Jack's indispensable integrated NavPac, but a fine Raytheon radar, though he insisted on a paper chart, eschewing the then pioneering use of electronic cartography.

So much for a rough outline of the condition of the boat. To attempt a sketch of the crew is less easy. After her intervention at the boatyard, Karen had divested herself of her city finery, and in jeans and shirt immersed herself in the work of preparation. Much of this was clearly to assuage the terrible sense of betrayal and its consequent bitterness following her dismissal from the BBC, for she worked with an almost demonic intensity, concentrating every waking moment into getting things ready, shopping, telephoning for delivery of required items, rushing back and forth to the boat.

This, incidentally, we had left at Walton. Neither of us wanted too close a replication of Guy's ill-fated departure from the River Orwell, and the extra fifteen minutes' drive, though irksome, was ameliorated by the fact that we left *Rolissa* in an alongside berth, a thing impossible at Pin Mill, but which greatly facilitated our preparations.

Although Karen referred to me for any decisions about what might loosely be described as the sea-side of our intended voyage and, acknowledging my actual ownership of *Rolissa* along with my previous experience as a seafarer, seemed happy with my being, as it were, the skipper, she had laid out her view of the voyage over dinner that night when we came back from the boatyard.

We had postponed talking about it until we were both sitting down in the hall's lovely old kitchen, which seemed, just for a moment, to echo with the laughter of a group of friends a year or so earlier. Increasing age shrinks the passing of each year, but this one had seemed so very short. We both began speaking at the same time, and both broke off.

'Go on,' I said.

'Oh,' she began, looking down at her plate, so that one curtain of her short, straight hair fell forward in its characteristic way. She turned her pasta over with a fork: 'I was just thinking it is about a year since we all sat here with Guy and – well, you know...'

'I was thinking exactly the same thing.'

'And now we're contemplating doing the same.'

'With happier consequences, I hope,' I said, not wanting our conversation to drift into maudlin sentimentality. It would have been unlike Karen to have allowed such a thing to happen, but then Karen at that moment was, in the aftermath of her redundancy, very unsure of herself. Although utterly bewildered by her wild project to replicate Guy's voyage north, I had been liberated from the past and the morbid contemplation of an uncertain future by Guy's post-mortal generosity. *Rolissa* had wrapped me up, emotionally and physically, and I was, I have to admit, a contented man. Moreover, after what I conceived to be months of indifference, Karen had invited me to dinner to discuss a joint project which would, whatever my misgivings, ensure that we lived in close proximity for an unpredictable number of weeks. Somewhat brusquely I added as I picked up my wine glass, 'Let's look forward, not backwards. Whatever Guy's motives in giving *Rolissa* to me, he wouldn't have wanted any voyage she made to be overshadowed by...'

'By what?' she interrupted, putting her fork down and looking directly at me.

'Oh, I don't know.' I was going to say 'any morbidity', but a look in Karen's eyes dissuaded me and I temporized with '...any regrets.'

She stared at me for a moment, then seemed to relax. Her expression softened as she picked up her own wine glass and held it up. 'You're right, Nicky; I'm sorry, I nearly sparked then. I don't know why...' She broke off and I saw the brightness of tears, which she quickly brushed aside with a sniff.

'Look, I was trying to toast our – well, our enterprise.'

I seized the moment. She had not often called me Nicky and the use of the diminutive now seemed to suggest a shift in her attitude towards me. Not that I seized this as any kind of licence, but we touched glasses and she smiled. 'You've been a good friend,' she said, and I blushed and felt thoroughly confused, so that it was she who had the initiative and, putting her glass firmly back on the table, she resumed her meal with a curt, 'Now, let us discuss this *enterprise* properly.'

It was at this point that we began the serious planning that, after the making of several lists, launched us into ten days of furious and unremitting activity. We did not finish our discussion until half past one in the morning and I stayed that night at the hall – in a guest bedroom, I should add, for towards the end of our talk she had said, 'There is one other thing, Nicky, and I want this to be quite clear between us. Perhaps I should have mentioned it earlier and – well, *Rolissa* is your boat and you may find this condition awkward...' She paused and I think I guessed what was coming.

'Go on,' I said.

'About us.'

'What exactly, about us?'

'I don't want you to think that by my railroading this voyage that our personal relationship is ... has changed ... I ... we've been good friends for a long time but...'

I was almost amused by the difficulty she was having, except that I felt a great pity for her. The unaccustomed intimacy of our situation might have made another man move towards her at this point and sweep aside her half-articulated misgivings, but I was not that man. I was frozen into my shell, half-fearful that anything I did would wreck this intimate moment and half fearful of the rejection that was coming. I had no desire to in any way influence the delicacy of the balance of her emotional state. I too had visited the lonely spot upon which she now stood, and I guessed I knew how vulnerable she was and how she was desperately trying to save something from the wreckage. I was the unknown quantity which she both required and yet wished to feel independent of. This had nothing to do with my title to *Rolissa*, nor the actuality of our proposed voyage, but it had everything to do with the manner in which we set out upon it.

Seeing me quiet, she rallied and smiled ruefully. 'Look, Nicky, whatever happens to us up there, I want us to be as good friends as we are now. I know that can be difficult in a small boat, but we are not strangers to that situation ... Only before Guy was there and Guy and I were...'

'It's all right, Karen,' I began, but she silenced me.

'It may not be all right. I mean – well, I know that you ... Oh, Nicky I'm not stupid and I know ... well if I hadn't gathered it myself, both Guy and Susan told me that you fancied me...'

I hated the banal expression and I think Karen surprised herself by using it, but it made me smile, the incongruity of it coming from Karen amusing me. 'I don't fancy you,' I said quickly, adding with all the brittle lightness I could muster, 'I've been in love with you for years, as Susan knew – though to know Guy had divined my passion came as a bit of a shock – but I can assure you that I have no intention of taking what I suppose you would call any *advantage* of you. In any case,' I added with brutal logic, putting my own glass down on the table for emphasis, 'we are going to be on watch-and-watch, so the only occasion I have to occupy your bunk may be when you are out of it, at the helm.'

She paused at this tirade; then, recalling earlier remarks about 'hot-bunking' in bad weather, when one bunk – that on the lee, or low, side of the yacht – would be preferable to a regular occupation of individual bunks, she laughed.

'You *are* a good friend,' she said and slid a hand across the table to touch my own briefly.

'Well, let's keep it that way,' I said with the masterful air of one assuming command of an expedition.

And that was where we left the personal side of things until the evening of our departure. In addition to the preparation of *Rolissa* there was, of course, the settling of our affairs at our respective homes. An absence of three months can complicate complicated lives and our departure was combined with Karen's personal leaving of the hall. She had ensured Catherine retained Tom Wilkins, for she was desperately anxious not to inflict upon him what the BBC had sprung upon her, and he kindly undertook to run over to my cottage and scoop up the unsolicited mail that seems to be an ineluctable part of our modern world. As for her own possessions, some I helped her move to Chelsea, the rest Wilkins was arranging to store.

As I drifted off to sleep that last night at home, I recall wondering, as I had thought every previous night, what we had forgotten. Normally I had remembered something, but now I thought that there was nothing poking itself into my consciousness. Anyway, I consoled myself, it was too late now. It was only at that moment that an insidious thought crept into my head. It sounds odd now to admit that it had never occurred to me earlier, but the simple truth was that it had not done so. In all the turmoil, the work and preoccupation, the intimacy with Karen, the intercourse with the boatyard and the detail of fitting out and preparing *Rolissa* for the cruise, I had never asked myself – or Karen, for that matter – what exactly we were trying to do and, if she knew, how on earth we were going to achieve it. If I had asked the question at the beginning, it had seemed only that, as it were, in following Guy's wake we should replicate his experience. I fell asleep pondering this conundrum and, to tell the truth, it did not greatly trouble me at the time. I was excited by the freedom Guy's bequest had left me and with the prospect of a long cruise in Karen's company. The eve of such an adventure was not a moment for doubt and I was so tired that I soon fell asleep.

And then, quite suddenly, we were off.

I think our predominant emotion, as *Rolissa* heeled to her sails and gathered way, slipping past the Pye End buoy and the houses of Dovercourt perched along the low cliff to windward, was that we were exhausted. I came aft and Karen unrolled the jib. As she made the sheet fast, I bent and switched off the engine and straightened up with a yawn.

'I'm tired too,' she said, in an unusual admission of weakness, adding, 'it's not a good way to start something like this.'

'No,' I agreed, 'it isn't.' I trimmed the main sheet. The ketch was on a broad reach and already doing six knots in the stiff breeze. 'If it blows up much more we'll be reefing,' I said, 'and the time to take a reef...'

'...is when you first think of it,' we both said together, echoing an oft-repeated adage that was as wise as it was tested. But I did not then take in a reef; instead I sat down in the cockpit and stared ahead. A large container ship, its blue hull proclaiming it belonged to Maersk Sealand, was rounding Languard Point ahead of us, about to cast off a tug and head out to sea. We would slip under her stern as we crossed the deep-water channel in and out of Harwich Harbour.

'Ugly brute,' Karen said.

'Oh, I don't know,' I remarked. 'I think they have a certain functional elegance, despite the boxes.'

Karen grunted her disagreement and I added, referring to our earlier exchange,

'This is too good a wind to waste.'

'Yes, I know,' she nodded. 'I brought some sandwiches; they'll have to do for our first lunch. I'll take the watch, if you like, and then you can put the kettle on.'

'Oh, I'll put the kettle on, but I'll stand the first watch and see us clear of the Harwich approaches. I'll get the grub too,' I said, ducking below to where I had seen the plastic container; 'but then I think you should get your head down.'

'I won't sleep,' she called after me as I pumped water into the kettle with the slight unease of one who is aware that the resource is finite.

'Maybe not, but you'll be resting.' And on that prosaic note our adventure began.

It is an axiom well known to cruising yachties that a voyage purposed in a certain direction will inevitably invite a contrary wind. Our friendly westerly had blown itself out by nightfall, by which time we had left astern the red-and-white-striped lighthouse on its long, low shingle spit at Orfordness. Moreover the bright flash of Southwold was already abaft the port beam and we were both pleased with our progress, to such an extent that we agreed to enjoy a glass of wine with our dinner. After an hour of uncertainty, the fickle westerly was replaced by a breeze from the north-west which, perversely, continued to veer until it headed us. We were not in a position to waste diesel fuel by hammering on under power, so we laid off our course more

84

to the eastward, arguing, as sailors had argued since they first set the wind in the shoulders of their sails, that the best course to take is the best course they can make. In the coming hours the wind slowly continued to veer until we were sailing due north-east, which was, at best, half-helpful, for while we were making northing we were making an equal amount of easting.

This proved to be a blessing in disguise, for *Rolissa* relished the challenge and snored along, close-hauled on the port tack, her lee rail occasionally burying itself as she leapt at the oncoming seas. It was not bad enough to greatly incommode us, but living at a steep angle so soon after our departure acted to remind us that we existed now in a world where our personal fate was a matter of complete irrelevance. A few insufficiently secured objects cannoned out of lockers or off shelves, and a certain number of domestic adjustments had to be made. But the wind held steady, the sun shone and the spray that danced away from our lee bow sparkled with all the colours of the rainbow. Best of all, *Rolissa* kept up a terrific pace and seemed to be striding across the North Sea with an eager confidence. The only drawback to all this, apart from our offset to the east, was the further attrition on our tired bodies, to which gradual decline was now added the burden of our unfamiliar watch-keeping. In time we should become accustomed to the motion, the watch-keeping and the lack of sleep, but with only two of us to maintain a vigilant watch as we progressed through the gas rigs and the busy shipping lanes that curved round the Frisian Islands along the northern coast of The Netherlands, we were kept at a high pitch of concentration. Moreover, it was not as though we were heading south, where a general improvement in the weather could be expected. While we might anticipate settled high-pressure conditions in the high Arctic – if we ever got that far – the Norwegian Sea which lay between was nothing more than a part of the North Atlantic, and a part moreover that lay on the downwind side of that notorious ocean. While we currently lay under the press of a northerly wind, the south-westerly wind that prevailed over these waters could, even in July, whip up a gale of rough, wet misery.

As I contemplated the chart on the evening of the second day, jammed in the doghouse while Karen rubbed the sleep out of her eyes and began peeling some potatoes for the evening stew, I decided to turn our situation to our advantage. Ahead of us lay the long, inhospitable coast of Danish Jutland. Sooner or later we should have to go about, but to tack meant that in this wind we should gain little northing and only recover our lost longitude. Granted, once we were back off Scotland, our next tack would allow us to lay a course for Norway, but I was temperamentally against wasting that time.

As if divining my dilemma, Karen called up

from the cabin, 'The glass is dropping a bit.'

I grunted acknowledgement. I had missed the forecast on the radio – almost deliberately I found myself thinking, as though we had imposed an embargo on having anything to do with the BBC even at the risk of cutting off our noses to spite our faces – but I had been watching the western sky during the late afternoon and there was a depression on the way.

'I think,' I began slowly, tapping the chart with the dividers and then breaking off as *Rolissa* took a lurch to leeward so that Karen called up, 'Well, what do you think?'

'I think we should take a day off.' *Rolissa* thumped another sea, though whether in protest or encouragement I was not sure.

'How on earth are we going to do that?' Karen asked, tumbling the peeled spuds into the pressure cooker lying on the cabin sole and then poking her head up next to the chart table so that she could just see over the fiddle and the chart exposed upon it.

'The Limfiord,' I said, poking the dividers' twin steel spikes at the narrow strait that lay between the main peninsula of Jutland and Denmark's northernmost part. 'We can tuck ourselves inside and anchor, or go alongside at Thyborøn.'

She stared at the chart a moment, then looked up at me. 'Good idea,' she said, before ducking below again to resume her preparation of the pot-mess.

★ ★ ★

87

It cost us a gallon or two of diesel, but the diversion, though it was not really that, was worth it. The depression brought with it a stiff wind, not quite a gale but strong enough to further weaken us had we remained at sea. Instead we rode it out tucked up under the shelter of Denmark's sandy west coast to the south of the rather unlovely town of Thyborøn. We had no contact with the shore and no inclination to have it. As the skies clouded and the shallow waters of the western Limfiord were provoked into vicious little waves, we put our feet up and dozed or read books from the excellent library we had brought on board. That evening we cooked a large meal, drank a bottle of wine and went back to bed, leaving the washing-up until the following morning, when it was twice as difficult to accomplish. We did not even rise early, but agreed to lie in, in a thoroughly un-seamanlike manner. The break did us good for it marked, as nothing else could have done, the transition in our lives, and its benefit was increased by our taking the break after we had committed ourselves to the expedition. In fact we relaxed for longer than we had intended, never doubting the break was worthwhile, for on the evening of the second day we were both ready to resume our voyage. By this time the wind had moderated to a steady south-easterly breeze. Powered by this good augury we weighed and sailed north, through the narrow buoyed channel, straight past Thyborøn and out into the

North Sea.

'We're really on our way now,' Karen said as I climbed back into the cockpit after securing the mizen halliard. 'I'm going to put her on self-steering.' And in the emotional, rather than the factual sense, that act has always struck me as being the true start of our voyage.

The Fifth Part

We settled easily into the routine of watch-and-watch after our break, enjoying moderate weather as we drove *Rolissa* northwards towards the land of the midnight sun. We sighted the coast of Norway and followed it until, off the great headland of Stadt rising grim behind the insular lighthouse of Svinøy, it fell back and was lost to us as we continued north-north-east. We should come in sightof it again in the region of the Lofoten Islands, but neither of us now wanted to stop, though we would put into a port in northern Norway before setting out across the Barents Sea – probably at Hammerfest, as Guy had done.

With a crew of only two the regime of watch-and-watch was rigorous. When conditions were fair, we stood four hours on and four hours off, breaking this routine between four o'clock in the afternoon and eight in the evening when we were both up and about. During this time we prepared, cooked and ate our main meal of the day. This shared occupation of what used to be called the dog-watches, still enabled us to rotate the periods we were on duty and made us share the main chores. It also enabled us to have a sort of companionable social life for a few hours. Should the weather turn foul, we intended to shorten our period on watch to two hours, but happily we were not called upon to do so at this time.

Somewhat to my surprise, on our fourth such dog-watch break after we left the Limfiord, when we were well on our passage, Karen produced a sheaf of papers and *Rolissa*'s old log book. She bore them into the cockpit, where she was nominally on lookout, as I sliced Frankfurter sausages, leeks and carrots for a stir-fry.

'We seem to have more or less caught up with Guy's outward track after our diversion to the Limfiord,' she called down to me (our conversations were often half-shouted out from cockpit to saloon or the doghouse, as we alternated the daily duty of cook).

'Yes, more or less,' I agreed, bracing myself against the lurch of the ketch and aware of Karen's shadow as she pondered the chart. We could follow much of Guy's outward track on the charts, for we were using his folios. Karen had given them to me some time ago when I had first acquired the ketch, remarking that they were part of *Rolissa*'s effects. Guy had rubbed off his pencilled course and the observed positions he had dotted along it, but many of his marks could still be discerned and, rather ghostlike in the circumstances, one or two were quite legible because his erasing had not been very thoroughly carried out.

'He seems to have favoured the Norwegian coast more on his way south,' I remarked, eager to hear what Karen had in mind, for it was clear that the appearance of Guy's records, which she had kept after his death, marked a watershed in our joint endeavour. I assumed that her bringing them to my attention now was of some significance.

'I expect that was because of the weather,' I added. I could imagine Guy working *Rolissa* south inside the Norwegian 'leads' – the straits, sounds and passages many of which lay inside the protection of islands.

'I don't think so,' she replied, 'from his log the weather was pretty good until he was well south, into the North Sea.'

'So...?'

'I think whatever upset him had already begun, or perhaps had already done its work.'

'You mean he was dragging his heels?'

'Well, yes. I've studied the log at some length and he shows no sign of pressing on. He's making passages of forty and fifty miles – that's the sort of progress one would count on when day-cruising somewhere hospitable like The Netherlands.'

'Well perhaps, as it was nice weather, he was enjoying himself. Don't forget that he *was* on his own and he had by then achieved his objective. He must have been pretty pleased with himself. Good enough reason for dawdling down that splendid coast, I'd say.'

There was a pause and then Karen said

92

slowly, 'Yes, I bet he was, and that's all very plausible, but...' I silently cursed female intuition which, in my experience, was nothing to do with prescience or instinct but bred of a paranoia.

'But?' I prompted, trying to keep the irritation out of my voice. After my acquisition of *Rolissa* I was apt to let Guy rest in peace; besides, I had something of a guilty conscience in respect of my regard for him. The aftermath of death is a complex business.

Karen was speaking again: 'There are a couple of lost days with no real data, nor a real locality or explanation as to where precisely he was.'

I frowned, then saw a possible explanation. I had never seen Guy's log properly, only ever having observed it on his desk, but I knew his habits well enough.

'It's true to say Guy never kept a *narrative* log,' I offered; 'but he was always meticulous in recording navigational details, though I recall his records were deadly dull.' I had seen and written hundreds of such pages during my career, and while they served to recreate the detailed passage of a vessel, they were never intended to withstand a cross-examination seeking the motives and passions of her navigators!

'As for the missing out of a location's name,' I went on, 'he may not have had a chart of the right scale to give the information. What exactly does he say?'

'*Anchored in seven metres, bent beacon and*

rock one-nine-three degrees magnetic, distant half a cable. Perfect anchorage,' Karen read out.

'Perfect anchorage,' I mused with a grin. 'That's pretty lyrical for Guy.'

'Yes, exactly.' As I mentioned earlier, I could not see Karen's face, and when I did peer up into the cockpit, she was staring out over the sea, but the attenuated way she said those two words lent them a memorable significance. At the time I said little more, largely because her next question seemed like a monstrous red herring.

'Can I trust you?'

I was dumbfounded, for it struck me that Karen – amazingly altogether and powerful Karen – had again descended to the use of a banality. Then I recalled she was no longer powerful and was very far from being altogether, so I took the question at face value: Karen was deadly serious.

'I beg your pardon?' This time I was four-square in the saloon doorway, peering up through the doghouse into the cockpit beyond. Karen regarded me over the fluttering papers she was holding against her knees.

'You heard what I said.'

I shrugged. 'If you intended the question, then I am unable to answer it, for it is unanswerable by me. Trust requires an act of faith on your part. You either trust me or you don't. What I do with your trust is something for my sense of morality. I mean, if you're about to tell me you've murdered someone, I don't want to know, because I don't see why

94

I should commit myself to placing myself in such a position as to take your guilt on board...' I shut up. I was being pompously heavy-handed and knew it was a characteristic of mine that Karen found odious. 'I'm sorry, I'll get on with dinner.'

I went below again, irritated that I had overplayed the matter and been so clumsy as to have broken the brittle but happy atmosphere that we had generated on board since leaving the Limfiord.

I put the wok on the gas and began cooking the stir-fry. As soon as it was dished up I poured two small glasses of wine and made a succession of lurching passes out into the cockpit bearing plates and glasses. *Rolissa* was humping along with the wind on her port quarter, doing a steady if unimpressive four or five knots under her big genoa, mainsail and mizen. We ought to have had the mizen staysail hoisted, but Karen had not mentioned it and had made no attempt to hoist it during her afternoon watch. After four o'clock I had read for a bit and then the preparation of dinner had occupied me. I thought I might hoist it after supper, for we were in constant twilight throughout the night now, but the notion was eclipsed by Karen's remarks and the production of Guy's documents which, sitting on the lee side, she now put beside her and half-wedged under her backside to prevent them blowing away.

'I'm sorry, that was patronizing and unkind of me,' I said, shoving the slopping glass at her; 'here, cheer yourself up.'

She turned back to me with a funny, compressed look about her face. I say compressed because that is the only way I can describe it. I'd never seen it before and it was a very long time before I understood what it meant. At that moment I just wanted to gloss over the silly little exchange, so I blundered on: 'Yes, of course you can trust me – if you want to, of course.'

'That's the point: I do. We have to understand each other a bit, otherwise this expedition, as you are so fond of calling it, is invalid.' She took the plate with its piled mass of vegetables and the slices of sausage.

'Oh dear,' I said, 'more evidence of my insufferable pomposity?' I tried to lighten the mood and she responded.

'I'll let you off.' After a pause while we both sipped at the Merlot and began to eat, she went on, 'If we've the slightest chance of discovering exactly what turned Guy into a misanthrope and...' She hesitated as though the recollection was painful ... 'a suicide, then I have to rope you into the quest – intellectually I mean, not just as the skipper of the yacht, but as one of Guy's friends.'

'I thought I was already roped in on that basis.'

She sighed. 'You are, up to a point, but one of the things that I know Guy liked about you was that you keep your mouth shut. He was ... Look, Nicky, out here at sea, just the two of us in this boat ... Well, all the normal rules of social behaviour seem somehow inappropriate, even inadequate. I guess that's why you have all the discipline and hierarchy and the arcane language and such stuff at sea, but it seems to be necessary to reinvent our rules of behaviour to suit our present situation; d'you understand what I'm driving at?'

I nodded. 'Yes, I think so. That's why such rules are invented in the first place. I understand that we may need to lay down our own, like your setting out the sleeping arrangements before we came aboard.'

'Yes. It all seems a bit silly but...'

'You were talking about Guy,' I insisted.

'And he was talking about you. And the reason I broke off was because ... Look, the reason I asked if I could trust you was because I want to say a few things that I wouldn't normally flatter you with but which, in view of what I know about you, and in view of our situation here, it seems to me have to be said.'

'Come on then,' I said a little impatiently, 'spit them out.'

'OK. Guy said that he respected you not least for your sense of discretion and that his respect had grown to admiration since he'd realized that you were – well, attracted to me but never sought to take any advantage. I also think,' she said with that ravishing slow and girlish smile from behind a curtain of hair, 'that he approved of your taste.'

I said nothing. My reticence was not really a feature of my inner character, more a product of what life had done to me. I knew where my obligations lay and I would have been a fool to ruin my relationship with Guy, as I have already explained. Anyway, I had been somewhat in awe of him, as I have also confessed, so this revelation that Guy actually thought of me in terms of *respect* was a concept entirely novel to me. I *was* flattered and it made some belated sense out of his gift of *Rolissa* and her accompanying bequest. 'That was kind of him,' I said at last, as Karen stared expectantly at me.

She leaned forward and touched me briefly on the wrist. 'So I have to confide in you, to let you into some of the secrets of our relationship, if you are to help.'

Help? Help with what? I was still unsure of what we intended. I sat in the swaying cockpit of the ketch with a lump in my throat. Then I coughed to clear it and my head. I turned to confront Karen.

'Look, I'm not at all certain what you really hope to achieve – in concrete terms, that is. I mean, are you really hoping to smoke out precisely what happened to him?'

'Yes,' she said, 'I am. Did you think I was doing all this for fun?'

'Of course not,' I protested, 'but...'

'But you thought – nice, admirable Nicky – that it would distract me from the horrors of contemplating my wrecked career and nursing my grievance at being kicked out of the hall, sitting all alone at home in Chelsea?' There was a nasty edge to her voice.

'I wouldn't have put it like that at all.'

'Well how would you have put it?'

'Well, simply that a northern cruise might give you some insight into what happened to Guy's state of mind and, anyway, it would be a fun thing to do – even with me,' I added with a hint of self-pity and a half-plea for understanding. I could see that Karen was spoiling for a fight, that she almost needed it by way of catharsis. In other circumstances I might have let her have her head and submitted to being her whipping boy; but, as she herself had redefined things a moment or so ago, we were in circumstances that would not admit such a therapeutic outburst. In an inspired moment I indicated the papers and log that she had laid beside her on the lee cockpit seat.

'I presume you've a load of clues tucked under your starboard buttock, like that *perfect anchorage* you mentioned.'

My diversion proved timely and she expelled her breath and nodded. 'Yes, I think so. Look, I'm sorry...'

'Forget it,' I said sharply. 'What have you gleaned?'

'Not a lot, I have to confess, but enough to give me a strange sense of conviction that I can't quite explain.'

'Well,' I conceded, 'you knew him pretty well, I suppose.'

'Warts and all,' she said enigmatically, and I sensed the presence of Guy's imperfections, not least of which was making concessions to

99

his sister.

'And that is why you must reveal some of your private—'

'Yes.' She cut me off.

'Well you'd better tell me then.'

'I'll finish this first,' she said, forking at the stir-fry; 'it's really good.'

'Don't sound so surprised,' I said with a grin, pleased that we had avoided a silly rupture.

We fell briefly silent as *Rolissa* shouldered aside a wave with a thump that swung the two booms snapping against their preventers. After we had both finished and I had put the kettle on for coffee, she seemed to gather herself.

'Right from the beginning he was reluctant – no, he actively *prevented* me from looking at this lot when he came home.' She indicated the gathered papers. 'It was only after he had killed himself that I had the opportunity to dip into the log and it is, as you say, pretty boring. But I didn't have the charts; I had already given them to you. Nor did I really want to waste my time recreating the voyage. I was too busy at work – then,' she added bitterly. 'Anyway, it was only after I – well, you know, hit the buffers, that I buried myself to any great extent in his notes and his type-script.'

'Go on.'

'Well I do know how Guy worked when he was writing a book. After all, he's written eight of them, so his method is predictable.

He firstly makes notes, salient points of the proposed story; then he works out his chapters, crafting the chronology into a narrative. He was very good at it...'

'Yes, I know; I've read several of his books...' It pained me to hear her unconsciously mixing her tenses, but I forbore from pointing it out to her.

'Well he was using the same method. The notes were succinct as far as his passage to Svalbard is concerned, and then there are some detailed jottings about the history of the archipelago; he had a first edition of Sir Martin Conway's book he had bought from Maggs Brothers, and he had copies of Dufferin's *Letters from High Latitudes* and Lamont's *Yachting in Arctic Seas*, with which he was contrasting earlier yachting voyages...'

'I gave him my copy of Frank Worsley's *Under Sail in the Frozen North*,' I added, Shackleton's sailing master being a personal hero of mine and the sacrifice worthy of note.

'Yes, he told me. He thought it particularly good of you.'

I was immediately embarrassed by the revelation; I had not intended to fish for a compliment, merely to oil Karen's diffidence and persuade her to come to the heart of the matter. But Karen had not noticed and continued as I forgot my blushes.

'Well all this had passed from notes into draft form. I think he had even polished this early part of the book, which was unusual at this stage, for usually he worked right through to complete a first draft before tidying things up, as he used to call it. I think he did this because he was unwilling to go on with it, or lacked the courage, or found the memory too painful. Anyway, I think it marks the beginning of some sort of process that led to his decision to take his own life.' She fell silent. What she said made a certain amount of sense. It was all quite possible and she, more than any other human soul, knew how he ticked.

'Go on.'

'Well, when we get to Svalbard, the whole thing falls to pieces. He can't sustain the narrative because he didn't keep up the log-writing. True, there are a few days of chrono-logical sequence, so that we know that he reported inwards to the Susselman at Long-yearbyen and that he coasted north, inside that long island...'

'Prince Charles's Foreland,' I put in.

Karen nodded. 'Yes, and that then he followed the tourist route north without en-countering much ice. But after he had visited Dane's Island and Virgo Bay there are five blank days.' She looked up at me.

I shrugged. 'Time off?'

She shook her head. 'I don't think so. That wasn't Guy's way and you know it. Then there's a latitude and longitude.'

'So?'

'Well he obviously recorded crossing the eightieth parallel of latitude...'

'That's fair enough, surely.'

'Certainly. Then there are a couple of words, each with just a note of the numerical date – and that's unusual for Guy, because he always meticulously wrote down the day of the week, the month and the year for every day's entry.'

'And these words?'

'*Muffin* and *following* and *bloody hand*.'

I considered the information while Karen added, 'I knew he had hurt his hand; it was quite badly scarred and he was reluctant to show it to me...'

I had a vague recollection of his hand being plastered on his return, though subsequent events had almost buried the memory. I concentrated on the mysterious words.

'Muffin?' I frowned, recalling the chart. 'There's an island, a curious atoll-shaped place off the north coast of West Spitsbergen, called Moffen. Could you have misread it?'

Karen shrugged. 'Yes, I suppose so.' She laid her empty glass down in the bottom of the cockpit, fished out Guy's stained log from under her bottom and riffled through the pages. I cast a glance round the empty horizon and *Rolissa* drove along. We were clear of the oil rigs west of Bergen and had thousands of miles of fetch to windward of us.

'Here.'

I stared down at the pages of Guy's log as she held them out. I took the book and scanned through it, seeing exactly what she meant. Not only had Guy's record become so abbreviated as to seem to peter out, but his handwriting – normally quite beautiful – had become slack. There was a definite sense that he had let go in some indefinable way. I saw what Karen inferred and it was difficult not to agree with her if one was seeking a mystery. But I was not so inclined, and there was a perfectly rational explanation that was, to me at least, blindingly obvious. I silently cursed that female paranoia that we had so obligingly christened intuition and wondered, not for the first time, how much misery it had caused in the world. However, I was not quite so foolish as to blunder into remonstrating with Karen, saved by a recollection of my earlier pomposities; so I took it one step at a time.

It was quite obvious that, if one knew the name Moffen, what Guy had scribbled could be read in that sense, as well as Muffin without a dot over the penultimate letter.

'OK,' I said, handing the log back. 'So he mentions Moffen and his hand. This comes last, so we may assume that his injury prevents him writing further. On the other hand, if you'll forgive the unintended pun, say he only curses his hand when he finds the pain intolerable. Say, therefore, that the injury to his hand occurred several days earlier, the day he stopped writing the log properly and just stuck in the numeric notation of the dates. That provides you with a perfectly reasonable explanation as to why it all falters. He would have been pretty depressed. Don't forget that for a single-handed yachtsman to injure his hand is pretty close to disastrous.'

'And *following*?' Karen was dogged in defence of her thesis.

I shrugged. 'I don't know, Karen,' I replied with a hint of exasperation in my tone. 'It could mean several things...'

'Such as ... Look,' she held out the page: 'it's not begun with a capital letter; he isn't beginning a sentence...'

'Oh, for Christ's sake! The poor bugger hurt his hand badly.' A thought occurred to me and I was about to voice it. Then I shut my mouth, aware of the intimate nature of my query. Karen noticed.

'What?' she said sharply.

'Nothing.' I rose and took another look round the horizon, the habit of keeping a lookout so ingrained into me from my earliest years at sea. I was rewarded by a blue nick on the horizon to the north-east. 'Ship on the starboard bow,' I said, sitting down again and bending to recover the washing-up from the cockpit floor.

'What were you going to say, Nicky?'

I put down the two plates and looked at her. What I had to say, the question I wanted to ask, was rather close to the bone. 'You said he wouldn't let you look at his hand when he got back.'

She shook her head. 'No.'

'But you slept together; presumably you made love...'

'No!' She shook her head violently and I thought I saw tears before she turned away and stared out as if searching the horizon for the distant ship. I had clearly put my foot well and truly into my mouth. With a sigh I resumed my task and went below to complete the dinnertime chores. When I had finished I stuck my head back up out of the doghouse. I could see the ship abaft the starboard beam and there was nothing else about. 'It's gone eight o'clock and I'm watch below,' I said briefly, forgetting all about the customary coffee. She nodded without looking at me and I turned back to the quarter berth into which I tucked myself. As I composed myself for sleep, I recall thinking that all that twaddle about making up rules for our behaviour and admitting me to an intimate understanding of her relationship with Guy had been – well, premature at best.

Karen was brusquely professional when she handed over to me at midnight. It did not seem like midnight, for at this latitude we were still in the twilight zone, not yet above the Arctic Circle and in full sight of the sun throughout the whole twenty-four hours. Muggy with sleep I let her go without any reference to our earlier conversation and settled down to the business of keeping watch. Since it occupied so much of our time and since you may not be familiar with passage-making under sail, perhaps I may divert for a moment to explain this routine background to our cramped life. It is important at least as the backdrop to our curious odyssey.

The routine of our life on passage I have already outlined; what is less easy to grasp is its relentless quality. We had a long way to go – over a thousand miles between the Limfiord and Hammerfest, and a further six hundred-odd to Longyearbyen. Within twenty-four hours one becomes dulled by the short spells of sleep, which accounts for our need of a break on the passage north from Walton after the frantic nature of our preparations before departure. This watch-and-watch routine of duty and sleep was punctuated by the business of living, of keeping the body and the ship reasonably clean, of answering nature's inevitable calls, of cooking food and of clearing up afterwards. First and foremost, however, came the ship: her welfare and progress had precedence over everything, and I mean everything, because our very survival depended upon her well-being, and upon her acquitting herself of the task we had set her. *Rolissa* could not do this by herself, for all her self-steering gear and electronics. Up to this point in our story the weather had been relatively kind to us. We had ridden out the strongest wind at a sheltered anchorage within the embrace of the Limfiord and our time at sea had required very little sail adjustment. We had put a roll in the jib a couple of times, but I had not yet had to reef down the main. Moreover, we had had the addition of the mizen staysail to boost our progress, though it was not a sail to carry if the weather freshened up, unless the main came down;

but had adjustments been necessary, as they would in the future, it was up to us to attend to them. In the nature of such things, such compulsion would be an unpleasant increase in the wind and a worsening of conditions.

Wind creates sea-state, and while an inexperienced sailor might have considered the sea rough enough to be unpleasant, that was not really the case. Nevertheless *Rolissa* lay at a more or less permanent angle of ten to fifteen degrees of heel, and she rolled beyond that from time to time. To this lateral movement must be added her endless pitch as she rocked bow-to-stern, depending upon her angle of attack to the waves. With a headwind and the little ship sailing close-hauled, the effect was the most alarming and noisy, for the wind speed over the deck was increased by her forward motion and this also affected the impact of the oncoming waves. With her sails hauled flat by tightening their sheets (paradoxically, the ropes that controlled them), she banged into the waves, butting them aside as they rolled down towards her. *Rolissa* sailed about thirty degrees off the wind – or 'pointed' at that angle to the wind – and with her deep keel she made a minimum of leeway. She was thus an able windward performer. With the wind on or near the beam she travelled, as all boats do, at her fastest. With the wind a little ahead, or forward, of the beam she would be on what is called a 'narrow reach'; with it further aft, abaft the beam and coming in broad over her

108

quarter, she would be on a 'broad reach', much as she was at the time I write of. With the breeze anywhere astern of this she would be running free, pushed along. Contrary to expectations, although the perceived wind speed over the deck is less than the forward motion of the boat, this is often the most uncomfortable point of sailing on account of it establishing a lazy and unpleasant roll. We could steady her with a spinnaker, had we carried one, but Guy hated the things and thought them too dangerous for single-handed sailing, preferring to boom out his genoa jib and have done with it.

The net effect of all this was, whatever the situation of the wind relative to our course, all movements through the cabin or along the deck required a constant bracing, balancing and a holding on – circumstances that often made the performance of even a simple task difficult, tiring and time-consuming. Of course we both wore safety harnesses in anything but the most clement weather and we religiously clipped these on to the jackstays that ran fore-and-aft along the deck. These last resorts to keep us on deck were imperfect saviours and a mixed blessing, which Guy always refused to use. I recall once, when crossing the North Sea with him, going forward to take a reef. We had left it rather late and I was struck by a green sea which came over the weather bow and clean-swept our deck. I was up by the mast, just about to tighten up the slackened main halliard after taking the reef in, when it happened. I was knocked down and, in holding on to the winch handle rather than lose it, lost my left-handed grip. The harness kept me on board, but I was washed along the length of the deck, cracked my head on the jib-sheet winch set on the cockpit coaming and fetched up abreast the mizen mast, winded, bleeding and exceedingly wet.

Regarding me from the tiller as *Rolissa* shook herself clear and the sea poured over her counter stern, Guy remarked sardonically, 'You are too bloody buoyant, Nick. Eat more beans and keep your feet in future.'

Such are the peculiar pains of sailing, necessary ordeals through which we voluntarily put ourselves in order to qualify for its richer rewards. Perhaps you would not agree, but that is no matter.

Outside these really exceptional moments there is the ever-present routine of 'keeping a watch' (and even here, sitting in the cockpit, the constant sway of the body is tiring). There are two principal elements to this: the maintenance of a good lookout and the conning of the ship. The former is self-evident, though the landlubber might be forgiven for not quite grasping its significance. To people to whom a speed limit of seventy miles per hour on land is insufficient, the notion of covering a thousand miles at four or five nautical miles an hour might seem pathetic in its slowness, even allowing for the fact that the nautical mile is longer than its statute terrestrial cousin. But even at four knots it only takes fifteen short minutes to traverse a mile and a ship approaching on a reciprocal course at, say, fifteen knots will cover four miles in that same time. Thus in a quarter of an hour the combined speed of the two vessels will be nineteen knots and, depending upon the visibility and the efficiency of the two lookouts, or the radar watches, or whatever means are being used on each vessel to determine whether or not the ocean in front of them is unencumbered, they are closing at something approaching a mile every three minutes. For one person to maintain a level of vigilance to ensure that such an approach is divined early enough to take avoiding action is tiring. And, of course, a vessel may very well not come down a reciprocal line to one's own course. She may be crossing, or overtaking, or passing clear like the ship I had spotted that evening when I upset Karen during our first delving into Guy's log.

The proper way to determine whether or not a vessel poses a threat is to take a compass bearing of it. If this remains constant there will be some point in time and place – perhaps sooner rather than later, but inevitable nonetheless – when the two vessels will collide. The geometry is simple and anyone who drives a car subconsciously makes judgements about the relative motion of other vehicles. It even applies when one foolishly drives into a stationary object and thus the only time a sailor deliberately places his ship and something else on to this 'steady bearing' is if he wishes to berth alongside it.

As for 'conning' – well, I use the term deliberately because we rarely steered *Rolissa*, using instead either of her self-steering arrangements. One of these was a wind-vane apparatus which kept her head constant relative to the wind. Once her sails were properly trimmed to take advantage of the prevailing conditions, *Rolissa* would romp along all by herself. The problem was that when the wind changed, she obligingly conformed and if one was not careful and failed to pay attention, she would be off on the wrong course. As an alternative we had a second device in the NavPac, which remained constant to the course. Under this automatic-helming device a wind shift made *Rolissa* protest and shake her sails, so that it was necessary to retrim them.

Thus the watch-keeper's duty to monitor the ketch's progress was a light, if serious one and, although not 'conning' in the strictest sense of the word – which derives incidentally from the ancient meaning of 'cunning', or possessing knowledge rather than mere craftiness – it will serve here.

There was one other important function and that was the navigation. Those who teach the subject to would-be yachties are apt to intimidate. It is indeed a complex subject which, in the days when I first went to sea, took a long time to learn, but is actually based on simple principles, even if, in its more recondite form, these are astronomically inaccurate. What do I mean? Well, in point of fact the determination of one's position on the surface of the earth using a sextant and a chronometer requires one to assume the pre-Galilean heresy that the earth is the centre of the universe. This is purely a convention which allows the sun, moon, planets and stars to be assumed to move against the inside of a sphere surrounding the earth at its centre. This enables one to measure angles and solve a trigonometrical problem and it is not as ludicrous as it sounds, for that is how we actually perceive such things, quite unable to see that the moon is any different in its distance from the observer than the stars surrounding it. Happily, however, science, and in particular Jack's wonderful NavPac, render redundant all the apprenticeship to which I had submitted myself. By utilizing time signals from a constellation of artificial satellites obligingly launched by the United States military, one is not only able to read out one's latitude and longitude with the same ease as one extracts a telephone number from a directory, but one is told of one's precise and true course and speed over the face of the globe. All this is marvellous and makes the matter child's play. Cynics will tell you that relying solely upon the US military and their Global Positioning System is un-wise and you will be in dire straits if the system is degraded or switched off. This may well be true, but in terms of navigating in the high Arctic, even the old method proves difficult. Just how difficult need not detain us here, but it serves to explain that Guy's ambition to sail in the polar seas was what had sparked poor old Jack's inventive genius in the first place.

Only when in sight of land – and recognizable land at that – can one fall back on simple compass bearings and the cold logic of geometrical navigation. Even then, many modern yachties prefer to stick to their GPS system and trust in the US military not to pull the plug on it.

As a matter of routine, when out of sight of land on a long ocean passage such as *Rolissa* was then engaged upon, we plotted our position on the chart once an hour. In this way we marked our crawl north-east, parallel to the indented coast of Norway sometimes eighty miles away to the east, following (there's that word again, which just shows how innocent it really is!) the imperfectly erased track of the ketch the year before.

So much for the didactic diversion. Now I must admit that there was another reason for expounding it, other than those I adduced at its beginning: it was to lull you into a mild disinterest in order to invest what I am about to relate with something of the shock I experienced when I made my discovery.

At 2300 – eleven o'clock that evening – I went to read off the latitude and longitude from the GPS incorporated in the NavPac. Then I noted it in our log, after which I took

114

up the parallel rules to lay it off on the chart. As I did so, I noted that, by an odd and, as it happens, entirely irrelevant coincidence, it lay very close to a similar position of Guy's. He too had been about here at 2300 on a night in July a twelvemonth earlier, heading to the north and east just as we were then doing. I did not trouble to ferret out the date, for Karen had removed all traces of the log and I was not sufficiently stirred by the congruence to take more than the most passing and trivial interest. What it had made me do, however, was linger over a chart that had become both familiar and vaguely boring, so far offshore were we and so far from anything of topographical fascination.

And in this lingering surveillance, casual as it was, my eye was caught by a tiny, faint cross surrounded by a circle about fifty miles to the east of us. It was a position all right, and a position which had been entirely missed by Guy's eraser. A faint abstract of a course, roughly parallel with our own appeared briefly a little further to the east, so that the position indicated showed the navigator to have been somewhat west of track. From the way it lay it looked like *Rolissa*'s homeward course.

'So what?' you are asking. Well, apart from upsetting the idea that Guy had come all the way south close along the coast of Norway, this very neatly pencilled position had alongside it the time of the fix, just as one would have expected. No, it did not read *2300*, as if

115

contributing to some slightly surreal hat-trick; it read, prosaically enough, *Noon*. Noon on which precise day was not adumbrated, nor did that matter. What came as a shock was the fact that it was not in Guy's distinctive and wounded handwriting. It was the mark of a complete stranger.

The Sixth Part

I mentioned nothing of this discovery to Karen when she relieved me at midnight, and the effort of holding my silence meant that my turning over of the watch was unkindly curt. Perhaps she did not notice, but she avoided my eyes as she accepted the mug of tea I had made her, suggesting that a rift still existed between us. I left her slumped in the cockpit, her face grey in the twilight. Not that too much should be read into this, for after a sleep of less than four hours, few of us are at our best. In the bucking saloon I kicked off my boots, took off my lightweight waterproof trousers and heavier foul-weather jacket, drew off my socks and sweatshirt, then in pants and T-shirt rolled gratefully into my quarter-berth. Ten minutes later I was fast asleep. It was only when Karen called me at four the following morning with a peremptory summons that I wondered if she had herself noticed that strange mark on the chart. While it had not been eradicated, it was rather inconspicuous and a bleary eye would have had difficulty noticing it, to say nothing of a preoccupied mind. I had, of course, left the chart exactly as I had found it, for there

117

would be no point in concealing the fact and the only reason that I had not mentioned it to Karen at midnight was that it did not seem an appropriate moment for such a distressing revelation. Furthermore, I think that at the time I was seeking a rational reason for this mysterious person being on board *Rolissa*, for I was certain that the neat hand was that of a woman. After I had taken over the watch and Karen had gone below, I childishly wished the ketch could tell me of her secret, a fancy easy to incubate in those solitary hours.

It was three days later before things between us were fully back to normal, by which time the chart in question had been returned to the drawer. The atmosphere had been steadily thawing, but our conversation had avoided any reference to Guy. To some extent this may be explained by the demands of the ketch, for we had hit a patch of fresher wind and a shift to the north of west that required first one and then two reefs in the main and a partial furling of the jib. *Rolissa* heeled to a steeper angle and began to bang through the seas, and though the sluggish roll had gone, the keener wind sliced the deck with spray which stung like the devil if it caught bare flesh and reminded us that we were slowly drawing closer to the Arctic, a reminder reinforced by the crossing of the Arctic Circle. The latitude of sixty-six and a half degrees north had rolled over on our GPS receiver, but the persistent cloud that had accompanied this wind shift prevented us

118

from seeing the now circumpolar sun.

The ocean too lost its benign ultramarine and assumed grimmer, greyer hues under the overcast. Ominously, one morning I saw a pair of storm petrels dabbling in our wake. Fulmars had been our constant companions, along with the handsome gannets and the dark and predatory skuas, but the rare sight of the petrels reminded me sharply of the great, indifferent natural world beyond the confines of our little craft with its silly tribulations.

It was that same morning that I had another reminder of the power of nature. I was nursing a mug of coffee at about six o'clock. Contemplating the bleak prospect of the boundless ocean and trying to recall some lines of poetry – without success, I might add – I saw a fin, not fifty feet away on the starboard beam. It was huge and vertical, like a black saw-blade cutting upwards from the depths and as the orca slowly dived, exposing a rolling section of his back, I noticed the pale crescent of greyer skin behind the upright dorsal.

'Bloody hell, a killer whale...' I breathed, glad that the big male was swimming away from us, for suddenly *Rolissa*'s hull seemed a fragile thing to be penetrating those remote seas. I had read of boats stove in by angry killers, and while the ketch was stout enough to take on the sea and I had spent some time considering and reading up about navigation in ice, I had entirely ignored any possibility of an attack by an unfriendly grampus.

I told Karen of the encounter over breakfast and she unwound sufficiently to say that she had thought she had seen one the previous day, but had not been certain.

'I'll make a note of it in the log,' I said. The following day, in a moment of idleness, I executed a tiny sketch of that rampant fin. I do not know what motivated me, unless it was relief that these supposed omens had been nothing more than chimeras in my own mind. Karen saw the drawing, remarking that we ought to do more of that sort of thing and thereby redeem our own logged account from the charge of being boring that Guy's so obviously merited. It was the first time Guy had been mentioned since our contretemps.

Next morning the wind had moderated and, although it had veered into the north and was correspondingly chilly, the sky cleared shortly after eight. Close hauled on the port tack, we found ourselves sailing over a blue sea dotted with sparkling white wave caps tumbling merrily to leeward. All the malice had gone out of the prospect and our spirits lifted unbidden in response. I had just relieved Karen after she had completed her breakfast when the sunshine made her pause before going below to turn in. She lingered a moment beside me in the doghouse, where I was perusing the chart.

I looked up in turn, feeling the immediate warmth of the sun through the glass of the windows. Suddenly my eyes were caught by something under the boom of the mainsail to starboard.

'Look!' I remember calling out, unnecessarily loudly; then both of us were scrambling with childish enthusiasm into the cockpit, Karen with the glasses snatched up in her hand.

'Wow!' she breathed as she peered through the binoculars. I stood behind her staring at the distant peaks of snow-covered mountains lifting into the sky above a low bank of hazy mist lying along the eastern horizon.

'The Lofotens,' Karen said, her eyes shining as she lowered the binoculars and handed them to me.

After staring through them for a moment or two I glanced down at the chart. 'They must be upwards of thirty miles away,' I said, 'that's remarkable.'

I think we both felt that the sight of those magnificent peaks marked the threshold of the Arctic with far more significance than the mere crossing of a notional parallel of latitude. The Norwegians have made of the troll a hideous, touristic icon, but looking at the grandeur of those distant summits one almost wanted to believe that gigantic and mythical creatures inhabited them.

'Quick! A sketch!' Karen commanded. I hesitated. It was her watch below but she was the better equipped for this task.

'Your watercolours!' I countered.

It was her turn to falter; then she said with a heart-warming and almost girlish glee, 'All

121

right,' and ducked below, to reappear a moment later with a small sketching block and a tiny box of watercolours. 'Water,' she ordered, picking up the chart pencil and swiftly outlining the mountain peaks. Ten minutes later she held out the finished work for my inspection. 'It's not very good,' she said.

'That's not true,' I said, delighted. 'Can I write the time and position?'

'Of course. Tear it off; you'll have to paste it in. I don't suppose we've got any paste.'

'No,' I laughed, 'but we can keep it until later. Well done.' And I meant it.

'Thanks,' she said.

'You ought to get your head down.'

'I ought to, yes, but it's such a lovely morning now; I suddenly don't feel so tired.'

'It'll catch up with you later.'

She paused, looking round, then agreed and went below. I was back in the cockpit, taking a bearing when she called, 'Nicky?'

I turned. She was standing in the saloon, staring up through the doghouse; stripped for sleep she wore only briefs and a T-shirt. 'I'm sorry,' she said.

I swallowed. 'For what?'

'Don't tantalize. You know *for what.*' She mimicked my voice.

'Forget it.'

'I'll talk to you later,' she said, smiling as she disappeared from my field of view.

The day continued fine and late that afternoon, it being my turn to prepare dinner – a pot-mess – I did so in the cockpit. The Lofotens remained in sight, their peaks brilliant in the sunshine as the sun, seen by us for the first time, swung inexorably west and northwards. It was the only cue that I could give Karen, but she took it.

'I'm sorry that I made so much of what I thought would be trivial,' she began. 'It's just that what you said and the way you said it – though I'm sure you didn't mean to – hurt rather. My fault really, after all that persiflage about rules and things.'

I looked at her and she stared back. I think that at that moment, all the 'persiflage' having been aired, we actually entered the new and more intimate stage of our relationship that she had tried to establish earlier. It was quite a day.

'He wouldn't let me have a look at his hand because it had been stitched up. He had sustained a bad gash and in the process of healing it was contracting the tendons, turning his right hand into a claw. Not only did writing the log book become very difficult, but I think even bashing his keyboard became a real chore.' She stopped and I was thinking about what she had said – a reasonable explanation of at least a contributing factor to Guy's depression – when she leaned forward and lightly touched my knee so that I looked up and she caught my eyes again.

'We never made love when he came back ... Apart from a kiss or two he never touched me, not in so intimate a manner as allowed

123

me to see, or to feel, his injured hand.'

I nodded. 'I see.'

'That's what you were driving at, isn't it?' I nodded. 'And,' she went on, touching me again to hold my attention, 'the estrangement was not new, Nicky. We hadn't made love for some time. We had been drifting apart physically for quite a while. Perhaps that is quite normal, I don't know. I'm never happy to measure my own experience against what I think is normal because I don't know what normal is. It strikes me that age and circumstances may naturally part couples from regular sexual contact, but I don't know for sure. I guess it is true for some and not true for others...' Her voice faded.

'I'm afraid it's no good asking me, but I suppose you're right.' I paused and then asked, 'Had you grown reconciled to this parting? I mean, did you resent it?'

She shook her head. 'No, not really, not before he left, certainly. I recognized that the demands of work were occupying me most of the time and that I hadn't much quality time to give to Guy. I don't think he found it easy, but he found it acceptable in much the same way...' She paused, then shrugged, as though having resolved an internal argument with herself. 'You see, I know he was ... well, he wasn't actually impotent, but...'

'He was having trouble...' I suggested.

'He was having trouble.'

'Twice. When it first happened, we made excuses like familiarity, lack of excitement, tiredness and too much to drink at dinner that night. But we never attempted to make love again until the night before he sailed for the Arctic ... up there ... up *here*...' She tossed her head with a gallant smile and I could see her eyes glittering with tears.

'I was a bloody fool. I should have let sleeping dogs lie but I felt a lot for him – and for myself, it has to be said, on that evening. I went to some trouble...' Her tone was rueful, even regretful. 'The full seduction routine...' She paused, and my imagination ran wild. In panties and T-shirt, her hair a little greasy, Karen had stirred me. I had no idea what precisely 'full seduction routine' meant, but I felt a dishonourable stirring myself.

'He came to attention all right,' she went on with a smile, 'but when I was vamping it up he got cross with me and...'

'And?'

'And that was that. We had a silly row and he said ... Oh, it doesn't matter.'

It did, of course, at least to my prurient sense of curiosity, but I forbore to comment and she did not enlighten me.

'He ought to have had the tenderest of farewells, really,' she added, and this time there was no doubt about her regret, 'in view of what happened, for I *had* loved him.' I was pondering the significance of her use of the past tense when she added, her voice low and intense, 'And he had loved me.'

When I spoke, my voice was thick with

emotion too: 'And at the end? Did you not both love each other then?'

She shook her head. 'We had already discussed parting.'

I think somehow that this came as the most astonishing revelation of all. Moreover, it seemed one more reason for Guy's terminal depression, as well as explaining his decision to deprive Karen of the hall. Then I thought back to the Guy of those last weeks.

'I ... er ... I understand about the physical element,' I said slowly, 'but I think that Guy did still love you.'

She shook her head. 'You're wrong, Nicky, you know. You're a nice Englishman, not a nasty one like Guy. I loved him – loved him for a long, long time – but in the end we just drifted apart. When he came home from his great achievement I thought that if I didn't make the break then, I would be trapped. It seemed at the time that my career was on the brink of new opportunities ... Bloody ironic, isn't it?'

'Yes.' I gave a short, unamused laugh. I was trying to square up numerous circles and said, 'Forgive me the frankness, but d'you think it was about then that he took the hall away from you?'

It was her turn to bark a brief laugh. 'Yes! And he took *Rolissa* away from me.'

'Oh shit! I never thought...'

'Catherine never wanted a bloody yacht; she's the horsey sort. Don't worry, *Rolissa*'s better off in your hands. God knows what I'd have done with her, but it was symbolic. As for the hall, yes, it was a sort of punishment, I suppose, but Guy was gentleman enough to leave me the flat and a hefty legacy.'

'I feel terrible.'

'Don't be silly. Now perhaps you can see why I was so screwed up about talking about it all. Look, Nicky, I don't *mind* this bloody boat being yours.'

'It's kind of you to say so...'

'It's true. I'd have been upset if you'd not invited me to sail aboard her, but even with my career down the pan, I can hardly claim to have any reason for keeping a *yacht*.' She enunciated the word with contempt. 'Guy wanted me to sell her anyway. He didn't want Catherine or her confounded brood to get their hands on her. His sense of the bloodline ended with the hall. *Rolissa* was different. He had indicated that I should sell her to you anyway, at a preferential rate, if it makes you feel any better.'

'Not much.'

'Well, it was just Guy making a point and being characteristically twisted and nasty.'

'What d'you mean, twisted and nasty?' I queried, recalling her earlier remark. 'I should have thought he was neither.'

She laughed – a genuine laugh – and explained: 'Oh, dear Nicky, what an innocent you are. Men like him are often beastly to their women. Guy was a professional soldier – trained to kill and brought up to believe in all that awful, legitimized military stuff. He was decent, according to his lights, and a responsible soul, but there was a streak of downright nastiness to him. Don't forget he'd seen action in Borneo – hand-to-hand fighting, I gather – and there was that period in Northern Ireland which no one talks about but which left a bad scar on him.'

'Did he never give you any clues?'

'Oh, plenty of *clues*, but precious little to go on in the way of facts. Not that I'd have wanted to know anything about that filthy business.'

'I recall you made an award-winning documentary programme about it.'

'Fat lot of good it did me,' she cut in bitterly.

'No, I know, not in the long run, but at the time it was sensational and Guy must have helped.'

She shook her head. 'Guy wouldn't tell me a damned thing,' she said vehemently. 'In fact it caused one of the first of our serious rows. He refused to come to the awards ceremony and would never let me display the award. Just as well, really; it was awful and quite out of place in the hall, but he never wanted me to get involved in the first place. In fact he tried to forbid me! Forbid, for Christ's sake!'

She was in a good humour now, oddly uplifted by unburdening herself, I guessed. I was not so unencumbered and without thinking I asked, 'But you cannot deny Guy was a tough character.'

'No, of course not. He was one tough bastard all right – that I do know.'

'Well none of this squares with his moral disintegration in so short a time. I really don't understand that. Notwithstanding a badly cut hand which left a permanent disability, I just cannot see how a man of Guy's stamp would crumble in such a way that would reduce him to suicide. Can you?'

I looked at her again as I asked the question and saw her mood shift as her eyes became at once dark and unfathomable. For one terrible moment I thought that she thought I was accusing her of some act that had precipitated Guy's solitary hell, but then the notion passed and she replied, recovering her brightness.

'Well that's why we're here, for heaven's sake, isn't it?'

And then I recalled the stranger's position marked upon the chart.

I have no idea why I now still failed to mention this to Karen except to say that the moment remained inauspicious. If, as I was certain, the stranger had been female, then it would have been unkind to have piled upon her personal confidences this exterior evidence of Guy's faithlessness; but how this fitted in with his impotence, if indeed he was impotent, I really had no idea. Anyway, it seemed too cruel a blow to inflict upon Karen now that the chart had been used and stowed away. On reflection, exposure of the fact at this moment might have saved us much time and trouble, but then equally it might not. Karen would have been in a receptive mood to take in evidence of Guy's perfidy, it is true, but it would not have solved the essential mystery, at least as far as I was to be concerned. But this is all speculation and a waste of time. The fact of the matter was that I held my tongue, having some vague idea that once we reached Hammerfest I intended to thoroughly study the log, Guy's notes and his draft typescript, all of which Karen kept in her locker and which in any case it would have been quite impossible to review while under way at sea.

In truth, like Karen's withdrawal of a few days earlier, small matters assume entirely different proportions aboard a ship, especially aboard a small yacht with a crew of only two. For this reason I had long, long ago learned to keep my mouth shut, as Guy had noticed. It was not a virtue, merely a survival technique.

Anyway, I said something to the effect that we would examine what we knew at Hammerfest, to which Karen replied, 'Yes, that's a good idea. We should have a clear picture before we leave for Svalbard and perhaps we'll learn something new while we're there.'

'Like what?' I asked.

She shrugged her shoulders and looked at me. 'How do I know?'

And with that enigmatic response I had to be content.

★ ★ ★

Perversely, we arrived at Hammerfest at one o'clock in the morning. The sun hung low in the cloudless northern sky and the gaily coloured buildings of the Norwegian town seemed almost toy-like as we motored to the berth close to a number of fishing boats where, according to Guy's log, he had secured *Rolissa* the previous year.

Despite the Norwegians being a seafaring people and familiar with all aspects of the life of seamen, the arrival of a strange yacht drew a number of curious onlookers who stared down upon our decks. They are not used to sailing yachts, which they tend to associate with wealth and leisure, themselves possessing a vast number of motor boats, which they consider as necessary as cars, enabling them to get about their sea-girded and islanded country.

If Karen expected someone to step forward and reveal themselves in some sort of re-run of the melodramatic 'Lo, I am your brother Jack, and I have come home to claim my love!' so beloved of the Victorian 'gothicks', she was to be disappointed. I am sure she anticipated some such circumstance, and it pricked my conscience a little that she seemed to be expecting not Jack, but Jill. Every time a comely blonde Norwegian female stared down upon our deck, Karen would scrutinize her sharply from the doghouse, entertaining some intuitive certainty that any strange Norwegian blonde beauty would be seeking her lost lover, a nasty Englishman

131

called Guy Edwardes.

Put like this it was all rather silly, but it did seem to me that Karen half-hoped for the emergence of a woman, and in the end I confronted her. We had eaten a good lunch and by tacit agreement were to huck out Guy's papers after washing up. Indeed, we were in the act of carrying the chore out when Karen, after a suspicious peering at one mature Norwegian matron on the quay, began stowing the crockery in the racks.

'I get the impression you think Guy picked up a woman here.'

She looked at me sharply and then shrugged. 'So?'

'And what have you concluded?'

'I know that he picked up a woman somewhere.'

'How the hell d'you know that?' I asked sharply.

She shrugged again. 'I do, that's all.'

I felt compelled to disarm her stupid female intuition. 'I think you're right, but unlike you, I think I've found real evidence.'

'*You* have.'

'Does that surprise you?' I asked, drying my hands and going up into the doghouse to rummage for the appropriate chart. I showed her the mark and explained.

'Why didn't you tell me before?'

It was my turn to shrug. 'Oh, there was all that silly upset between us and I really didn't want to tell you at the time. I wasn't trying to conceal the matter from you, just waiting for

132

the right moment. That's why I suggested we review everything here in Hammerfest.'

She seemed content with this explanation, more interested in the mark, as though from those four letters she could divine the identity of the writer.

'That was definitely written by a female,' she said, and I grunted agreement. Then she turned to the log book and turned over the pages. I saw what she was doing, trying to match up that *Noon* with the chronology as revealed in the log.

'I can't remember, but would Guy have used *Noon*, or *1200*?' she asked.

'In army mode he'd have written *1200*, but afloat he'd observe the old sailing-ship habit of writing *Noon*.'

'Not many people would observe the old sailing-ship habit' – again she mimicked me – 'unless instructed by Guy to do so,' she observed. As I pondered the shrewdness of this she found what she had been looking for in the log. After a moment she looked up at me and remarked in a low voice, 'I sort of wish you hadn't pointed it out to me, though I think I knew it all along...'

'I'm sorry.'

'It doesn't matter.'

'But why, if you already thought you knew?'

'Because, my dearest Nicholas, this position on the chart' – and here she turned back the log book and tapped the pencilled mark – 'is after Guy's oh, so bloody *perfect anchorage*.'

'And you think...'

'And I know the bastard was screwing her!' she said sharply.

'So...'

She caught my drift. 'I didn't say he couldn't get it up; I only said he couldn't get it up with me, for God's sake!' She looked at me fiercely for a moment and then her face relaxed and she ran her hand down my cheek. 'I had no idea what an innocent you were, Nicky.'

'Thank you,' I said, thoroughly confused and not a little humiliated.

But Karen was undaunted and referred back to the log book. 'Let's have the Svalbard chart out,' she commanded.

'Aye, aye, sir,' I responded, playing on my new-found and innocent status. Sweeping the chart on the saloon table I said, 'All's well until he's up north, beyond the Norways,' as two lesser islands off the north-west shoulder of West Spitsbergen were confusingly called. 'And here's Moffen.' I planted my index finger on the curious atoll-like island. 'I've read that it's home to walruses.'

'You've read all the books; where and when would he encounter ice?'

'Well, it works its way round the south of West Spitsbergen's South Cape' – I pointed to the southernmost tip of the main island that made up the complex archipelago and was the only one that was actually called Spitsbergen – 'and it can trap a boat in any of these southern fiords.' I indicated Horn Sound, Bell Sound and Ice Fiord. 'Further north, up here by Prince Charles's Foreland, which is actually an island not, as Willem Barents first thought, a mere headland, it is relatively clear during the summer. Up here' – my finger ran further north to where a cluster of offshore islands, including the Inner and Outer Norways lay – 'is where the old whaler's port of Smeerenburg used to be. Ice-free during the summer.' I pointed to the flat peninsula that lay opposite the anchorage of Virgo Bay, named after the ship attending an ill-fated Swedish polar expedition. 'North of the Norways' – my finger traced the 80th parallel and rested upon the walrus haven of Moffen – 'well, I guess it depended upon the particular conditions last year, and I'm afraid I don't know what they were like.' I paused, then added, 'And the log doesn't tell us.'

'I suppose we could have found out.'

'I suppose we could, but we were in an awful rush and that sort of detail simply got forgotten. It's difficult to judge from the state of ice-damage to the boat,' I finished lamely.

'But if he got to Moffen, then it was clear, or clear enough for him to take *Rolissa* there.'

'Certainly,' I said, 'we know he crossed the eightieth parallel and we know *Rolissa* wasn't *badly* scarred by ice-damage, so it's fair to assume that, knowing Guy too, he would not have hazarded the boat.'

'No, he loved the boat all right.'

'Karen, I didn't know...'

'It's all right, Nicky, of course you didn't know. I'm just having a little whinge.'

We went on as the log entries petered out. I peered at the charts and made out a whole series of positions, all unmistakably in Guy's bold script impressed into the chart, though most of the graphite from the 2B pencil had been erased. At this point there seemed to be nothing wrong with his hand or his hand-writing. It was possible to trace *Rolissa*'s track east-north-east for a while on the general chart of Svalbard, number 2751 in the British Admiralty series, an erratic track which suggested the presence of ice. But after that all we had to go on was that lower-cased word *following*, and then the trail ran cold, just when *Rolissa* was entering the most unpredictable phase of her voyage. Thereafter we had a few clues as to her progress south-wards, down the Norwegian coast to some-where in the region of Bodo before she had headed offshore, to that odd position marked by the hand of an unknown female. Then we had a few disjointed GPS positions, mere occasional notations of latitude and longi-tude. I did not have to refer to any chart; they were clearly the homeward passage south down the North Sea.

'*Following*? But following what?' Karen mused.

'The following day, following my hunch, following a whale, following ... Oh, I don't know! You're getting fixated, Karen. Look,' I said, trying to cement the thing with cold logic, 'I think we can assume that at the very least Guy hurt his hand at the time the log entries go haywire, but *after* he passed Moffen. He wrote them retrospectively. I suppose he was busy navigating through ice – difficult enough for the two of us, very difficult for Guy alone. I reckon he kept the navigation plot going but neglected the log.'

'That's pretty obvious ... and there was a girl on board by the time they reached his *perfect anchorage* miles to the south on the Norwegian coast ... What we want to know is what happened in between? What happened to screw up tough-guy Guy? Was it the girl and who was she? Where had she come from? Where is she now?'

I smiled at the play on words, but Karen looked grim. Suddenly I had the feeling that I was being swept along on a tide of obsession and, for a prescient moment, there was a danger in the quest. I seemed suddenly like a man come up for air and granted the boon of a cool, fresh indraught.

'Karen,' I began slowly, 'I feel a trifle like Ishmael...'

She looked up from Guy's notes with a quizzical look. 'Ishmael? What on earth are you talking about, Nicky? Ishmael who?'

'I don't think we know his surname.'

'Excuse me?'

'In *Moby Dick*, Ishmael is the sole survivor of Ahab's obsession, his hunt to the death of the white whale ... Melville's masterpiece...'

'I know who wrote *Moby Dick*, for heaven's sake, but what in God's creation has that got to do with us?' Then the penny dropped. 'You

137

think I'm mad, like Ahab?'

'Ahab wasn't mad, Karen, and no, I don't think you're remotely like Ahab...'

'Well that's bloody good of you, you condescending shit!'

'Shut up, Karen,' I responded sharply, 'and listen, just for a moment.'

She subsided into silent fulmination. I think it was the first time she had ever heard me in full professional mode. 'Look, I understand everything about your need to unravel the mystery of why Guy killed himself and what exactly made him unhappy enough to take his own life. I'm curious myself, or I wouldn't be here,' I added though it was not strictly true. 'I know he left no suicide note and therefore he denied you any explanation, though I read somewhere that suicides, like all autobiographers, write only what they want to be remembered by...'

'That's unworthy...'

'I read it somewhere. It may be true, it may not. In any case, the absence of any explanation suggests Guy didn't want you to know...'

'That's exactly why I want to know, you idiot! Why I *must* know!' Karen's face was thrust up at mine, her eyes wide, her mouth drawn back as she almost snarled.

'Well you're not going to know, are you?' I snarled back. 'Not for a certainty, not beyond all reasonable doubt.' I stabbed the chart with my right forefinger, out of my own tree by now. 'Not going on the paltry evidence here!'

'That's why we've got to come up here!' she

138

almost shrieked at me, stamping her foot on the cabin sole as if it represented the entire Arctic.

'And you think it's going to jump out of the bloody rocks and bite you on your nose, do you? You've been working in fantasy-land for too bloody long, Karen. Get real!'

'You bastard!'

And I realized what a foolish and hurtful thing I had said as she turned and stamped out of the cabin, up through the doghouse and ashore. I followed, calling out my apologies after her, but I was treated to the sight of half a dozen Norwegians staring at her as she shoved between them. Then they swung their collective gaze upon me. Some just stared; two women who had obviously been discussing our noisy row turned away; a dog barked at my appearance and one old man laughed.

'*Kvint!*' I thought he said, which I think means 'women!'

I smiled wanly and he nodded his head complicitly then said something else which I did not understand. He muttered again and turned away too, which was the signal for the little crowd to break up. Feeling a complete fool, I went below.

Back in the saloon I swore with a deep sincerity and reached for the grog locker to pour myself a large gin. Fortunately I stopped myself. Just in time I recalled the mizen staysail halliard was frayed and I went back on deck and renewed it. I had calmed down by the time I had finished the task.

I went down again and put the kettle on. Back in the cockpit I stared along the quay. There was no sign of Karen. I had been going to suggest that we simply went on with the cruise to Svalbard, enjoying it for the grand adventure that it was, or could have been. Now, it seemed Hammerfest would be our furthest point north; the two of us together could not even equal what Guy had accomplished alone.

Guy would have laughed at that and I could almost hear him saying, 'It's a metaphor for the whole disaster of the human condition, Nick. Without ruthless order, nothing is ever accomplished.'

'How right you bloody well are,' I replied to his ghost.

The Seventh Part

Karen had not returned by late afternoon and I became increasingly worried about her – not on account of her safety, but about the ridiculous situation we found ourselves in. I thought at the time that I had grossly under-estimated the effect of her dismissal, coming as it did after the horrors of Guy's suicide and the unhappiness caused by his will. I did not, however, go looking for her. Why? Well, partly pride on my own part. Put crudely, I had rather given up on Karen and with this con-clusion came the subsidiary alarm that, in truth, I wanted no repetition of all the misery that the breakdown of my marriage to Claire had entailed. Karen was a big girl, and in my pique I simply wanted a line drawn under everything. We were not going any further than Hammerfest. I even considered putting *Rolissa* up for sale the moment we arrived home. Beyond that, the cottage would be sold and I would move away – to Wales, Ireland or some remote part of Scotland. Like Jack, I would retreat, though I hope with a little more success and a little less booze.

So I did not run ashore after her. Hammer-fest failed to attract me. I had been a seafarer too long, and I was so entirely wrapped up in the conclusion that nothing was going right that I simply did not care. I knew Karen would be safe enough and that, when she wanted to, she would come back. My guess – rightly, as it turned out – was that she had gone for a long walk. Besides the replacement of the mizen staysail halliard there were several other minor tasks to occupy me. That, as any boat owner will tell you, is always the case. Dinner time came, and with it a sleeting drizzle from an overcast sky that matched my mood and would, I thought, bring Karen back the quicker; but it did not.

I gave in to the impulse to have a drink and had several. The rain stopped and left behind it a sodden and silent calm. The oily water of the harbour lay smooth and dark, the rising land a darker shade of the same monotone, the coloured buildings of Hammerfest drained of their bright hues. Not a wavelet lapped the hull of the ketch until a fishing vessel went past, but the rocking soon subsided, lending emphasis to the returning gloomy silence. About ten, unfed and a little drunk, with the prospect of a full night's kip ahead of me, I damned all women, rolled into my bunk and fell fast asleep in minutes.

There is a developed habit in seamen that allows them to fall asleep easily and to do so in the most appalling conditions. They are capable of sleeping through bad weather, through the regular roar of fog sirens and the thunder of machinery; but let a single discordant exception, or an unpredictable movement, upset any such inhospitable environment, and they are awake. Drink will modify this instinctive response, as drink modified mine that night, for Karen had been back on board for some time before she succeeded in initiating this professional alarm and woke me. I think that in my befuddled state she had aroused me earlier and I had simply rolled over in the knowledge that she was back, a sleep-and-drink-sozzled pride preventing me from coming fully awake at her first intrusion. But when she was clearly doing something unusual, I woke properly, peering blearily at her back from my quarter-berth. For a moment, I said nothing, certain that I should stir an unpleasant response, and I watched her for a moment. She was bent over the saloon table, which was once again spread with charts, and Guy's log, notes and typescript. Whatever Karen was doing, she had decided to do it after stripping off what must have been sodden clothes to turn in. I was treated to an arousing view of her long legs and her bottom, and confess I let my senses respond before I asked, 'What on earth are you doing at this hour?'

Despite her unconsciously inviting stance I was expecting invective, abuse, a diatribe on the male sex in general and myself in particular, so I was surprised when she swung round, her eyes alight with enthusiasm and almost barked, 'Get up! I've something to show you!'

So astonished was I, so infected with this change of mood and so relieved that she appeared to have recovered her temper that I extracted myself from my quarter-berth with alacrity, so much so that my priapic state emerged with me. For a moment she stared at me and then, with a still-wild laugh and a flick of her hair, she demanded my attention at the saloon table. My tumescence subsided instantly!

For the next half-hour we bent over in close and faintly ridiculous propinquity as she elaborated her so-called discovery. Still sleepy, somewhat embarrassed by the revelation of my now subsided but protrusile tissues, it took me some moments to catch up with her exposition.

'While I was ashore I decided that the only way to decide the extent to which we could resolve any of this matter was to come back and go through all the data. We'd only played with it up to now and, in fact, we actually have much more information than we first thought.'

'Oh, have we?' I think I muttered.

'Yes. You got the key to it by discovering that imperfectly erased position. In fact, with the charts inevitably getting a bit damp and with people leaning over them in waterproofs, they soon lose their pristine quality, even when only used once. As you know, it's a tedious task rubbing all the positions off. It struck me as odd that Guy had done it at all. He didn't normally do so, preferring to have the record of his voyages on a chart unless, like those of the North Sea, it was a commonplace trip and he was going to use the chart again. This case was entirely different: it was his one-off lifetime exploit, and in addition he was going to write a book about it. Rubbing the positions off seemed perverse. From this it is clear that he had something to hide and he therefore broke his normal habit.'

'I agree, but he didn't do it very well,' I said, moving to put a kettle on and rid my mouth and my head of their accumulated fur. 'And that is very *unlike* Guy. He was usually so meticulous, even for a Sandhurst-trained pongo.'

'Yes, that puzzled me for a bit until it occurred to me that he might not have done the job properly for a number of reasons.' She straightened up and struck off the points on her fingers as I put the spoonsful of coffee into the two mugs. 'Firstly, it might have been difficult: he's doing it on board and his hand hurts; second, he is reluctant to do it because he knows it will make things difficult later and he is doing it as a kind of nod to some imperative; and third, that imperative is a variable.'

'I don't understand. What d'you mean?'

She frowned and bit her lip. She seemed to find it difficult, and the old suspicion about female intuition rose unbidden into my mind.

'Look, something happens that makes him feel he's got to rub the positions off. He doesn't actually want to do it and, apart from finding the task actually difficult, thinks, from whatever happened, that he *ought* to do it. That's the imperative.' She looked at me to see if I had grasped her contention.

I nodded. 'OK, anything else?' I asked, taking the boiling kettle off the gas and making the coffee.

'Yes, there's a fourth point and it seems to me that it's crucial and it's why he felt he had to rub out all those positions. I mean, what difference does it make?'

'And?' I handed her the mug.

'Thanks.' She took it and went on. 'They were laid down by *her*, the girl.'

'The female,' I corrected, but Karen ignored me. To her *girl* implied desirability, sexual infidelity and the final dissolution of her relationship with Guy. It seemed to preoccupy her to an unreasonable degree now that Guy's death by his own hand had done the same job so efficiently.

'So you are convinced the erasing was done at sea, under some form of psychological pressure. It wasn't done at home?'

'Yes, I am. I didn't see all he did, but just after he came back home I was also doing some work at home on a proposal and we were both knocking about the place. I made him coffee and tea, as I always seemed to do despite his protestations about us being a working team. That was claptrap: he bought a dishwasher so that he didn't have to do the one chore that he willingly undertook when we were first together.'

146

I laughed. Sandhurst had never been strong at teaching its acolytes the dignity of menial labour, not like my own alma mater, which had insisted that mercantile apprentices cleaned lavatory bowls and scrubbed decks before they had the moral authority to insist others did the same.

'So he went to all this painful trouble to prevent you discovering he had been shagging some girl he'd picked up in Norway?'

I do not quite know why I used the crude verb then. In Karen's presence I was usually careful to avoid the vernacular of my calling. Somehow the intimacy of the white night, the sight of her, her breasts moving freely under the insubstantial T-shirt and my own vengeful and put-upon self made me literally thrust it forward, a metaphorically penile intrusion.

But the word's crudity suited Karen perfectly. 'No,' she said, 'he was destroying evidence of something else.'

'What?' I remarked with a wry grin over the rim of my mug. 'Evidence of something worse than adultery? What on earth are you suggesting?'

For a moment I thought, somewhat fantastically, that her lips moved to form 'm' for murder, but she merely made a moue and then said, 'That's what we're going to find out.'

'How? I mean you're saying we're going on?'

'Yes. We're going up there.'

Up there. The once familiar words rang with

147

new import. 'To Svalbard?'

'Yes,' she said, and before I could remonstrate further she added, 'There's one more thing...' She sorted through the charts, the heavy paper crackling. 'If you look carefully at this chart...' She drew out Admiralty Chart number 1504, *Cromer to Orfordness*, pointing at two faintly visible positions. 'These are in Guy's own hand.'

'So?'

'Where's the girl?'

'Powdering her bloody nose, Karen!'

'No, she's gone.'

If I had hoped, or even thought, to end the matter there and go back to bed, I was wrong. In what I can only really describe as a kind of fury, I recall Karen within a whirl of paper, from which she produced in succession a chart, then a page of the log, then a note or a sheet from Guy's now thoroughly dog-eared typescript. Finally she laid out all that she had discovered.

'I have been through and cross-referenced *every* allusion I can find. OK there are some vagaries and I'm not *certain* of their exact progress after Moffen, but I've a pretty good idea. You can make the best judgement about the nautical side of things, but they came south through the Hindlopen Strait, skirted Bear Island and returned here, to Hammerfest. While I was going walkabout I found someone who had recognized the boat. She remembered seeing *Rolissa* and Guy with a young woman – a blonde, about twenty-six or

148

so, certainly under thirty.' This was said with incontrovertible firmness and I felt my objections wither under assault. 'Then they coasted south...' Here she paused to shuffle charts, turning to me, her eyes afire ... 'further south than is suggested by the appearance of that position you discovered.'

'You mean they turned and went north again?' I asked, more puzzled than ever.

Karen nodded. 'Uh-huh, so it seems, and then finally headed to the south...' A succession of charts followed. I was familiar with them, since we had so recently covered much the same ground in the opposite direction. Karen resumed her speculative narration. 'South ... south, with the girl plotting the fixes. If we turn to the log...' There was a further flurry and Karen flicked over the pages of Guy's log, holding each one in front of me ... 'we get the date and a position. There's the odd addition of a notation about the wind, but note they're all in Guy's hand. It's bloody shaky and awkward, but it's unmistakably his; the girl isn't allowed to write up the log and' – her voice stressed emphasis – 'the wind seems only to be noted when it's above Force 6. You and I know that *Rolissa* definitely needs reefing between Force 5 and Force 6 and that reefing means labour, work, and Guy's got a septic hand.' I forbore asking how she knew Guy's hand was septic, though the continuing shaky handwriting seemed to suggest all was not well. On the other hand, sufficient time seemed to have passed for it to be healing, but then I was being seduced by Karen's conviction, if not her argument. Moreover, I was not untouched by the intensity of the moment, by her striking looks, which her present fervour seemed to enhance. I was quite bewitched.

'Then...' she seemed to assume an air of triumph as she strained back the log book's spine. In the central fold the remains of a carefully torn-out page were just visible. 'Then we lose a day, perhaps two...' She was turning the log over again ... 'but not much later there's a position...' We transferred our attention to Admiralty Chart 1504. '*Rolissa* is approaching the East Anglian coast and Guy is again putting positions on the chart. Look, he hasn't even bothered to attempt to rub this one out.'

I saw what she meant. 'But the girl could still be powdering her nose,' I said.

'Don't trivialize this, it's serious.'

'I'm not trivializing.' I raised my eyes and they fell on the bulkhead clock. 'D'you know what time it is?' I asked.

'I've no idea, with this eternal bloody daylight.'

'It's five in the morning.'

'I'd never have known. I don't feel at all tired.'

'No, it does have that effect on one, but you're living on adrenaline. You ought to get some sleep.'

'I will, but let's go, let's get under way. I'll turn in when we're on our way.'

I shook my head. 'No, we need water and diesel and some stores. I should have done it yesterday.' She dropped her eyes as I referred obliquely to our public row. 'I'll deal with all that once the natives are up and about. You turn in and we'll sail when you've had some sleep and all this lot is put away.' I indicated the mass of paper on the salon table, adding with a hint of irritation, 'I'll have to sort out the charts anyway.'

She considered the proposition. 'All right,' she said, and turned towards her berth.

'There is just one thing, Karen.'

'What's that?'

'I still don't understand how going north will help.'

She came back towards me. 'I don't either,' she said, 'but I've nothing better to do and – well, I just have a feeling that I have got to retrace his last voyage.'

I shrugged. I was not convinced we could stand each other's company and the far north was faintly intimidating. 'I don't know how frequently the Hinlopen Strait is free of ice,' I prevaricated. 'I mean Svalbard isn't the Solent. Replication may be impossible.'

She became shamelessly seductive, standing there before me, eyes cast down, the dark curtains of hair fallen forward, her damned nipples heaving up and down and so close that the warm smell of her filled my nostrils and stirred me again. Then, with that bloody shake of the head, she looked up at me. 'Humour me, Nicky, there's a darling,' and

151

she placed a hand on my arm and, on tiptoe, kissed me. As I responded she twisted away. A moment later she was in bed, and I was standing there like a loon, half-tumescent in the Arctic morning.

Before the town was awake and I could ferret out sources of stores, water and diesel, I sorted out the charts and paperwork, lingering over the notes in particular. Interesting though they were, they revealed little and the typescript even less. Karen had quite properly discounted them. They were written after ... Well, after what I could not say, but after whatever it was that had *happened*.

To tell the truth, I was perplexed by Karen's theory of the singular event. My own reconstruction ran thus: at some time Guy hurts his hand badly and his previous disciplined approach to log-book keeping and navigation is consequently slackened. It has already been circumscribed by the difficulties of navigating solo through the ice. He is, however, determined to achieve his objective and accomplishes a creditable passage round West Spitsbergen and, I assume, south through the Hinlopen Strait. He's in a lot of pain and this alone takes some doing. Then he heads south, returning to the Norwegian coast. The hand isn't healing and instead of going into hospital, he decides to continue homewards. In the meantime he's met and, we must assume, picked up a girl. What she looks like, we don't know, although Karen's witness

152

might be able to enlarge, but we assume they got on.

I was drifting into the realms of fantasy now, the residue of my arousal fuelling my speculations. Images of Guy's *inamorata* fused with images of Karen as I slumped on the saloon settee and I was in something of a half-doze over the log. I had become Guy and the girl had turned into Karen, an easy fantasy given that I was in the very spot where their love-making had taken place – it was significant that I now thought of it as love-making and not the shagging I had earlier called it. Guy and I were coasting down the beautiful Norwegian coast in a sexual idyll, finding en route our perfect anchorage, contemplation of which stirred me to the extent of suggesting masturbation.

The notion that I should do something woke me fully. Of course! They – Guy and the girl – had had a row and Guy, in one of his famous furies, had fired off some ultimatum and headed out to sea. I was wide awake now; I could almost hear him in the cockpit, his clipped diction sharp and staccato with menace and wicked intent. Indeed, Karen was right: Guy *could* be a nasty bastard when he wanted to.

'All right!' his ghost exclaimed, reminding me of an occasion in Ostend when he had thundered at Karen, 'You want to sail and get home before the bloody BBC ring you up on Monday even when the weather is so bloody foul, we'll damn well sail. But don't complain

153

when you don't like it offshore, my girl!'

And off we had gone, into the teeth of a rising gale that had raged for two days, past the deadline of Karen's commitment (for an overdue script, I think), and into one of the worst North Sea crossings that we had ever experienced. I recalled the row so well, and how bloody-minded Guy had been, enlisting my complicity with a 'We'll show her; she'll never make the same mistake again.' He knew that I and *Rolissa* were quite capable of taking the punishment, but that it was, nevertheless, a foolhardy thing to do. Afterwards – after Karen had gone off home ahead of him in a rage herself by then – he had said to me, 'I'm sorry about all that, Nick. It's just that there are times when the world seems mad and I have to face its madness head-on.'

I had never quite understood what he meant. Clearly he was contemptuous of Karen's imposed and, to him, unnecessary imperatives, just as he had clearly relished the challenge of the gale as well as frightening Karen. I had thought she might never sail again, for I knew of wives for whom such an experience would have proved terminal in so far as sailing was concerned; but Karen was tougher than that. The matter was never afterwards referred to – at least, not in my hearing.

Awake now, with recollection of Guy's worse side, I found myself holding the log book. I began to flick through it as I completed my reconstruction of the final phase of

154

Rolissa's previous trip. After this clash of personalities in which, so I argued, the age and experience difference cut in, Guy had headed south, intending to repatriate the girl from England. With his bad hand he would undoubtedly have required her help. I tried to recall the details of his return. He had phoned me himself.

'Hullo, Nick, it's Guy. I'm back.' And I had responded with congratulations. 'Got back to Pin Mill early yesterday morning and home about lunch time...'

I turned to the log and found the terse entry: *29th Pin Mill mooring @ 0554. Came ashore.*

I did not expect the log to tell me how he got home from Pin Mill, but Karen should remember; otherwise there was nothing to help there. I supposed the girl could have been taken to Colchester station where a bus ran to Stansted. From there I knew she could get a flight to Bergen. Anyway, Guy was certainly not going to advertise the method by which he quietly disposed of his clandestine girlfriend even if she had long since ceased to be his bedfellow. Besides, as I have explained, working watch-and-watch is not conducive to running a torrid affair. He had been doing that during his leisurely cruise down the Norwegian coast at forty or fifty miles a day. Anyway, Guy was a brilliant improviser; a man with so *English* a gloss as Guy, who could survive under cover in Northern Ireland, was not going to find the business of

155

spiriting a young woman out of the sight of his friends very difficult. For all I knew he had set her up in an hotel for a week or two, until he could attend to the matter at his leisure. Good heavens, my imagination ran on and on, perhaps he had renewed the sexual side of his relationship, rediscovered his impotence and this horror had formed the core of his final despair...

Shaking my head at my own credulity, I returned to the pages of the log and curiously inspected the fragments of the removed page – or pages. The hiatus occurred in the second half of the book and a brief inspection showed that Guy had not removed all the evidence of the missing material because he did not wish to remove the opposite sheet, which bore the fully inscribed data of an earlier day. This must have confronted him with a dilemma, for a missing page earlier would have been almost as suggestive. It was a canon of my profession that one never tampered with a log book, but not every sailor is a paragon of virtue and we were only talking about a yacht's log. Was the matter, the singular event, the *thing that had happened*, as important as Karen claimed?

Guy had carefully removed the page he did not wish to be retained well enough to make its absence obvious only to someone with a suspicious turn of mind. Then there was another question that now arose: if he had had to remove the page it must have borne something he did not wish anyone else to read. Did that mean someone reading it after the end of the voyage, or after he had written his book? Did it mean the information on that page was, in itself, something that he did not want others to see, or merely that it was evidence of the girl's presence? Though I was disinclined to believe it, either might be incriminating. Stimulated by this train of thought I took the log book up into the doghouse and, placing it down on the chart table, picked up the magnifying glass from its place in the wooden rack. Then I switched on the chart light with its focused beam. Moving the log book underneath its restricted pool of light, I perceived the faint outline of script.

My heart was now hammering and I tried very hard to make out what had been written down and caused such offence. I did not succeed – at least, I was unable to make any coherent sense of it – but for what it is worth, and since it has some relevance to the way things fell out, I was reasonably sure of several things. The first of these was that a paragraph of six or seven lines had been scribbled over – comprehensively scribbled over as though the scribbler had wished nothing to be readable. Both the scribbling and the initial imprint, little flourishes of which emerged at the extremities of the hatching, gave me the impression of having been executed in ballpoint pen. Most of the log book was written in fountain pen – a curious idiosyncrasy of Guy's, but a fact, nonetheless – although some of the shakily

157

written positions belonging to the period after his hand injury were in pencil. The point was that this entry was not capable of erasure, or of spoiling with water; it was in ballpoint. Below it, however, there was a pencilled paragraph; the imprint was wider and softer – a 2B chart pencil, I surmised. I have no idea what its relationship to the paragraph above was, but I was sure it was in Guy's handwriting. This conviction took me back to the emerging flourishes which had escaped over-scribbling and it took but a second glance to persuade me that these were not Guy's and were, at least by inference, those of the girl. Had she simply broken Guy's rule and written in the log book? or had she been trying to write something of importance in the yacht's permanent record, even challenging Guy's mastership? I had no idea; one thesis seemed reasonable: Guy was unwell – perhaps by now feverish – and had found out to his intense annoyance that the girl had meddled (I could hear him accusing her of the very crime!). On the other hand, he must have arrived home not long afterwards, and while he had been depressed – terminally so – he had not been in a fever, or not to my knowledge. I wanted to wake Karen and ask her, but one glance in her direction showed her deeply asleep after her long and soaking trudge ashore.

Though I thought I could make out a few letters here and there, the contents of the first paragraph were quite illegible. To decipher the second I brushed over the page very lightly with the chart pencil and then smudged my finger over the graphite. It was not a success, but I experienced a sort of feeling of relief, as though Guy was at least vindicated in part. You see, I quite clearly read the personal pronoun *I* several times; the word *love* figured twice and this, on one occasion, came before a full stop. The second time, however, it preceded the initial letter *K*.

I looked again at Karen's sleeping form. Surely, I thought, the whole affair had a plausible if grubby explanation: a sordid and adulterous liaison, the most improbable facet of which was that somehow an injured hand had precipitated it.

Well, stranger things had happened, I thought, closing the log and stretching. I roused myself and began to tuck all the charts away. There were signs that Hammerfest was waking up and I had work to do. Karen was paranoid and stressed out. As I turned out of the doghouse I found myself reconciled to her plan and I hoped a cruise *up there* would lay all her ghosts and restore her spirits.

More to the point, I thought that my chances with her were very much improved.

The Eighth Part

We left Hammerfest at four o'clock that afternoon. I had woken Karen at two and served up a cold lunch, which we ate without reference to the events of the previous night, though it was difficult to reconcile the word with the continuous daylight. I suspected that Karen did not want to resurrect the matter in case I repeated my arguments against proceeding further, whereas I, for my part, having come so far, now wanted to press on. I had never ventured into the polar seas before and I was putting the business of Guy behind me, considering privately that I had solved the conundrum, if conundrum it was. So far I thought we had done pretty well and I saw no reason to curtail the cruise, which gave us a sense of purpose and would, I hoped, give us in due course a real sense of achievement.

Oddly I did recall some words of Guy's, but only because they seemed to fit the bill. 'The pleasure of *having* something is fleeting,' he had said when we were discussing why people like us went off in sailing boats and subjected ourselves to such wretchedness and discomfort, 'but the pleasure having *done* something

160

is lasting, for time enhances it, rubbing off its unpleasant aspects to mellow it in the memory.'

I hoped all this would mellow in the memory, but perhaps it was this intrusion of Guy's metaphysical soul that prevented me from quite letting him go. Even so, it was only after we had got clear of the land that I referred to him.

We had cut the engine and lay ghosting north under drooping and dripping sails, for it had begun to rain again and the wind, though favourable, was light. Under her autopilot *Rolissa* glided north while all about the tiny wavelets were pocked with the widening concentric rings thrown out by the plopping of an infinity of raindrops. Having hoisted all plain sail plus the mizen staysail I was sweating under my heavy-duty waterproofs.

'Breathable, my arse,' I remarked as I wiped the perspiration from my forehead and Karen, sheltering under the doghouse, handed me a cup of tea.

'Aren't you wicking away?' she asked with a grin.

'Am I hell,' I responded.

'And you don't think I'm mad?'

'Did I ever suggest you were?'

'I think it was your sub-agenda.'

'I don't even know what a sub-agenda is.'

'And you don't think going on up there is barmy.'

'I think you may be disappointed in one

161

sense, but I don't regret what we're doing.'

'You're equivocating.'

'You're provocating...' She put her tongue out at me. 'Just satisfy me on two points arising from last night's discussion,' I said.

'Go on.'

'Tell me exactly what state Guy's hand was in and whether he was in any kind of a fever when he arrived home.'

'I told you, he wouldn't show it to me...'

'Come on, Karen, think,' I interrupted; 'he must have told you about it, even if he didn't want to show you – I suspect because it was pretty bad.'

She nodded. 'OK, yes, he did and I did actually get a look at it, after which I didn't want to look...'

'Pretty horrible, eh?'

'It had been septic, he told me; only constant draining had prevented the whole thing from going really bad. I guess being at sea and in the relative purity of the Arctic saved him from what, in other circumstances, might have proved fatal.'

'Septicaemia?'

'Yes, or toxaemia or gangrene – one shudders to think; but Guy knew about battlefield wounds and was quite capable of administering self-surgery,' she said, adding, as a cloud passed over her expression, 'until the girl could do it for him. Anyway, I think the thing was slow healing because, apart from the initial infection, he would keep using it.'

'I suppose he couldn't avoid that.'

'No. And he wasn't the type to give up ... too much of the Stoic.'

'And the fever?'

She shook her head. 'No, he was a bit fever*ish* – you know, running a bit of a temperature – but he wasn't incapacitated with a real fever.' She paused, then said, 'Why d'you ask?'

'Oh, I don't know; I was just trying to put together my own picture of what happened after all that you'd told me.'

'And is that all?'

I nodded. 'Yes, I think so. No, there was one other thing. The day he came home, how did he actually *get* home? I mean were you there?'

'No, I was in London. He rang me from the hall and was there when I got home.' She frowned. 'I don't recall asking him how he got home, but I think he said something about being lucky and getting a lift. I don't think I thought about it much. Why? D'you think it important?'

I shrugged. 'Not really. I was just curious.'

She looked for a moment as though she wanted to say more and I anticipated a question about the girl's fate, but she obviously thought better of it and let the matter drop. Whether she was suspicious that I doubted her story, I have no idea. Certainly I did not think it sensible to advance my own rational theory about what had happened. At the time I think I thought that the failure of our wild goose chase *up there* would lay the ghosts and incline her to accept a more plausible if less

163

dramatic explanation than she seemed to have embraced in her notion of the singular event.

As Eliot said, a cold coming we had of it, for the Barents Sea proved a snare. As we drew away from the Norwegian coast, the rain gradually ceased and the wind filled in. Slowly the air cleared, the overcast broke and the sun shone fitfully. I thought the halcyon idyll had returned with the sunshine but, despite the rising barometer, this was not to be. Slowly the wind veered again into the north and drew down a freezing stream of polar air, which in turn, blowing hard over a warmer sea, raised a low and impenetrable fog through which *Rolissa* raced unchecked. In brutal conditions I double-reefed the main, single-reefed the mizen and furled the jib. In its place I was compelled to set the storm jib, for the wind rose to a whole gale and beyond. Within hours it had become a storm of Force 10.

I went forward again, a staggeringly cautious figure, swept by spray, the wind pressing my heavy waterproofs against me as with a giant hand, as I inched my way, dragging with me the carbine hook of my safety harness along the webbing jackstay. Grabbing the mast I set up the topping lift and let the main halliard go. The wind tore at me while the spray stung the exposed portions of my face. I can still feel the awful cold of the wind ache, a terrible pain induced by the wind chill that in time led to a numbness that was the terrible harbinger of frostbite. Lord, did it hurt!

In the cockpit Karen hove in the last inches of the mainsheet and I stood up, stretching my safety lanyard and, legs wide apart in an attempt to steady myself against *Rolissa*'s dido, I pressed my chest against the boom and forced myself to pass the sail ties round the vicious cracking of the mainsail's stiff fabric. Weakened by the effort I regained the safety of the cockpit with relief, hunkering down in the shelter of the spray hood, which now augmented that provided by the doghouse.

I closed my eyes to squeeze the unwanted moisture out of them, catching my breath and trying not to wince as the blood forced its way back into the contracted capillaries of my near-frozen face. Karen watched anxiously.

'Look,' she called to me above the noise, pointing forward. My gaze fell upon the first rime of ice where the wind chill was freezing the seawater as it collected along the pulpit and guardrails. We stared at this manifestation of the true Arctic and then I turned to her.

'Go on,' I almost shouted. 'it's your watch below.'

She went reluctantly, after making me a cup of packet soup, leaving me to contemplate the grey waves which rushed at us out of the fog and over which *Rolissa* thrust herself, bursting up and through the tumbling crests

165

as they were shredded in a smoking spume that flew to leeward with the force of gunshot. It was now a test of endurance in which Karen and I were by far the weakest part. *Rolissa*, under storm jib and reefed mizen, behaved like the thoroughbred she was, all her elegant beauty bent upon the grim purpose of disarming the storm in a demonstration of what a wonderful thing a well-balanced yacht was.

As I sat there, with intermittent glances at the course, peering into the fog and periodically looking at *Rolissa*'s Raytheon radar screen, it seemed inconceivable that a greater world lay beyond the tiny compass of my circumscribed vision. I began to half-sink into that brown study that besets a yachtsman aware that he has done all he can, and must leave matters to his little ship. I began to chase the muse – hence my earlier reference to Eliot – that had eluded me a few days ago. What moved me to this inappropriate detachment, I cannot say, beyond admitting that such distractions whiled away the monotony of tedious watches. Perhaps it was because we were now headed for the island of Spits*bergen* and in my musings I had considered Bergen as the likely destination for Guy's totty. Certainly I had previously been trying to recall the verses simply because the city of Bergen had been marked upon the eastern margin of the chart then in use and its appearance had reminded me of a poem. It was a very, very long way away now that I fumbled my way towards the remembrance of Chesterton's lines in which Bergen featured: 'The wind blew out of Bergen,' I declaimed out loud in the triumph of my recollection. How much more appropriate were the words now, at the howling height of the storm:

> *The wind blew out of Bergen from the dawning to the day,*
> *There was a wreck of trees and fall of towers a score of miles away,*
> *And drifted like a livid leaf I go before its tide,*
> *Spewed out of house and stable, beggared of flag and bride.*
> *The heavens are bowed about my head, shouting like seraph wars,*
> *With rains that might put out the sun and clean the sky of stars,*
> *Rains like the fall of ruined seas from secret worlds above,*
> *The roaring of the rains of God none but the lonely love.*
> *Feast in my hall, O foemen, and eat and drink and drain,*
> *You never loved the sun in heaven as I have loved the rain.*

I struggled a bit with that first verse, but then the next flooded back. I had long ago learned it by heart to console myself at sea and ward off the megrims that threatened me as I thought of Claire's infidelity:

167

The chance of battle changes – so may all
battle be;
I stole my lady bride from them, they stole
her back from me.
I rent her from her red-roofed hall, I rode
and saw arise
More lovely than the living flowers the
hatred in her eyes.
She never loved me, never bent, never was
less divine;
The sunset never loved me; the wind was
never mine.
Was it all nothing that she stood imperial
in duress?
Silence itself made softer with the sweeping
of her dress.
O you who drain the cup of life, O you
who wear the crown,
You never loved a woman's smile as I
have loved her frown.

And the next verse came to me as I thought I had shifted that female displeasure from Claire to Karen. I wondered, briefly, if she could hear my declamation and found I did not care. In the exhilaration of my solitary watch and the high, rousing sentiment of the poet's words which cast our struggle in embattled metaphor, I went headlong on:

The wind blew out from Bergen from the
dawning to the day,
They ride and run with fifty spears to break

168

and bar my way...
... Yea, I will bless them as they bend and
love them where they lie,
When on their skulls the sword I swing falls
shattering from the sky.
The hour when death is like a light and
blood is like a rose, –
You never loved your friends, my friends, as
I shall love my foes.

Finally, I realized, it was not that distant Norwegian city that had wrenched Chesterton's words from my memory, but our unhealthy obsession with Guy's fate and it was he, not I, who seemed to claim the grand image conjured up by the culmination of 'The Last Hero':

Know you what earth shall lose tonight,
what rich uncounted loans,
What heavy gold of tales untold you bury
with my bones?
My loves in deep dim meadows, my ships
that rode at ease,
Ruffling the purple plumage of strange and
secret seas.
To see this fair earth as it is to me alone was
given,
The blow that breaks my brow tonight, shall
break the dome of heaven.
The skies I saw, the trees I saw after no eyes
shall see.
Tonight I die the death of God: the stars

shall die with me:
One sound shall sunder all the spears and
break the trumpet's breath:
You never laughed in all your life as I shall
laugh in death.

I was as exhausted after my delivery as I had been after dousing the mainsail. And now Guy's spectre seemed very real and close, for this poem, which had once consoled me in the bereavement of my lost love, seemed totally grabbed by him. His was an all too real blow – a blow that had indeed broken his brow – and, leaving his meadows and his ships, I could almost hear him laughing in death. Guy the golden, Guy the hussar officer, Guy the landed and the fortunate!

The uncanny resonance hurt – hurt with that strange twist in the guts made worse by the powerful emotions the poem naturally raised in me. There were more and different tears in my eyes as I finished my crazy recital. For a moment it seemed there was a great silence, but it was only in my head, and the storm roared back into my consciousness. Words possessed a power greater even than music to move me, a private and concealed weakness, or vice, of mine. I am never sure which – only that it is a reprehensible thing for a man to be so rocked upon the bearings of his normal equanimity.

And now the shade of Guy – Guy laughing in death – was sitting upon my shoulder or – I almost started – by my side, as he had done so on so many wretched foul-weather passages in *Rolissa*. The wild thought crossed my mind that he had gifted the ketch to me in order to haunt me. I turned, half-expecting to see his face peering at me from the shroud of his oilskins, half-defying his ghost to show itself.

The howl of the storm-force wind, the roar and hiss of the breaking seas, the defiant thump-thump of *Rolissa*'s hull – were they the only sounds to be heard? Lone yachtsmen spoke in their memoirs of strange voices, where no voices could possibly be. Joshua Slocum had been visited by the Pilot of the *Pinta*; Odysseus had heard the Sirens; why could I not be hearing Guy's sardonic laughter after death?

Mad fancy, you might say, and you might well be right; but the sequel was as odd, and emphatically owed nothing to any self-inflicted delusion. As I dashed aside my tears I was unaccountably prompted to take another look at Guy's log. This impulse was executed before it was fully formed and my attention focused not upon the three-quarters of the volume filled, perfectly or imperfectly, by the record of Guy's voyage, but upon the empty residue. Why? Again, I have no idea; it is simply where I looked. I suppose we had neither of us seen what I had found before because we had ignored the vacant pages at the end, thinking them unused or, in flicking through them, had failed to see what Guy had half-hidden.

Perhaps Karen *had* seen the words, and was concealing the fact – I do not know; but what I found was, I think, Guy's missing suicide note.

Moreover, its discovery upset all my notions of a logical explanation for Guy having taken his own life, though not with any specific reason, for it actually explained nothing, even while it hinted at the explanation of everything.

In that moment of discovery, amongst the elemental tumult of a raging storm, my thinking had been turned upside down. Now I knew that I sailed north, to *up there*, invested with the same sense of hope and conviction as the sleeping Karen.

What had I found? Well, not much, on the face of it. Only a line tucked away, written at right angles along the line of the book's spine and deliberately hidden in the fold of the thing. It bore witness to his wounded hand, but was written with painstaking care. Moreover, I knew Guy had left the words there deliberately, just as I guessed they were his last message to the world, for he had been at some pains to amend them. They appeared like this: *I am all there is and it is ~~completed~~ finished.*

There was both a resonance with that poem of Chesterton's, which had uncannily risen into my memory, and an irony in his having placed those last words in almost the same place from which he had removed the others with their burden of incrimination. No wonder he had been unable to write his book, for after having written this corrected sentence he had not been able to commit another word to paper with any satisfaction. His book could make no progress for, do you see, he was already hell-bent on killing himself. In his own mind he was already dead. He had taken his own life before he had ever brought *Rolissa* up to her home mooring.

The Ninth Part

Looking back, our progress further north seems an act of madness, yet at the time I recall our joint conviction, for I shared my newly acquired views with Karen as soon as the weather moderated. From the purely psychological point of view it can of course be argued that Guy's death and our individual personal situations had left us both with purposeless lives, at least in the short term. The so-called mystery surrounding Guy's end, which had taken root as an obsession in Karen's mind, had now infected mine. The only sane gloss that I can retrospectively put upon my own conduct up to this point rested on two things that I hesitate to call facts, neither of which will make much sense unless you are a yachtie or in love. The first was that I wished to pursue our voyage, since it was gratifying to me at a personal and, I suppose, professional level. The second was that I wished now to spend as much time as possible in Karen's presence and see where our relationship was going.

To win Karen – if the verb is not too sentimental – for I can think of no alternative to describe my confused motives, I first had

174

to wean her off Guy, and therefore I was not unwilling to go along with her, since it seemed that Guy's infidelity might prove to be to my advantage. Thus far we had had a couple of spectacular rows and I had, as I have admitted, been reduced to contemplating giving up the whole enterprise. But actually we got on rather well most of the time and I was emotionally blown around like a rather despicable weathercock. To this you now have to add my Damascene conversion.

As to the personal and professional dimensions, despite my long experience and my master-mariner's certificate, my rollercoaster career, culminating in redundancy, had prevented me from ever actually *commanding* a ship, a fundamental ambition of every youngster who goes to sea as a cadet. Somehow, taking a yacht up into the Arctic mollified this deep and embittering frustration, while convincing me that I might live thus in the future, at least until my body began to rebel with age.

The 'foggy-storm', as we afterwards called it, lasted about thirty hours. It appeared to have been a locally generated phenomenon, a whirling collision along the fringe of two air masses, the one warmly temperate and maritime in character, the other convincingly polar. In my inexperience of Arctic conditions I had to go on what I had read and I feared a strong and persistent northerly airstream would bring the ice down the eastern side of the Svalbard archipelago and fling it round the South Cape, blocking the deep fiords along the normally accessible coast of West Spitsbergen itself. More significant to us, if we were to stand any chance of following *Rolissa*'s track of the previous year, it would be forced down upon the north coast, blocking our way to Moffen and the Hinlopen Strait beyond. In the event this was only partially the case, but the anticipation, combined with the fog, induced us to lay off a course on the starboard tack, clear of Bear Island, which lay approximately halfway along the three hundred and fifty-odd miles between Hammerfest and Spitsbergen's South Cape. Such a course also took us clear of the main shipping lane round Norway's North Cape, much frequented by Russian vessels going to and from Murmansk, Archangel and the ports of the White Sea.

'I wonder,' Karen asked as she patted the cockpit coaming beside her, 'if *Rolissa* knows we are trying to follow her voyage of last year?' It was on the evening after the foggy-storm, when our routine with its pre-dinner tipple in the cockpit had reasserted itself with the improvement in the weather.

I stared out over the grey sea, still heaving under the impetus of a northerly swell but disturbed only by a moderate westerly breeze which had us gliding along at six knots under all plain sail, and smiled at Karen's fancy. Then I turned to her and told her of my curious notion of having had Guy sitting next to me during the blow.

'Oh, that's happened to me several times,' she said. 'I keep hearing his bloody voice.'

'Do you?'

'Oh. Yes. Quite clearly.' I held my peace, as I could see she was going to say more and I had learned that interrupting Karen's thought processes often led to her abandoning them. 'It was a bit spooky at first but then, as you get a bit lonely and fanciful at times on watch, I found I rather welcomed it.'

'It's not unusual,' I said, explaining about the phenomenon affecting lone yachtsmen.

'Yes, I've read the same somewhere.' She paused again, then added, 'He used to enjoy holding forth,' with a smile of reminiscence playing about her mouth.

'He certainly did,' I agreed.

'He used to say that he could lift himself on to another plane of existence just by standing still and contemplating something natural. He said that in looking at a blade of grass, a leaf, or a spider, he could feel a unity with the natural world and the pure joy of being alive. The tragedy of man, he said, was that the illusion was momentary, that he was soon brought down to earth again, usually by something that irritated him.'

'Like the fact that the leaf ought to be swept up,' I added, recalling the same lecture with a grin. 'He was a militarily conditioned stickler for tidiness.'

But Karen was not listening to me. 'Or that I had interrupted him.'

'You?'

'Oh, yes.' She looked at me directly. 'Do you ever feel like that?'

I nodded, meeting her gaze. 'Yes, sometimes, though often I can't escape the depressing conclusion that the leaf's and the spider's days are numbered, that somehow we've screwed up the natural world and that I am unable to take that pure delight in it that still seemed possible to Guy.'

'Well,' Karen said with a nod, 'he couldn't face it, could he? His type never give up the reins, do they?'

It had never occurred to me that she saw herself as separate from Guy's 'type', that she perhaps suffered something of my own sense of difference, if not quite inferiority. But these things are not obvious; they excoriate internally and the subject was too embarrassing to pursue. Besides, she had given me another opening, one which I could not resist.

'I'm surprised that *you* upset him.' It was clumsily said, but it hit its mark.

'Constantly,' she said, looking away.

There was a moment of awkward silence and I was about to extend my hand and simply touch her, but she rose suddenly and went below to check on the progress of our dinner. I was unwilling to let the moment of intimacy pass and, when she reappeared, I asked, 'Do *you* know what he meant by this sense of fleeting contentment?'

'Yes, of course,' she said, 'but in my case such moments are not so easily lost.' She broke away from further self revelation and after a moment added, 'You see Guy was really a solitary, a real solitary.'

I knew she was right. It was the reason he had never married her, the reason he had had his successes in the army with his intelligence work, or whatever dark deeds had earned him his quiet glory. I said, 'For me it's not so much the untidy leaf that affronted Guy, or really the sense that we live in some final, terminal era, but the immense and terrible disappointment that one cannot cling longer on to that heightened state of wonder and contentment. It's like a little glimpse of the Promised Land, taken away as soon as given; a trick of God's, a lifting of the Almighty fingers to the immanent nose, a gesture of humiliation to all mankind, the announcement of the limitation: "This far and no further." Most assuredly it belongs to this world, for that is where all this nature exists. Perhaps Guy, like me, *did* realize that it was too late – too late for him and too late for all of us. Nature and the multiple zillions of existences within it have slipped beyond our wonder, we have been like children trying to hold sand, we end up with nothing – individually and collectively. Mankind has taken a wrong turn, science has misled us and we are all in a cul-de-sac. Perhaps Guy, as a man with an active mind and body and the certainties of soldiering, felt all this.' I paused; then, thinking of something else, added, 'But I doubt it.'

Karen seemed not to be listening to me.

179

'Guy, like most of us,' she said, 'failed to see that he was not what he thought he was, but what others thought he was.'

'That makes him sound like something invented ... a construct.'

She shrugged. 'We're all invented' – dismissing my objection. 'Anyway,' she said with conviction, 'it's why he killed himself.'

'I don't understand.'

'He discovered the fact for himself, about himself. It destroyed him.'

I frowned, having completely lost the thread of Karen's argument. She saw my lack of comprehension.

'Guy could not stand the fact that he was something other than what he wanted to be – what he himself thought he was.'

'You mean he couldn't stand what *you* thought he was, how *you* thought of him?'

Her shoulders rose and fell again. 'Me, you, everyone...' It did not square with my image of Guy at all, but Karen had the advantage of intimacy with Guy, and she went on, 'He was a failure in the eyes of others...'

'Not in mine,' I began to say, but Karen was not brooking any interruptions.

'Men find that hard to live with; men like Guy find it impossible.'

'Well I suppose this voyage might have confronted him with the discovery that he was not quite what he supposed. You alluded to his...'

'His impotence?' Karen laughed. 'No, that wasn't it; besides he wasn't impotent and he would have accepted the attrition of age, for he was a dignified man.'

'Then what?'

'Someone was a mirror to him; someone showed him what he truly was.'

'The girl he had an affair with?'

'Yes, of course.' She looked at me with a dismissive expression of surprise at my stupidity.

Hurt and confused I shook my head. It was all conjecture, of course, but on that passage north it was of Guy that we talked incessantly, recalling him again and again as one memory triggered off another. In the end his presence seemed very real and *Rolissa* so thoroughly haunted by his ghost that I once produced three sets of cutlery for dinner. Karen saw what I had done and met my eyes as I too realized my foolishness, but neither of us mentioned it out loud in case we broke the spell.

It was Karen who first sighted the peaks of West Spitsbergen, sharp summits which had inspired Willem Barents, a Dutchman from the flat landscape of The Netherlands, to name his spiky discovery a land of needle mountains. This is something of an exaggeration, but the effect of the jagged range was spectacular enough to engender an intense excitement.

Karen called me half an hour early to see this magnificent sight. It was a morning of high Arctic splendour, for the sky had cleared and the sea lay like a deep-blue carpet to the eastern horizon where the rim of the world rolled away. The actual coastline was not then in sight and the mountains hung above this delimit of our surface visibility. Dark where the gradient was too steep to support snow, the summits were sundered by the awesome and contrasting glitter of glaciers. Under all plain sail and on the port tack, *Rolissa*, with a lazily graceful roll, bore down upon this distant and almost ethereal prospect.

'Nifelheim...' I breathed, as struck with the magic of the sight as Karen, the hairs on the back of my neck standing up in primitive reaction.

'What?'

'Nifelheim,' I repeated, my voice oddly low. 'The old Norse name for a remote and mythical stronghold inhabited by ice-giants which lay far in the polar north. The Vikings touched here in their longships long before Barents arrived in 1596. *They* called it Svalbard – the cold coast – in contrast to their own chilly but foggy and unfrozen countries. When the ownership of the islands was settled on Norway in the twenties, the Norskies reverted to the ancient Viking name.' I felt Karen's eyes on me and confronted her. 'What?'

She smiled. 'You're really moved, aren't you?'

'Sorry, I was lecturing...'

'That's not what I said, Nick.'

'OK,' I nodded, my voice catching. I felt foolishly exposed. 'Yes,' I admitted, 'I'm

182

moved.'

She gave me a strange look that would, I thought, have melted half the glaciers hanging amazingly above that distant horizon. 'Dear Nicky,' she said; then, leaning suddenly across the cockpit, she kissed me briefly upon the lips, retreating immediately and throwing up a diverting barrier of words before I could recover from my amazement. 'Sorry I woke you early, but I just wanted to share the sight with you.'

'I'm bloody glad you did' – swearing to recover my manhood and immediately feeling silly for having done so.

By the afternoon we had the coast properly in sight and met the first icebergs, small jagged or eccentrically shaped chunks which varied from pale blue to strong green, shot through with streaks of red or rich brown moraine, for this was not sea ice, but glacier ice. By the evening, as the sun bore north-west and dipped towards mountains now almost surrounding us, we entered the wide mouth of Ice Fiord. The smooth water was dotted with these small bergs – 'bergy-bits' they are called – which had broken off the glaciers that enter the sea at the head of the score or so of lesser fiords which are tributary to the great inlet of the Ice Fiord. Just as I had thought of the trolls in connection with the Lofoten Islands, I kept thinking of the only possible inhabitants of this fantastic landscape as being ice-giants. Anything else seemed inconceivable. I do not wish to bore you with endless descriptions of the scenery, even supposing I was capable of avoiding a tedious repetition, but there was – is – something so utterly otherworldly about the majesty and magnificence of Barents' needle mountains and their glacial slopes that they constantly overawe and confound, stirring an endless wonder all the more overwhelming to an old cynic like me who has seen a great deal of the world. I knew Karen was similarly moved, for her silence was of the bitten-lip sort, and her eyes were bright with wonderment – and on that repetition I had better cease, except to impress upon you the strangely fairy-tale impression it left upon our souls.

As the 'night' drew on and the sun swung further to the north, we fought the strong current which flows seawards out of the great fiord, passing the distant sight of the Russian mining settlement at Coal Bay. Under engine and with the Norwegian courtesy ensign flapping bravely from the starboard crosstree we approached the 'capital' and seat of the Norwegian administration, Longyearbyen, a name which, given that 'by' means town, might have some romantic connection with the midnight sun but which in fact refers to the name of an American mining engineer, John Longyear, who came hither to exploit the coal deposits now being worked to un-economic exhaustion by the Russians.

About two o'clock in the morning we secured alongside the concrete jetty at
184

Longyearbyen. Near us lay a Norwegian coastguard corvette and the rumble of its generators reminded us that we were not actually in fairyland, but still resided in the troubled world of men – and women too. Particularly of women.

Once in sight of Spitsbergen we had broken the watches by consent and so we slept until we woke of our own accord, with no hint of the actual time from the sunlight flooding into the cabin. It turned out to be about one o'clock in the afternoon and as we roused ourselves, Karen reminded me we should report our arrival formally to the office of the Governor, or Susselman.

'We don't want to hang around here,' Karen said, hitching a pair of jeans up and peering out at the rather desolate, semi-industrialized landscape of Longyearbyen. 'This is *not* what we came up here for.'

'It would be sensible to give the engine a good looking over, though,' I said. 'I thought the overheat alarm pipped twice just as we berthed.'

'Oh, that's probably only some muck in the intake.'

'Let's hope that's all it was. Anyway, I'd like to change the oil...'

'OK, then give me your passport and I'll go up to what passes for a town hereabouts and do the business with the Susselman's office. I must have a cup of tea, though, and I expect if we talk nicely to the officers on the coastguard boat we can get a shower.'

And so, half an hour later, I was bottom-up over the engine and Karen had departed with the yacht's papers, having discovered that the coastguard 'boat' was on the point of departure for Tromsø.

I have a love–hate relationship with engines and am ridiculously nervous whenever I am compelled to touch them. Beyond the simple routine of checking oil and water, I am in foreign territory. I am convinced engines have a wilful life of their own and that the best way to treat them, providing they are working, is to ignore them. That way they constantly seek your approval by working hard. The minute they have your attention they go wrong and let you down. At the moment *Rolissa*'s was playing up, having sounded that brief pipping alarm, indicating an overheating of the cooling water. As it had only occurred in the last seconds of our manoeuvre alongside, I had switched the engine off and turned in. Now, running the engine to warm the oil up, I found it cut in again, and this time it was a full-blown alarm.

It did not take a moment to find the intake clear, whereupon, with a mounting irritation, I unscrewed the plate from the water-circulating pump, only to find that the neoprene vanes had broken up. I had a replacement, but extracting the fragments from the adjacent pipework took long enough to frazzle my equanimity and I scarcely acknowledged Karen's presence when she returned. To be fair, by this time I had finished work on the pump and was completing the operation of changing the oil, sucking it up from the sump and managing to get the old oil everywhere.

'You're not listening, are you?' she said, with a hint of truculence in her voice.

I grunted and then, as the pump sucked air, I straightened up. 'No, I'm not listening, though I think you said we had a problem...'

'Yes, we have.'

I set the container full of the old oil down on the cabin sole and tried to clean my hands up. 'What's wrong with the paperwork?' I asked testily. I had gone through the extravagant process of paying the British Registrar enough money to effect the transfer of ownership of a medium-sized merchant ship when I had acquired the boat from Guy's estate. This turned out to be difficult enough, since the previous owner could not simply sign the bill of sale, and it had had to be part of the process of probate. Now to have a polar bureaucrat challenge...

'There's nothing wrong with the paperwork.'

'Well, what's wrong then?'

'We haven't got a gun.'

'We haven't got *what*?'

'A gun.'

'A gun.'

'Yes, a gun.'

'Why would we want...?' I recalled the fuss Guy had made about taking a gun – not a piddling twelve-bore but a pump-action thing that fired heavy slugs. Since Guy was part of

the gun culture that was so alien to me, I had
never given the matter a moment's thought.

'Polar bears,' said Karen.

'Polar bears?'

'I do wish you wouldn't keep repeating
what I say. Apparently they're a very real
danger. He won't let us proceed north without one.'

'So I've got to buy a gun?'

'He recommended a Husqvana.'

'That's a bloody sewing machine.'

'They also make guns, apparently. He said
he would arrange for one to be available at
Ny Ålesund and that you might pay for the
hire by credit card.'

'That's jolly good of him.'

'It means we will have to stop there.'

'Why can't we pick up one here?'

'This is the base for the tourists who go
snow-catting and they're all required.' Karen
adopted a rather serious tone. 'He did emphasize the animals are dangerous, very
dangerous, and that although they're pro-
tected from casual hunters after their coats,
you should not mess about with them. They
will outrun you and kill you if they are
hungry. You must shoot to kill. The only thing
is that you must report any such death here at
Longyearbyen on our return.'

I digested this news. 'We may not come
back this way; in fact, it's highly unlikely.'

'I don't know, Nick.' She shrugged dismissively. 'Let's just go along with it, shall we?
It's not worth making waves. You can put it

on my credit card if you like.'

'No, it's all right.'

'Not a very girlie thing to do, eh?' she said, looking at me from under a curtain of hair as she sorted out *Rolissa*'s documentation and held it out to me.

'Not necessary either,' I replied, indicating the state of my hands and the chart table.

'When are we sailing?'

'You don't want a run ashore then?'

'No. You wouldn't if you'd seen the place. One-horse town. Hotel, bar, lot of young people and coal tips. Besides, go ashore and the next thing is you're inviting people back. You know what the Norwegians are like once there's drink around.'

I looked at the engine. 'Right, we'll run this up, have something to eat and then go.'

'Good. I've bought some reindeer steaks.'

We gave the engine a good test on our way north to Ny Ålesund, for the wind had dropped to a flat calm and we motored the whole way. Our passage lay by way of Foreland Sound, which lies inside the island erroneously named Prince Charles Foreland by Barents, who failed to realize it was an island. In fact, a shallow patch almost forms an isthmus linking it with West Spitsbergen and, since the whole tectonic plate upon which Svalbard lies is still rising from the relief of the ice shelf, which in prehistoric times lay heavily upon it, it may well become a peninsula in due course.

Once clear of this, our course swung more to the east of north, rounded the headland of Kvadehuken and entered the King's Fiord. There was much more ice here, nasty little bergy-bits some of which were true growlers – old bergs which lay awash and required a careful lookout to be kept to avoid running into them. The ice had broken away from the King's glacier that lay some miles away amid spectacular scenery at the head of the fiord. We saw none of this, running alongside the jetty at Ny Ålesund. On the outside of this lay the *Orion*, a small expedition ship flying the Swedish flag; inside was a large, very substantial Colin Archer type cutter. These handsome double-ended boats look ideal for ice navigation, though in fact they were not built with this purpose in mind but as replications of the famous Norwegian sailing rescue boats stationed along Norway's rugged and much islanded coast. There was no one aboard her, though she was unlocked and I could see, nesting in a rack against the inside of her cabin, two heavy-duty pump-action shotguns.

'We have to go to the North Pole Hotel for the gun,' Karen explained, and we both walked up to the village of brightly painted wooden huts, past the notice announcing that at just under seventy-nine degrees of northerly latitude Ny Ålesund was the world's most northerly village. Neither of us mentioned this as we walked past. I think we both felt this pandering to the tick-box instincts of tourists was not part of our quest – a thing to be eschewed and ignored. We could not ignore the touristic atmosphere of the hotel, nor the party from *Orion*, who might not have seen themselves as tourists but were seduced by the soft luxury of the seal pelts on sale there. Marketed under licensed control, the white skins of the babies were heartbreakingly seductive, so that even Karen was ambivalent about them, fondling them as I made enquiries about a gun.

They were expecting me, and in no time at all I was in possession of a heavy and ugly monster, along with fifty rounds of ammunition: 'Some small shot cartridges to frighten him off and some heavy shells to kill him if he doesn't go avay,' the young man said in excellent English, referring to a particular polar bear which, he seemed to suggest, was out there in the icy fastnesses waiting for me. The young man looked at me as I gingerly picked up the cartridges and peered at them. 'You loads one shot and two slugs. One for the warning, which won't kill him; then if he does not run avay you kill him. Quick. Bang! Bang!' He paused. 'You haf fired a gun before, yes?'

I shook my head. 'No,' I confessed.

'OK.' The young man drew out the syllables, as if struggling with credibility.

'I shall be all right,' I said.

'I hope so,' he said, shaking his head.

Putting on the boots we had shed at the entrance, Karen and I walked back to *Rolissa*.

She had bought a pelt and was troubled by the morality of her purchase, so I sought to reassure her. We were so deep in this futile examination of her ethical dilemma that we were almost back at the boat before we noticed the tall man on the quay. A few stragglers were making their way aboard *Orion* so we had reached the ladder down to the yacht before we realized the tall man was nothing to do with the Swedish expedition ship.

'You are from the British yacht?' he asked, surprising both of us. He was obviously Norwegian, a huge man of about forty, with a handsome, sunburnt head topped with white-blond hair. Karen was clearly taken with him, for she answered first, with an irritatingly girlish eagerness, 'Yes, we are.'

'Where is your skipper? I have called him but he did not come.'

'I am the skipper,' I said combatively, missing the allusion to Guy, which only dawned on me as he said with a frown, '*You* are the skipper?' in a tone which suggested disbelief. I was clearly scoring well in the insincerity stakes with the natives today.

Karen, already alert and engaged with the stranger, quickly asked, 'Did you know Guy?'

'Yes, Guy Edvardes, was it not? We became quite friends when he was here last year. He said he would come back, I thought...' He looked at me suspiciously.

'He was unable to come,' Karen said quickly, 'and we were due to sail with him, so Nick here is acting as skipper this year.' She began to descend the ladder and threw her head back so that she looked up at the towering figure with the bright smile that made her so extraordinarily beautiful. 'Please come aboard and have a drink.' Then she looked at me and said, 'Nick, will you pass my parcel down when I'm on deck?'

Her face had gone suddenly hard, and my feelings of extreme jealousy as she flirted with the blond giant were for an instant sharpened by this contrast, until I recalled her observation about Norwegians and drink at Longyearbyen. She had 'ploy' stamped across her forehead.

'Yes,' I said expansively, waving him ahead of me down the ladder. 'Come aboard and welcome.'

In the saloon he folded himself into the starboard settee and waited for the bottle and glasses.

'I'm Nick,' I said; 'whisky or gin?'

'You have some Scotch?'

'Certainly. Laphroaig or Glenmorangie...'

He shrugged his enormous shoulders as though confused by twin gates to paradise. 'I'll have a small Morangie, Nick darling,' Karen said, and I could have kissed her for the endearment.

'Right.' I busied myself as Karen sat opposite him and introduced herself: 'I'm Karen.'

'I'm Lars – Lars Foyn.'

'D'you live here?' Karen asked.

'Yes.'

'Just in the summer?'

193

'No, all the year round. I work for the Norwegian government here.'

'Your English is perfect,' she said, adding 'Skol,' as I handed out the tumblers.

'Water, Lars?'

'Er, is it good manners to say yes?' he said with a charming smile.

Karen shrugged. 'Not at all, if you don't want it.'

'Then I am fine, thank you.'

'Guy would have loved to see you again, I'm sure.'

'He was quite a guy ... Oh, I'm sorry...' Lars flushed at his unintended pun. 'My English is not so good.'

We laughed and Karen reassured him that the joke was an old one. This and the whisky relaxed us all.

'He was certainly quite a guy all right,' Karen said, a hint of manufactured reminiscence in her tone.

'You were close to him?'

'Oh, yes,' I put in; 'didn't he mention us?'

'He mentioned that he and his wife were not too happy.'

'Oh yes,' said Karen without batting an eyelid; 'that was rather sad, wasn't it, Nick? All his friends were so upset. We liked them both, you know; that makes it very difficult.'

'Oh sure. We have a lot of trouble with that sort of thing here. It is a small community, you know.'

Karen topped up first her own and then Lars's glass. 'Nick?' She held the bottle out to me. I was still standing, leaning against the galley. 'Especially in the winter, I should think,' Karen prompted with a broad and knowing smile, 'all that darkness.' We laughed, a loud, slightly louche adult laugh. 'You were lucky Guy was here in the summer,' Karen added.

'Oh he did all right.'

Karen looked at me. 'There, what did I tell you? You men always bounce straight back.' Then she smiled at Foyn again. 'I suppose he upset one of your local husbands,' she said.

Foyn laughed, a deep throated roar, so that I was reminded of the fabled Viking ice-giants. 'Oh no, he was much fascinated with the German boat ... You did not hear? No, of course, he probably would not tell you...' Infuriatingly, Foyn continued to laugh and then sipped his whisky.

'He certainly didn't,' Karen said brusquely, and I thought she was going to close the subject, but she was far more clever. 'And I'm not certain you should tell us either.'

'No?' Foyn looked from one to another of us. My jaw must have been hanging open, for he smiled at me and said, 'Nick would like to know about the boat full of German women, I think.'

'Sure,' I said, pretending to sip whisky, a drink I am not fond of. I thought Karen was also toying with hers. 'A boat full of German women seems to offer a good story. Where were the German men?'

Foyn gave a huge shrug and allowed Karen

to top up his glass again. 'They were on some sort of expedition – the women, I mean. They wanted to circumnavigate Svalbard. They arrived the day after Guy in this boat.' He patted the saloon table. 'Tied up alongside of him and he complained about the noise, so they invited him aboard. There were five of them, two about thirty, maybe about thirty-five, and three a little younger. One of the older women was a very experienced yachts-woman, the other was a doctor – no, a psychiatrist or some sort of scientist, I think. Two of the three younger ones were students under her and the third was a nurse. Guy wanted the nurse...' Foyn laughed again. 'He was much too old for her and the yachts-woman was very jealous. She wanted Guy. I think the psychiatrist was a lesbian, but then I am not certain. There was some dancing up at the hotel and...'

'Don't tell me, Guy made a scene,' Karen said.

'No, no. The yachtswoman made trouble because Guy would only dance with the nurse; then the psychiatrist made some trou-ble because the yachtswoman was making a fuss over a man and – well, it is not unusual up here...' Foyn's story trailed off as he laughed again. 'They had been at sea too long. All those women in a small boat. Crazy.'

'Not as crazy as Guy being on his own,' Karen said, and I could see where she was trying to nudge Foyn.

'That's true, but they left a couple of days

later. The place was quite dull after that.'

'And Guy stayed behind?' I asked.

'Not for long. He had some work to do on the boat and then he left. I did not see them again.' Foyn sipped his whisky, emptying his glass and putting his hand over it when Karen offered him some more. Shaking his head, he added, almost as an afterthought, 'Not until this year. And then you come too, but without Guy.' He laughed and pointedly added, looking at me, 'But *you* cannot cheat on your wife. *You* have brought her with you and' – he stood up and, bending beneath *Rolissa*'s cabin roof, bowed from the waist – 'you would be foolish to deceive so beautiful a lady.'

'Why thank you, kind sir,' Karen said, smiling radiantly. 'But tell me: d'you mean the German yacht is here again?'

Foyn withdrew from behind the table. 'Yes, they told me that the ice was too bad to get up to the Sjuøane – sorry, the Seven Islands, which are all named after Englishmen – and they could not get to the east. I think they will be unlucky this year too.'

'Are they the same women?'

'Not quite but almost, yes, though the psychiatrist is not with them. There is an older woman in charge. Helga, I think her name is. Not as good-looking as before; but the nurse is back. I saw her but not to speak to. They were not here long. They heard the ice was clear in the Hinlopen Strait and decided not to waste time here at Ny Ålesund. It was bad in the strait last year.'

'What is the name of the boat?' Karen asked. 'Perhaps we might see them.'

'It would be fascinating, eh?' Foyn said, smiling. He looked at me, 'The curiosity of the female.' I echoed his chauvinism with a little relish and laughed too. 'The boat is called *Adler*, Eagle; so very German, don't you think? We still don't love them in my country.'

'We drive their cars,' I said. 'You are too young to remember the Occupation, though.'

'Sure, but my father lost his eldest brother in the war and some of us have long memories.'

'That isn't fair on the Germans today, though,' Karen said, 'especially the women.'

'No, but then life is not very fair, eh?' Foyn ducked his head and made his way past me, turning when he got to the doghouse. 'Thank you very much for the drink. It was very kind. How long are you staying in Ny Ålesund?'

'We only came in for a gun. We forgot to bring a gun with us and the Susselman's office in Longyearbyen—'

'Yes, I heard. That is how I knew your boat was to come here. I remembered the name *Rolissa*.'

'You liked Guy, then?' Karen asked. I detected the slight catch in her voice – an effect of the whisky, I hoped.

'Yes, he was a nice man.' Then he laughed again: 'She was very pretty, that nurse.'

'Are you married, Lars?' she asked.

'Female curiosity,' I added, thinking Karen

198

a little importunate.

'Yes, I am married and I have five daughters. As you say' – he laughed again, a loud and genial roar – 'all that darkness!' He turned to go then said to me, 'Be careful of the polar bears. They are dangerous, particularly if they are hungry. The young males are the worst. They lack experience and do not understand the risks. Goodbye. Nice to have met you.'

And with that he left us. For a moment we stared at each other, both aware that he was not yet far away, and then Karen let her breath out in a sibilant hiss. 'God, I've drunk too much too fast and on an empty stomach.'

'Not much liking the stuff, I hardly touched mine,' I said, setting the half-full glass down on the saloon table. 'What do you think?'

She shook her head. 'I had not expected to find the trail so hot...'

'Nor me,' I agreed.

'Now we know who he was *following*.'

'Of course! I had forgotten that other word in the log.'

'And what an insult Guy would find a boatload of women up here, amid the land of your bloody ice-giants!'

Karen's observation was absolutely correct, and it would have been all the more confusing when lust triggered off his chase of a ridiculously young woman.

'I suppose,' she went on, 'it was the desire to reduce the achievement of a female crew that led him to pursue one of them, as much as to prove to himself he could still pull.'

I remember grunting a sort of agreement, though I was not so sure myself. 'I take it, then, we are going to do our own following...' 'Yes, of course. And what are we waiting for? You've got your gun.'

The Tenth Part

The encounter with Foyn was fortuitous, but less fantastic than might at first appear. The permanent community on Svalbard was tiny and concentrated at Longyearbyen and Ny Ålesund. A few scientific out-stations existed elsewhere during the brief Arctic summer and the Russians were evident in some strength at Barentsburg, but the apparently civilized cruising area of Spitsbergen's west coast was an illusion. Frank Worsley, a former apprentice with the New Zealand Shipping Company, Shackleton's magnificent navigator and a personal hero of mine, had brought a brigantine up here in the nineteen-twenties. He wrote of this coast that it was 'a pleasant place in the summer time', and this pleasaunce has since that time attracted a number of large cruise ships. We saw one coming out of Magdalena Fiord as we left astern on the starboard quarter the tremendous spectacle of dark and serried peaks intercut with the blue-white glitter of the Seven Glaciers. Magdalena Fiord was one of 'the sights' of West Spitsbergen, situated just south of the cluster of islands on the north-west corner of the main island. Among these were 'the

Norways', and within the sounds running between them lay the site of Smeerenburg, the Dutch whaling settlement of the seventeenth century. Once inhabited by hundreds of whales, these sounds now formed the most northerly destination of the cruise ships. Beyond lay the unpredictable Arctic Ocean and the cruise liners left it to the occasional expedition, the scientists and the odd yacht owner with a perverse taste for personal discomfort, probable hardship and possible disaster. One emerged from the straits between the fractured rocks of the Norway Islands about sixty nautical miles, or one degree of latitude, to the north of Ny Ålesund. The north coast of West Spitsbergen stretched away to the eastwards, the mountains, invaded by fiords, receding into the distance and the land falling to a peninsular plain, the 'Reinsdyrflya'. Twenty miles beyond its terminal point lay the low circular atoll of Moffen. From the Norway Islands to Moffen lay some fifty miles of possibly iced-up sea. From Moffen, on a course of about north-east and at a distance of roughly one hundred miles, were the Sjuøane. The Seven Islands marked the most northerly group of the Svalbard Archipelago, situated to the north of the second-largest island, known as North-East Land. The summits of this remote and mysterious place are covered with a permanent ice cap which runs off its southern coast in an immense ice cliff over 200 kilometres in length, entirely obscuring the actual, geological coastline.

The Seven Islands are named after the members of a British Admiralty expedition sent hither in 1773. It was led by Commodore John Constantine Phipps, afterwards Lord Mulgrave, and Phippsøya is the chief island, but the location is famous as being the location in which the young Horatio Nelson had his encounter with a polar bear. In fact a chasm separated Nelson from the animal, but the image of the diminutive and youthful proto-hero are part of the iconography of his later apotheosis, and along with islands named after Parry and Ross there is also a Nelsonøya. I mention all this only because it touches me, not that Nelson himself came here, but that he, and Phipps, and others, like the whaling captain William Scoresby (whose name may also be found on an island forty miles south of Sjuøane), are part of the now largely forgotten maritime history of my country. In Nelson's day the area was solid with ice and the expedition's ships, *Racehorse* and *Carcass*, failing to find a north-east passage to the Pacific, had some difficulty extricating themselves from its embrace.

To circumnavigate Svalbard, one has to pass the Seven Islands and, intending to stop briefly at Moffen, this was now our objective. Clearing the dark and forbidding slopes of the Norways, which culminated in a rock split as by the sword blade of an ice-giant and known as Cloven Cliff, we emerged upon a sea bearing a deceptively placid appearance.

The breeze filled in from the north-north-west, a seductively easy sail. *Rolissa,* under main, mizen and jib, seemed to delight in the challenge and, as the engine fell silent – and I in equal silence thanked the demons that resided within it for their acceptance of my newly fitted circulating pump – she quickly picked up a couple of extra knots.

The only ice in sight was a faint gleam along the coast. To the north and ahead of us, to the east-north-east, the Arctic Ocean was clear.

'How far ahead of us d'you think the *Adler* is?' Karen asked.

I shrugged. We had both forgotten to ask Foyn when she had left, though both had come away from our chance meeting with the impression that it had not been many days earlier. Nevertheless this serious omission annoyed both of us, once we realized we had made it. 'I simply don't know,' I replied. 'The trouble is that things are so uncertain up here. If she is held up by ice, we might catch her up; on the other hand, we might run into ice ourselves, in which case we will fall behind and – well, you know...'

'We *will* catch her up,' Karen said with passionate conviction.

'Well we do know that they have got to pass between the North Cape of North-East Land and the Seven Islands. They then have to pass across the bay named after Nordenskiöld...' I could not pronounce the native names, nor that of the Norwegian explorer for that matter. 'If we really crack on, I'd say we've a pretty good chance of catching them up, particularly if they stop and go ashore for specimens, or whatever they're doing on the scientific front.'

'You don't think they're just hell-bent on the circumnavigation?'

'How the hell do I know, Karen? I presume they'll want to stop...'

'What? Because they're all girlies?' she asked with a dangerously accusing edge to her voice.

'Oh, for God's sake...' I began, then broke off, about to lose my temper. We had been running an intermittently bickering argument about the distant German yacht ever since Foyn's revelations. I had been walking on eggshells, a model of conciliation and understanding, as Karen privately dealt with the additional details of Guy's infidelity; but at that moment I had had enough. 'Look, Karen, we are doing all we can to catch them up. Maybe we'll get another stroke of luck; in the meantime let's hope the *fräuleins* have all gone shopping.'

It barely qualified as a joke, but it was enough to make her laugh. 'I'm sorry. I've been beastly to you.'

'Yes, you have.'

'It's my watch and time you turned in.'

I went below. With the Refleks stove on, *Rolissa*'s accommodation was warm enough, but I could not sleep. The constant daylight was oddly invigorating and although I turned

205

in and tried to cover my face, my brain went on turning over the same old facts and suppositions. I was already forming an image of the *Adler* and her company.

How the discovery of the German yacht and her all-girl crew would have stung Guy! I could imagine his fury, his feeling that women had no place up here – or if they did, it was to warm the huddled wooden houses at Longyearbyen and Ny Ålesund, not force a passage through the ice in the wake of Phipps and Nelson. That was a male preserve! And then there was the culminating irony that these were not Brits, but *German* women. Guy must have been incandescent with rage and yet I could see him wanting to remain in company with the Germans, not just because he was chasing tail, but because he would want to be on hand to prove himself better. He must have seemed like an old fool, a huffing and puffing elderly exaggeration of the male adolescent show-off!

Now I could understand the charge in that single word *following*, for it seemed so bound up with the complexities of Guy's situation. It implied both subordination and a perverse, misapplied and wholly redundant chivalry; a pathetic and rather prurient eagerness and a loss of rationality. Had Guy been off his head? Had he taken risks? Is that how he had hurt his hand?

That was it! Of course!

I was about to leap out of bed and tell Karen, but then I thought better of it. We had

206

done nothing else since leaving Ny Ålesund but occupy ourselves in fruitless hours of conjecture. Besides, it was only more of the same. I had no evidence to support my thesis and I was fed up with attaching a mystical value to any conjecture that metamorphosed into 'conviction'. It was all so bloody silly. The main thing upon which I felt I should now focus was that, for whatever reason, we were aboard our little wooden world on the broad and heartless bosom of the Arctic Ocean. Notwithstanding the presence somewhere ahead of us of a crew of German women, we were surrounded by a hostile environment which, benign enough at the moment, could turn nasty in an instant. The wind was fair for our purpose, but it was out of the north, blowing down from the pole only six hundred miles away. As it grew in strength, the air temperature fell, although at the moment in the sunshine it was quite warm. Ominously, the surrounding sea was only a few degrees above freezing. No, I had better things to think of than the psychological state of the dead lover of the woman I was smitten with. This *was*, after all, my self-chosen chance to prove my professional worth as a seaman and it ought to take precedence. We too would attempt to complete a circumnavigation of Svalbard and if, as seemed entirely possible, it would also be accomplished by a group of German women, it would not bother me personally. Our achievement would not be diminished by theirs. Besides, they outnumbered us, so ours would be marginally the greater success.

And with that consoling conceit I fell asleep.

I was badly shaken a few hours later when I nearly lost *Rolissa* on the island of Moffen. Having talked about this odd and lonely spot on and off for weeks, to stumble over it in such an inexpert manner was totally reprehensible. Mercifully, I extricated us from disaster with a whisker to spare. What made it worse, however, was my personal culpability: I had been dozing.

The ketch had been on a broad reach since we cleared the Norways and was bowling along at seven to eight knots in a moderate sea. Her motion had been easy. Away to the south lay the distant and receding peaks of West Spitsbergen, including one improbably named Ben Nevis. The Reindeers' Plain lay below the horizon, which was sharp as a knife edge for the full three hundred and sixty degrees round about us. Our course converged at a shallow angle with the 80th parallel, a few miles beyond which lay Moffen. Today this strange island, which nowhere rises more than a couple of metres above sea level, is a ring surrounding a lagoon. In earlier times it was possible to anchor a ship within the encirclement of the low reef but, perhaps due to the inexorable rise of the Arctic tectonic plate, this is no longer the case. There is a beacon marked upon the chart on the southernmost curve of the island and to the south-west an exposed anchorage in three and a half fathoms, or six and a half metres. I had planned to celebrate crossing the 80th parallel, shortly after which we should have sighted Moffen; but I fell asleep.

Although the wind made a lee shore of Moffen, it also cast a low swell down upon the shallows and humped up a ground swell of slightly greater steepness than farther out. Thus *Rolissa*'s motion underwent a subtle change as she ran blithely down upon the reef under her auto-steering. Perhaps my inherent seaman's instinct was alerted to this change; perhaps my conditioned reflexes kicked in at this point; but that is not what I remember.

What actually woke me I recall vividly, for the snort and stink of the bull walrus was no more than a few feet from me. We were mutually surprised, for he was an old bull, all whiskers and tusks, and had been asleep on the water. These monstrous beasts possess the ability to inflate the fatty tissues of their necks with a reservoir of air. With this natural lifebelt they are able to rest, though why this old devil chose to do so a matter of a stone's throw off an island where his mates had hauled out, I have no idea. I heard them grunting, a great heap of males, separated from their females who, once delivered of their annual progeny, leave their brutish male partners for fear of them damaging the young.

I was on my feet in an instant. Ahead of me

the swell broke on the low shore, which seemed to my distracted eye to stretch from the port to the starboard beam and disappear under the very bow of *Rolissa*.

'Shit!' I swore, dislocating the auto-steering and throwing all my weight on to the tiller as if that would ensure *Rolissa* answered her helm the faster. I felt the stern lift under an incoming swell, felt her hull respond by scending forward with increased speed, taking us to our doom all the quicker. I thought of Karen, I thought of the liferaft, and I thought of the appalling situation we would be in in a matter of seconds.

The moment of hiatus was truly terrifying. Things may happen comparatively slowly at sea, but there is an inevitable quality about them. I was too late to avert disaster and I paid for my inattention in those attenuated seconds as I closed my eyes, waiting for the keel to strike and for the masts to come down round my cowering head. I made to shout a warning to Karen asleep in the cabin, but all that came from my throat was an ineffectual croak: terror had robbed me of moisture in my mouth.

Then *Rolissa* rolled with a heart-stopping lurch so that I thought she had struck. This was where it was all going to end, on this remote stony beach, my incompetence witnessed by a herd of male walrus. Pride, my self-conceit, had brought us to this pass. I could almost hear Guy, in an extremity of rage, roaring at me, 'You stupid cunt!'

Suddenly there was a terrific shudder, the ketch almost fell on her port beam and I knew it was all up with us. I croaked Karen's name again, with what effect I was not certain, for in the next instant I realized that we were not ashore, but *Rolissa* had gybed and was even then picking up speed with the wind coming over the *starboard* quarter. I steadied the helm and straightened up. With my heart hammering painfully in my chest I looked ahead: it was clear; I looked aloft: the masts still stood, the sails drew hard; I looked to port: the dull red-brown of a stony beach raced past us. A stone's throw away the backs of curling breakers humped up and broke with a roar upon the unforgiving beach, above which a hundred walruses regarded me with suspicious curiosity. Hauled out and cooling themselves, they were pink in the sunshine, their white tusks and grey bristles quite clear to my amazed and sheepish gaze as *Rolissa* tore past them. I looked at the echo-sounder which, unusually – for the Admiralty Chart 2751 had not been metricated – had been set to read in fathoms. It was reading 0.8, 0.9...

'Christ! Oh, Christ!'

I leaned again on the helm and hove on the main sheet as I dragged *Rolissa*'s racing bow west of south until I had 1, 2 ... 5 on the echo-sounder and finally took proper stock of my position. We were no more than a mile north of the southern extremity of Moffen, and I could see the iron beacon erected by the

211

Norwegian coastguard, but it might have been a mile too far. As I brought *Rolissa* slowly back to a course to clear the island, Karen appeared in the doghouse. Her hair was tousled and as she clung on with one hand, she rubbed the sleep out of her eyes.

'What's going on? I felt her roll right over and then...' She looked aloft and then at me. 'We've gybed.'

'Look over to port,' I said, my mouth still dry, adrenaline flooding my system and my heart still doing a dido in my ribcage. 'I bloody nearly wrecked her,' I confessed.

'What happened?'

'Simple: I fell asleep.'

'Nick!'

'I'm sorry.'

She shook her head. 'It's all right. I know you wouldn't do it on purpose.' A silence fell between us.

After a little I repeated, 'I'm sorry,' adding, 'I let you down badly. I feel a complete fool...'

She was shaking her head. 'How on earth did Guy manage?' she asked in so low a voice that I thought she was talking to herself.

'It's this bloody endless daylight.' I tried to mitigate my conduct by explanation. 'You feel so energized. I couldn't sleep for a long time when I went below and then up here, bang, I went out like a light.'

'We'll both have to watch that,' she said, and I blessed her for her lack of recrimination. 'I'll make some coffee.' And she went below and put the kettle on while I altered

212

course round the south point of Moffen and afterwards hauled *Rolissa* up for the Seven Islands.

After this near-catastrophe there seemed little point in a celebration of having crossed the 80th parallel. Nevertheless I felt the need for some mood-changing ritual and tucked away instead the notion of toasting our furthest north, wherever that happened to be. Wrapping up, Karen joined me in the cockpit and we sipped our coffee. I reset *Rolissa* on auto-steering and sat opposite her, on the starboard seat facing out to port. After a few minutes, during which I had become aware that she was staring out to starboard over my shoulder, she asked, 'What's that?'

I turned, half-expecting to see a yacht flying the German ensign; instead I saw a grey-white fuzz along the horizon. Clear of it were some white dots.

'Ice,' I said. 'Iceblink in the distance, with some bergs visible near the horizon.'

'Between us and the land.'

'Yes.'

Possessed of a single thought we both looked ahead. The iceblink seemed not to extend further than about four points on the starboard bow. 'It's built up against the land,' I said, reaching into the doghouse for the chart and drawing it out so that Karen could see it. 'See, the coast is entered by this deep fiord.' My finger traced the sixty-mile length of Wide Fiord, which almost split West Spitsbergen in two. 'I guess the northerly winds have driven the pack from all around here into Wide Fiord and Wood Fiord next door.' I pointed to another massive fissure in the coastline that ran deep into the interior behind the flat peninsula of Reinsdyrflya.

'I feel like a little fly up here, amid all this ... this immensity,' she said, waving her hand about her in a gesture I found full of a terrible pathos.

'I think the Arctic gets you like this,' I said with unintentional sententiousness.

But this time she did not notice my pomposity, or chose to ignore it, for she replied in a low voice, 'It's terrifyingly wondrous.'

Then I remember thinking that the BBC had lost an extraordinary person, and that this was not Karen of the business suit and the briefcase.

An hour or two later we saw the dark shadow of a distant headland, the extremity of Ny Friesland, a peninsula which formed the eastern side of the Wide Fiord. Then, a few hours after the iceblink had appeared ahead, a glance at the chart convinced me that the pack had drifted up against LÅgøya, or Low Island, and the coast of North-East Land, which lay beyond it. I hauled *Rolissa*'s course a point further to the north, away from the coast, reasoning that if the ice lay against the land, we might have to pass north of the Seven Islands, rather than cut inside them. All depended upon the northerly wind continuing as, so far, it had.

Apart from my dangerous gybe, we had hardly touched the sails since we cleared the Norways. Indeed, had it not been for that moment of deep humiliation and near-disaster off Moffen, I should have remembered the passage as one of the easiest and most enjoyable of my life. Those inclined to a belief in Providence will explain my fright as not simply well deserved, but fortuitous, for I was thereafter tuned to a new and nervous sense of my surroundings. Only in port did I afterwards sleep deeply; I had reached the mature stage of my profession. Despite the fact that I commanded a small and insignificant craft with a crew of only one other human soul, I thereby removed myself into the lonely existence of a fully fledged commander. It took a while for this altered state to dawn upon me, but now I understood the foibles and apparent eccentricities of all the masters I had ever sailed with. I know all this does sound pompous, but such things are very real to those who understand.

It was just as well the incident off Moffen acted upon me in the way it did, for the cushy, halcyon days of our cruise were behind us. Not that we knew it at the time, of course, for our difficulties increased slowly to start with. Halfway between Moffen and the Seven Islands, somewhere with Low Island roughly upon our starboard beam, we began to run into ice. This was not the bergy-bits of the fiords, but broken pack, some of it hummocked and old, a fusion of rafted ice and

215

small bergs, all melted and then refrozen over several winters. Elsewhere the generally flat plates of fragmented pack began to appear. There was plenty of open water and it was only necessary to make minor adjustments to the course to avoid them. There was no sense that we were in any danger of being beset. Rather, we thought, it was merely a function of our proximity to the land and our increasing latitude, for we were now passing the eighty-and-a-half mark, a mere 570 miles from the North Pole.

But the sunshine was intermittent, and from time to time clouds bore down upon us, bringing a sleeting rain which soon turned to snow, and the vicious sting of squalls. Still, they were not bad, and it was often only necessary to ease the sheets and spill wind, for we could see brighter weather coming and there was no compulsion to reef. Of course, mindful of keeping healthy reserves of fuel, we kept *Rolissa* under sail and the boat performed well. She was always easy on the helm and responded quickly, as I had had cause to be grateful for off Moffen.

Apart from the gulls and skuas, we saw a few seals and more walrus, and one imperfect sighting of a small school of white beluga. There were no polar bears. It was, though, growing much colder. Despite turning up the stove and working up a fug, condensation began to form inside the boat. If working on deck, our hands quickly became cold and we had long since learned to work in gloves.

Fortunately our modern layers of thermal garments topped with heavy-duty weatherproof 'oilskins' kept our bodies pretty warm. I was personally delighted with such technological benefits, whatever Guy might have thought of them. But ominously, once or twice I now began to feel seriously chilled, recalling lectures about core temperatures, frostbite and the difference between hypo- and hyperthermia. Ears and noses proved highly susceptible to the colder, damper air.

This slight deterioration in our conditions began, imperceptibly, to drain morale, so there was no sense of triumph when we sighted the Seven Islands and the passage to the south of them seemed free of any seriously obstructing ice. We made an effort to keep our calorie intake up, maintaining our ritual of a hot meal every day and supplementing this with hot snacks, soup and beverages throughout the day. Our biggest problem was the fact that there were only two of us; in the colder weather, this made every chore an effort and such tasks occupied every waking moment. Our brief moments of social relaxation seemed all too brief.

But I must not make too much of all this, for it was to get worse once we had passed the Seven Islands. The decision to press on, which proved all but fatal, was driven solely by the fact that we had not yet overtaken the *Adler*. I remember saying to Karen that perhaps they had gone through the Hinlopen Strait between West Spitsbergen and North-

East Land despite the ice, and that it was unlikely that circumstances had conspired against them a second time...

'No, that's nonsense' – she cut me off – 'they will have pressed on.' I looked at her for a moment and then relented. There was no obvious reason why we could not press on to the eastwards, for the wind still remained obligingly in the north, though with less west on it, giving us a fine reach. Without stopping at the Seven Islands, though we scoured the coast through the glasses, we passed the North Cape of North-East Land (a lack of imagination seems to have infected the first explorers who named these remote places), hauled round to due east and headed across Nordenskiöld Bay, heading for Cape Platen. Twice now *Rolissa* hit growlers. The collisions appeared to do little damage, though they might have done had the wind been stronger at the time. As a result I suggested we should heave to and rest periodically, for I was convinced from my own experience, that Karen had dozed off, or at the very least, failed to keep a sharp enough lookout.

'No. If we heave to,' Karen argued with incontrovertible logic, 'the *Adler* will get further and further ahead.'

I think by this time I had given up entertaining any serious hope of actually catching up with the German yacht. I was, however, now upon my mettle and intent upon completing a circumnavigation of the whole of Svalbard. We had, after all, come a bloody long way, and the thing seemed in my grasp – an achievable goal, unlike the so-called 'quest' after Guy. Looking back, I suppose I had begun to lose touch with reality, but then I might argue that without such an objective no explorer would have achieved anything. Not that I considered myself an explorer, though I was most certainly engaged in a private expedition; but I felt a sense of culmination in my life, as though after the wreckage of my marriage and career, this crazy voyage might give me something to look back on in the way of attainment. Most of all, I felt a tremendous urge to press on. I suppress the phrase *at any price*, though it lurked at the back of my mind. I am not quite sure what a psychiatrist would make of all this: on the one hand lay the difficulties – the problems of ice, the limitations of a two-person crew; while on the other lay the oddly seductive path of glory – albeit a very small and personal glory, but a glory none-theless.

And the bottom line was that we were so far in that there was no other way out.

The Eleventh Part

With continual daylight I have no clear recollection of the passage of the days. Somehow reference to the log book fails to bring recall, and while logic tells me the period was actually quite short, the cold, the increasing damp and the routine of watch-and-watch soon blurs such things. Since this is no dry recounting of a log, and other demands had begun to make our own log as cursory and uninteresting as Guy's had been boring and deficient, I have to rely upon memory. I had turned in as Karen took over for the crossing of Nordenskiöldbukta, Nordenskiöld Bay. As I lay in my bunk and waited for sleep to claim me, I heard the occasional scrape of brash ice down the side of *Rolissa*. It was nothing bad, just old slushy stuff that barely scraped our enamel paint, but it kept me awake and I fell into a half-dream, remembering stories of the loss of ships in the ice, of the splendid cadet-training barques *København* and *Admiral Karpfanger*, the first owned by the Danish East Asiatic Company and the second by the German Hamburg–Amerika Line, both of which had vanished from the face of the earth, thought to have been sunk by icebergs. These disasters had happened on the far side of the world, but we might sink up here and no one would be any the wiser. It had never occurred to me to ask Foyn – or anyone else, for that matter – to keep a watching brief on us. In fact, we had decided this whole matter was 'private' and now this lack of sensible precaution gnawed at me. The truth was that in this remote corner of the Svalbard Archipelago we were totally isolated.

I must have dropped off, for the next thing I knew was that something had changed. *Rolissa* was trembling faintly and the rapid click of a jib sheet winch and the flog of sails told me Karen was altering course. At first I attributed my sense of alarm to my earlier semiconscious anxieties, but then the ketch heeled alarmingly and I heard Karen swear as she struggled in the cockpit. A second later she bawled out: 'Nick! Nick! I need a hand!'

I was out in the cockpit in an instant. She was struggling with the starboard jib sheet, having caught a riding turn and jammed the thing. It was the lee sheet and, with the sail full of wind, it was bearing a terrific load.

'I need to take a roll in the jib!' she said as *Rolissa*, over-pressed, dipped her lee rail right under.

I grabbed the jib sheet from her and shouted, 'Ease the main sheet!'

She spun round and struggled with the jamming cleat. A second later the boom was leaping about as the sail thundered above our heads. I succeeded in getting the rider off the winch, easing the sheet. Karen threw her weight on the furling line. As the jib decreased in size *Rolissa* began to luff and I eased the main sheet. Only then did I take a look about me, wondering if we should put a reef in, or if this was a squall that would soon pass. What I saw alarmed me: to starboard loomed the mighty shoulder of Cape Platen, its dark summit hidden under a veil of cloud; to port lay the pack, an almost unbroken line that pressed down upon us; a quick look ahead showed more ice in our track.

'What the...?'

I looked at the compass. We were heading almost due south. Karen straightened up from belaying the jib furling line.

'I can't help it, Nick; the wind jumped right round to the east and all this ice was suddenly crowding down upon us.'

'Shit!' I felt a great hole in my gut and wanted to be sick. Fear, pure and visceral gripped me. Almost as a reflex I grasped the chart table and bent over the chart, hoping Karen had not seen my moment of weakness. I stared down until the chart swam back into focus, though I had already guessed what had happened. The veering wind had compelled Karen to alter course to starboard, an alteration augmented by the sudden westward movement of the ice. Fortunately for us we had doubled Cape Platen and the Dove Fiord lay open to us, but this in truth only offered us a breather, for we would as surely be beset in the Dove Fiord as anywhere along this unforgiving, iron-bound coast.

222

In pants and T-shirt I was shuddering as the cold gripped me. Karen saw my predicament. 'Get below and get some proper clothes on!' she commanded. 'You're losing body heat!'

I had the sense to do what I was told quickly, piling on my thermal layers as fast as my numb hands could answer. I also had the sense to shout up to Karen, 'Ease sheets, Karen. Spill wind; we don't want to be driven too far down into this fiord!'

'Aye, aye,' she called back and a moment later, as I drew on the second pair of long johns, I almost fell as *Rolissa*'s heel eased. The ketch began to tremble again as the sails flogged, spilling wind. Concentrating on the business of dragging on my gear gave me the respite I needed to master my terror. I emerged into the cockpit booted and spurred, determined to fight back. I had wanted to be an expedition leader and fate was taking me at my word. Curiously, I now felt imbued with a sense of exhilaration.

'This isn't a squall,' Karen said.

'No, so let's get two reefs in the main. You take the helm.'

I was up by the mast in a jiffy as Karen luffed. My hands were still cold and I fumbled with the topping lift and the main halliard, but once they were dealt with I got both reefs down without too much trouble. Hauling the halliard tight again proved more difficult, but I did it in the end and let fly the topping lift again. I would leave the mizen for the time being. As I came after down the

223

starboard side I glanced out on the beam. A bay had opened up. On the heights above it a glacier hung, a magnificent and mighty sight. It was then the crazy thought entered my head that this was a great place to die and that to die in such a manner, overwhelmed by the tremendous forces of nature, would be a splendid death, infinitely preferable to being slowly murdered by a tumour. Or blowing my brains out.

Oh, I was bedazzled by the stupendous magic of the high Arctic!

Karen had swung *Rolissa* back off the wind again and it was time to consider how the hell we were going to get through the ice to windward. Swinging into the cockpit I dived below, opened the seacock and went to the engine starting panel. I counted to thirty after switching on the coils then turned the key another half-turn. For a long moment the starter motor turned the big diesel ineffectually before it fired. When it did, I set the engine in gear at 1,200 rpm then clambered back into the cockpit. I felt warm again.

Grabbing the binoculars from their teak box I swept the ice edge as a grunting Karen leaned on the tiller and bore away. A bergy-bit suddenly swam into my field of view and passed astern of us. Having studied the ice I took stock of our exact position in relation to the closer ice round and through which Karen was nursing *Rolissa*.

My heart was beating, partly from exertion, partly from apprehension. The pack ice, though extensive, proved not to be as bad as it looked. There were leads through it, and while the wind would be pressing it down on the western coast of the Dove Fiord, we had perhaps a short opportunity to escape being trapped.

'OK, let's close-haul her on the port tack. The engine'll help; we should be able to find a way through.'

'There's a gap there,' Karen said with courageous optimism.

'Go for it,' I said, adjusting the sheets.

Rolissa swung and drove at the gap. On her port bow a hummocked floe of rafted ice grew larger; to starboard lay a group of flat floes. As we closed the distance, I noticed with alarm that a ground swell rose and fell, causing the ice to move vertically, the low edges of the flat floes slopping and scooping up water. At the same time the invasion of so much ice was cooling the sea temperature so that the surface of the water was taking on a viscid appearance, evidence that it too was not far from freezing. Should such a thing happen around about us, we should be beset.

The sky had clouded over and the ice was no longer reflecting the light. Gone were the bright hues and the sparkling brilliants. Now the ice was grey or white, uncompromising in its forbidding presence – pallid at the presumption of our intrusion, indifferent to our fate.

I have difficulty recalling the succeeding hours, except to say that they were composed of relentless endeavour. I cannot claim that they even approached the effort made by the polar heroes as they man-hauled their sledges over frozen pack ice, for it did not go on and on over hundreds of miles, but it gave us a tiny insight into the stamina and determination of Nansen, Shackleton and their ilk. These considerations did not occupy us at the time, for then we were concentrating upon the bare business of our own survival, which seemed serious enough. *Rolissa* was tacked countless times; she was run off before the wind, then hauled about again. She was turned short-round in a score of dead-ends and she brushed and bumped a hundred floes, half a dozen times with breathtaking impact. At first I winced, as though the wound was inflicted upon my person, but then I found that risks had to be taken, and on two occasions we stormed through closing leads, the narrowing gap shutting behind us while floes ground at our very chain plates as we drove through. Anxiety waned as a furious determination to succeed forced us onwards.

Karen was magnificent. She stayed on the helm as I stood and conned, calling out instructions, then ducking down to handle the jib sheets and check our course. From time to time I caught sight of her face, and it was the face of a primitive, teeth bared and breath hissing as she hove the tiller this way and that, stooping to adjust the engine revs on my instruction. Not once did she quail or query and, as the time passed, we gained confidence. We owed much to the engine and its internal demons must have been as scared as we were, for it was the engine that forced *Rolissa*'s head round when we tacked with insufficient way to stay properly, and it was the engine that, full astern, dragged us from numerous collisions. Mercifully the ice was old and when it did encounter the propeller it was churned to mush. Thus, in a succession of thrashing tacks, of false starts, of backing and filling, and of wild dashes, we slowly worked our way to the north-east. Not that it was all dramatic action. Several times we found ourselves stuck, the lead astern closing and no apparent escape ahead of us. *Rolissa* was no ice-breaker. Once, confronted with this hopeless situation, we let fly the sheets, took the engine out of gear and put the kettle on. As we ate a wedge of bread pudding and tinned tomato soup in a gloomy silence surrounded by the creak and grind of ice that moved upon the dark and undulating ocean, a small opening appeared on our beam. As we watched the swell make the ice dip and roll, the slow separation of a larger, leeward floe opened an increasing gap. The windward floe being lower was thus less susceptible to the influence of the strong wind. An instant later, with no word exchanged between us, we were driving through the opening. We were fortunate, for beyond lay an expanse of clear water, which led roughly east for about a mile, after which we found another lead and gained some northing.

In this slow and testing manner, often going in a direction contrary to our wish, we crossed the wide mouth of the Dove Fiord. On the eastern side the entrance culminated in two islands, North and South Repøya. The strait between the mainland and South Repøya was choked with ice, but the gap between the two islands seemed clearer. North Repøya is a lower island and we were deceived. For two hours we were compelled to turn to the west-north-west and go with the drifting pack before, almost halfway back across the mouth of the Dove Fiord, we reached clearer water to the north.

Although dotted with ice, this was open pack, clear enough for us to shut off the engine and sail, though we kept the reefs and rolls in main and jib, for the wind was a cutting Force 6 and now bore upon it an occasional snow flurry, causing a periodic lack of visibility. To our astonishment we found we had been fourteen and a half hours in the ice. That I do remember, partly because it astonished us, but also because the clock said two and it took me some time to work out whether it was two in the morning or two in the afternoon, a decision complicated by the sun being masked by a thickening overcast.

'You must be exhausted,' I said to Karen, and she nodded mutely. 'Turn in,' I said. 'I'm going to heave her to and doze in the cockpit. If we do bump into anything, it shouldn't be catastrophic.' Without a word Karen went below, exhaustion in every movement of her body. Despite my advantage in the matter of sleep I too was completely knackered so, having backed the jib and lashed the helm a-lee, I hunkered down in the cockpit. I felt a huge satisfaction in our achievement and, strangely, drifted into sleep feeling light-headedly happy. *Rolissa*, held in thrall, curtseyed to the oncoming waves, alternately edging up into the wind, and then falling off again. If she hit any floes I was oblivious to it.

I woke stiff and fuzzy. For a long moment I hung between sleep and full consciousness, unwilling to abandon the release sleep gave from the cares of our situation. But my chilled and aching muscles dragged me back into the real world and I noticed immediately that *Rolissa*'s motion had changed. Standing up and stretching, I found her lying alongside a large floe. Roughly flat, its edges were wet and slushy, its surface irregular, evidence that within it was old ice, an accumulation of many years of the freezing-and-melting cycle, the surface worn by the attrition of high winds and the ice spicules that, in time, eroded any jagged eminence. I wondered idly how many years it had been circulating round the Pole, for the polar circulation, established beyond doubt by Nansen, tended to push ice down, past Svalbard, where it met the warmer waters of the North Atlantic drift, then melted and sank. This produced what was called the North Atlantic conveyor, whose corollary was the warm flow of water north-eastwards out of the Gulf of Mexico thousands upon thousands of miles away. I was just about to go and consult the GPS to determine our position when I noticed something more immediately pressing. Across the floe and quite unmistakable to my untutored eye, was a series of huge paw-prints – the mark of the polar, or ice bear.

Slowly I stared about, for the spoor came towards us. Of course it might have been days old, except that a fine snow was falling and it had scarcely dusted the crisp imprints. Then I saw her: a female, by the black teats that swung beneath the loose yellow-white fur of her belly and the solitary cub that stood indifferent at her tail. She was staring at us from a floe astern and had clearly swum between the two ice islets shortly before *Rolissa* had gently come alongside the larger.

It seemed that we stared at each other for a long time. I suppose my sudden movement, or perhaps my smell (I have read since that *Ursus maritimus* has an acute sense of smell capable of detecting a human six or seven miles away), made her regard me as she emerged out of the water. I have no idea whether she was hungry, though I suspect not, for the open water must have been productive of seals and we had seen several whilst working through the ice. At all events, she did not approach. After a while, as my heart hammered and I wondered whether to go below for the gun, she turned full circle so that her nose nudged the cub at her rump, and the two walked away, dropping into the water on the far side of the floe. I watched their heads as they swam powerfully away from me until they were lost in the snowy gloom.

Fearful that they might not be alone, for I then knew absolutely nothing about the habits of such animals, I gingerly worked *Rolissa* off the floe until we were making way again. The wind had dropped a little and had veered more into the east, so it became important that I got a fix. Setting a course and connecting up the self-steering gear, I let the wind drive the ketch on the best course I could achieve, something close to north-east, thinking to tack to the south later.

Below, the condensation was bad and I found myself dripping all over the chart. This is annoying, for charts are expensive and a single cruise can reduce the things to a stained and sodden mess. I found that we were within twenty miles of the rather grandly named King Charles XII Land, a small island named after the famous Swedish king which, upon its discovery had consisted of two islands. However, in the intervening period – not long in geological terms – the tectonic plate has risen so much that a saddle now linked the two peaks. Since deep water appeared to lie round about, though soundings were sparse in this area, I determined to continue on our present course before turning to the south-east. My reason was simply that I rather wanted to sight this oddly diminutive 'land', a reason engendered, I think, by a lazy reluctance to tack *Rolissa*. There might have been another, more seamanlike reason – that a group of islands lay to the south-east of us and it might be best to work to the east of them – but I cannot really claim that I gave this much thought. The truth was that, sleep or not, I was still dopey after the ordeal in the ice, and my head was contemplating the real risks entailed in encounters with polar bears. On the evidence of my recent experience I thought the warnings of Foyn and the young man at Ny Ålesund to be exaggerated.

I labour all this because the delay in turning to the south-east had a curious consequence. Looking back, it was a critical moment. I have described my own motives as honestly as I can; I am left to consider whether what occurred was pure coincidence or the workings of Providence. I still do not know, nor do I think I ever shall, for such things are among the great mysteries of life, the meanings of which are beyond our grasp. If I was a mystic, I should claim it proved the existence of God and that this revelation proved that God was good. But I am not a mystic, nor am I persuaded by any religious faith. My life experience suggests to me that beyond all human thought and comprehension lies a cosmic intelligence, and one might call this numen 'God' or anything else one cared to, but there is no link between this and our individual and petty existences. Hitherto I had thought that coincidence, luck and misfortune, were the arbitrary engines of human destiny and that their function was best explained – if that is the right word – by the Greek notion of three blind Fates who arbitrarily played around with our lives. However, confronted with the reality of our Arctic experience, I am less certain and, in consequence, remain confused.

The strange outcome of my lazy decision was not revealed immediately. Having cleared the floe and stood away to the north-east, I went below and, bobbing up and down, prepared a corned-beef stew, trusting in *Rolissa* to sail gently along at some four knots. Occasional attention was required to avoid floes and some small bergs, but there was no real danger, provided a lookout was kept – hence my bobbing up and down. I left Karen to sleep until she woke, at which point I lit the gas under the pressure cooker.

'Feeling better?' I asked when she finally emerged into the cockpit.

'Actually, I feel bloody awful and that's *after* I cleaned my teeth.'

I laughed, then yawned. 'The dinner's on. I hope you're hungry.'

'Mmm. Now you mention it, I'm starving.'

We ate and then, after I had put a fix down, we tacked *Rolissa*, laying her head about south-east. We had not sighted King Charles XII Land, but then the light snow kept the visibility down to about two or three miles.

On the chart I pointed out to Karen the cluster of islands that lay fine on the starboard bow. 'Keep an eye on our position. Both wind and current will set us down that way.'

She nodded her understanding and I went below to turn in.

For some hours we ghosted through a world circumscribed by a light snow and bounded by the loom of ice, occasionally enlivened by seals or walrus. The vicious white burgomeister gulls were much in evidence, once on an ice floe red with blood, tearing apart the remains of a harp seal left presumably by a satiated polar bear. We were approaching the island of Storøya, off the north-east corner of North-East Land, still dodging round loose pack ice, when the snow stopped and it began to clear. Above us a patch of blue sky broke through and I turned in again, leaving a more cheerful Karen anticipating a brightening in the weather.

I was deeply asleep when Karen gave a shout. 'Nick! Come quick!'

Out in the cockpit again in T-shirt and pants I stared south, where she was pointing. 'My God!' I was already reaching for the binoculars, but I didn't need them. The red parachute flare hung in the sky, descending out of the receding cloud bank. I took a bearing, put a fix down and gave Karen a course.

'It's a distress flare, isn't it?' Karen asked as I doubled back, jumped below and dragged my clothes on.

'Give me a moment,' I called out from the inside of a sweatshirt. 'I'll start the engine.'

A few moments later I was back on deck and had rolled the jib, lowered the main and was standing up on the cabin top staring through the glasses. An unarticulated question hung between us: was the flare from the *Adler*?

But what else could it be?

Under mizen and motor we headed down the bearing of the flare. Although it was brighter to the north and east, to the west and south the snow and clouds had yet to clear. Ahead of us the ice lay denser, an obvious accumulation about the island of Storøya. A second flare went up and I thought I could see the yellow of an oilskin or survival suit. A few moments later we were surrounded by ice, which soon became impenetrable. It was clear that the people sending up the flare were beset. Karen, once more on the helm, set the gear lever into neutral and eased *Rolissa* alongside a floe. With a scrunch the ketch came to rest and I fished a large red ensign out of the flag locker. Taking it forward to the burgee halliard, I ran it up to the main-masthead.

'They can obviously see us,' I said as I belayed the halliard; 'this might help.'

'It's the *Adler*, isn't it?'

'I think it must be,' I said, wondering what to do next, and staring round at the ice. 'I suppose one of us is going to have to cross this stuff...' I said uncertainly.

'We'll make her fast and go together,' Karen said.

I shook my head. 'No, I don't think that's a good idea.'

'If we're going to fall in, let's do it together, Nick...'

'No, Karen, that's silly. It's better if I go.' I looked round again and selected a more rugged floe which seemed to offer a better landing place. We moved *Rolissa* and I carried out a rope, belaying it to the anchor windlass handle, which I drove into the ice. I found it difficult walking on the ice, even in my sailing boots, but I had little choice. Returning to the ketch I picked up two bars of chocolate, the hand-bearing compass and the gun. Then I turned to Karen. 'Look,' I said, 'while you were asleep and we were in the ice, I saw a bear. You'd better keep a sharp lookout and if you see anything, go below and shut yourself in.' I was suddenly less confident about the harmlessness of the animals.

Karen stared at me. 'Why didn't you tell me?'

I shrugged. 'Didn't want to worry you. You'll do as I say, won't you?'

'Yes, of course.'

Then I bent and on impulse kissed her. 'Bye.' I swung myself over the rail and, slipping somewhat, began my trek over the ice.

It was farther than I had thought, though I might have guessed it would be, and the going was tough. The generally flat appearance of the ice at a distance was belied by the experience of crossing it. I formed the opinion that the pack had been stacked up by wind and current, for it was obviously rafted, and the mass of ice had been building up for some time – perhaps months, perhaps years. After a while I could see the darker rock of the island above the ice, and then, quite suddenly, there was a human coming towards me, progressing with equal awkwardness, muffled up in orange oilskins, their head covered in a yellow woolly hat. Having clambered up on to a low eminence, the figure stopped and watched me approach. I noticed the gun slung across the shoulder. When I was ten yards away, the stranger called out. I was not certain, but it appeared to be German.

'I'm very sorry,' I puffed, *'nein sprachen Deutsch...'*

'You are English?'

'And you are a young lady,' I riposted, feigning some surprise.

She nodded and I noticed beguiling but troubled blue eyes and wisps of dark-blonde hair emerging from beneath the woolly hat. 'I'm German ... We saw your mast ... Thank God you have come. Thank God.'

'Your English is good,' I said. 'What has happened to you?'

'Our yacht – we got caught in the ice. She is being...' She gestured compression with her mittened hands.

'Crushed?' I suggested.

'Yes, exactly – crushed.'

'And the name of your boat?'

'In German it is *Adler*; it means Eagle.'

So our quest was alive again. My heart was suddenly thumping. I stared over her shoulder, trying to sight the stricken boat, but all I could see was some dark spots on the ice. I looked at the young woman again and smiled. 'How many of you are there?'

'Three of us.' I wondered what had become of the other two and wondered if I had misunderstood Foyn. She seemed to be struggling with something, and then she said, her breath coming out of her in wreaths of steam, 'There were five of us, but it was bad, very bad. You have a gun.'

'Yes, in case of the bears.'

'They are very dangerous. Come.'

I followed her as she slithered down the floe and set off towards the black dots. 'What happened?' I called after her as I followed.

'We were stopped by the ice and Leni, our leader, went out on to the ice to see if she could find a way out. She did not take a gun and very quickly was found by an ice bear. We heard her scream and thought she had fallen into the sea – that had been our big worry. Kirsten ran after her. She came to the ice bear...' The young woman stopped and turned round so abruptly that I cannoned into her. I felt her breath on my cheek, damp and warm and sweet. I backed off. 'The bear was eating...'

It took me a moment to grasp what she was saying. I shook my head. 'I'm sorry...'

'Kirsten came almost back to our yacht but another bear caught her. I had a gun out but Greta took it from me to fire at the bear...' She heaved a shuddering sigh. 'Greta hit Kirsten and the bear dragged her away.'

'Dear God!'

The girl lowered her head and turned away. We resumed our march in silence and ten minutes later came to the scene. The dark dots were the remnant evidence of the story I had just been told: a dismasted yacht, a dark bloodstain which trailed away alongside great paw-prints, and the shredded remains of an anorak. I unslung my gun, for I could not imagine the bears were far away, the wrecked boat being a convenient source of food for them.

The *Adler* was about forty feet in length, a white, heavily built glass-reinforced-plastic boat. She was a wreck, having been nipped so that her topsides were already split, while her tall mast lay over her starboard side in a tangle of spars and stainless-steel wire rigging. In her cockpit sat another woman, an older woman whom I afterwards learned was Greta. She held a gun and stood up as we approached.

'That is Greta,' my guide said. 'She doesn't know English. The other girl speaks a little but you will have to speak through me. My name is Karina.'

'OK.' I forced a reassuring smile at Greta,

who looked grimly back at me, as though unsurprised by my sudden and fortuitous appearance. She seemed frozen into immobility, a consequence, perhaps, of having shot her shipmate. 'I don't think we have much time. I am worried about my own boat and yours is not going to last much longer.' I omitted saying that I was also suddenly bloody scared of polar bears. 'Get what you need and what we can carry, and let us go.'

My interpreter began to gabble at Greta. I recognized the repetition of the word *schnell*! There seemed to be a brief exchange of opposing views as the third survivor appeared in the cabin entrance. Greta finally moved her head to look at me, then asked something, which Karina translated.

'She asks how many crew you have and whether you can help to save some of our equipment.'

I shook my head. 'My crew consists of a friend – a girl friend. If I am to take the three of you, we will have little room, little space. If you have some food, perhaps I could carry that, though I think we have sufficient.'

Greta received this news with ill grace. Looking round me at the obvious signs of a lack of any organization or attempt at self-help, I formed the opinion that the strain of their desperation, exacerbated by their leader's horrible death and Greta's accidental killing of the would-be rescuer Kirsten, had poisoned the atmosphere and sapped morale.

It was, of course, impossible to condemn them for this, but it did not help my impatience to be off and to rejoin Karen. Somehow, although as prone as *Adler* to a similar fate, the distant *Rolissa* seemed a veritable oasis of safety compared with this unhappy, blighted wreck.

'Greta says will you keep a watch for bears?'

'Of course.'

I took my station in the cockpit. After a while the third girl, whose name turned out to be Margit, passed me up a knapsack full of tins of what I took to be food and I placed them and other bags on the seat beside me until they were ready to move. Even as I sat there, I felt the hull tremble and groan. Peering down into the cabin, which seemed a complete mess of clothes, oilskins, charts and other debris, I could see the dark swirl of water seeping into the *Adler*. There really was no time to be lost and my impatience grew. To steady my nerves I stared about me. Twice I thought I saw a bear, but a second glance proved my fears groundless. Then my eye was caught by the red, yellow and black ensign and I took it down and folded it up. Karina was the first to emerge and I handed it to her.

'Thank you,' she said solemnly, placing the German ensign in her pocket.

She was followed by Margit and then Greta emerged after passing out their bags. We clambered down on to the ice, shouldering our weapons, and I began to lead them back towards *Rolissa*. After a few minutes I could make out the big red ensign flying at her masthead, bright in a patch of sunshine.

I could scarcely contain my apprehension, for I was desperately worried lest the ketch had come loose from her imperfect mooring. Not that it would have really mattered with Karen on board, for she was more than capable of bringing *Rolissa* alongside again, but I had a deep-seated fear of being too far from my ship that went back many years.

The biggest threat to our survival came from the rear of our little column for, without warning, the report of a gun barked suddenly, echoing off the low slopes of the ice all about us. I spun round, clumsily unslinging my own weapon.

The bear had dropped to his fore-knees, a pathetic sight, and Greta fired again, whereupon the great animal slumped sideways. I saw Karina and Margit exchange glances and wondered about the internal tensions of this little group of women. Greta was scrutinizing the bear and Margit said something to her. I heard the name Kirsten mentioned, but apart from looking up, Greta said nothing and an instant later she walked past the younger women – and past me too – her face like stone. I was left for a moment, staring back at the dead bear and wondering if Greta had had her revenge and whether it was, as I supposed she had been trying to determine, the same animal that had savaged their

242

leader, Leni.

It suddenly occurred to me that I might look like a hero, but I had no real idea of how to shoot the gun I held in my hand and I quickly followed in the footsteps of the three Germans.

The shots had brought Karen out into the cockpit, and as I came up to *Rolissa*, I pulled the windlass handle and its rope out of the ice. Karen was already smilingly shepherding the Germans aboard, telling them in her own German, which was pretty good, that they should take their bags below and we would sort them all out after we had got under way.

'I'll start the engine,' I said, shoving myself into the doghouse as the women, with Karen's help, struggled to manoeuvre their traps down into the saloon. I leaned across the chart table to turn the heating coils on. As I did so, I became aware of Karina. She was standing next to me, waiting for her colleagues to sort themselves out and staring about her. Feeling my gaze upon her, she swung towards me. She was frowning.

'What is the name of this boat?' she asked, her voice low.

'*Rolissa*,' I replied, though I knew I was confirming what she had already guessed.

'*Mein Gott!*'

'Don't you want to know where Guy is?' I asked softly.

She stared at me for a long, penetrating moment. 'He is here?' she asked with a tone transparently incredulous.

'No, he is dead.'

'Ahhh...' She seemed to sigh, her face softening in relief. Then her expression grew sharp, intelligent, and her eyes quizzed mine. 'And who are you?' she asked, but her face was already turning to regard Karen waiting in the cockpit.

'I am...' I began, but Karina was no longer looking at me, but staring below where Karen was still helping the others.

'Karen...' I heard Karina breathe, and at that instant I recalled Guy's words about *K*. He had been referring not to Karen but to Karina. I gunned the starter and the engine obeyed me. It was just as well, for as I looked up again, my attention was caught by movement on the ice. I shouted a warning: 'Bears! Two of them!'

The Twelfth Part

Once again I find it difficult to describe in detail what happened in the next few hours. There seemed to be several priorities and these competing demands were shot through with human tensions and the merciless cold. I have to confess that a full appreciation of all these factors only occurred to me later, for I was myself deeply involved. First, there was an instinctive desire to escape from the prowling bears. Mercifully, this was soon accomplished, for they seemed not to like our engine, nor the disturbance caused by our propeller in the water. Then there was a degree of confusion aboard *Rolissa*. Suddenly our ordered little world of two fairly integrated personalities was disrupted by the influx of three complete strangers, only one of whom spoke anything like fluent English. The interior of the ketch was turned into an untidy muddle, anathema to me as a seaman at any time, but made apparently worse by the incomprehensible methods of women, even those imbued with Teutonic efficiency. This, of course, was rampantly unfair chauvinism, but it stung me at the time, for I was trying to negotiate the ever shifting pack

245

ice and *Rolissa*'s safe extraction from her enclosed predicament seemed to me to be paramount. The state of affairs reigning below struck me in my heightened state as a distracting affront. My own tension was made worse by indecision – not a thing I like or care much to admit to – for after escaping the bears I was worried about continuing our attempt to double the eastern coast of North-East Land. It seemed to me that to the southward the ice only got worse, but at that moment I was still in the process of assessing this, being in those first hours only confronted with mounting evidence that this might well prove to be the case. My state of mind was influenced by having witnessed the wreck of the *Adler* and by a proper appreciation of the enormity of my responsibilities. It was not helped by the parallel thought that ego had trapped me as I now feared the ice would. The truth was that our plight was desperate and my predicament was further complicated by our having become involved in a rescue mission.

As far as I knew at the time, Karen was herself preoccupied with dealing with our guests, though I was not really paying any attention to the babble of English and German as she sought an account of what had happened, as Karina either spoke on her own account or translated what Greta and Margit had to say. From time to time the German women's voices were raised, and there were angry and recriminatory sparks

flying between them. This frequently distracted me and I shot the odd glance below. They
had all taken their outer heavy-weather
clothes off and I saw for myself what had
attracted Guy to Karina, for she was spec-
tacularly beautiful in a sturdy, out-of-doors
way. Greta was in her late thirties or early
forties, a biologist of some distinction from
Hamburg, it turned out. She was a paler,
more classic blonde than Karina, regular-
featured and striking enough, but no beauty.
Nor were her looks helped by her recent
ordeal which, it appeared, had excited
vociferous animus from Margit. It transpired
that Margit had been a close friend of
Kirsten, and the two had been students of
Greta's. Judging by the dark, puckishly
intense face of Margit, the distance between
preceptor and pupil had been broken down
by the wrecking of the *Adler* and the death of
Kirsten; indeed, it seemed likely that the
strains of a voyage in the Arctic had long been
eroding it, though I do not know for sure.
Certainly the warm sanctuary of *Rolissa*'s oil-
heated saloon unravelled the last of the bonds
of respect between these two. Even above the
noise of the engine, the occasional explosion
of anger was quite clear to me and I
wondered how these people had been getting
on before disaster struck. I assumed that the
dead Leni must have been both a yachts-
woman and a leader of formidable skill.
Sadly, I never quite understood the ramifica-
tions attached to this all-woman, low-key

expedition to Svalbard, except that it had academic and environmental backing. It seemed to be intended as an annual event, originally established under the aegis of the dead Leni who had been, I *did* learn, a German yachtswoman of international reputation, better known to the cognoscenti as Helga Leni Reisenburg. There was about their interaction a hint of lesbian intent, but I sloughed off this latent whiff of Guy's paranoia. So what? I thought; even supposing it to be true, so bloody what...?

Besides, my overriding consideration remained the extrication of *Rolissa* from the ice. Many years earlier the two great axioms necessary to any seafarer had been rammed into my young brain – namely that the ship *always* comes first, and the ship is always your best lifebelt. In our situation the second was certainly true and to ensure it, the first had to take precedence over everything else. Perhaps I have mentioned this already, but I can recall it forcing itself into my consciousness as I shrugged off the intrusive dissension down below.

The situation in the saloon gradually simmered down, though the dynamics between the three Germans remained fraught with tension for some time to come. As the immediate pressure eased, however, I became aware of Karina's guarded attitude. I caught her several times peering about the boat, looking for God knows what, but seemingly seeking some touchstone of the past. To what

248

extent she felt Guy's ghost I then had no idea, nor for the time being did I have any chance of discussing the matter with Karen.

We were still under motor, making slow progress through the ice girdling Storøya, and it was around this time – when Greta finally fell asleep and Margit sat slumped in the saloon wrapped in a black mood – that I began to worry seriously about getting through the ice to the south. Karen had sensibly decided to cook a large stew, knowing a meal was what we all wanted and that the eating of it would bring a measure of civilization to all our disrupted existences. At first Karina seemed to hold back, but after a little she quietly began helping Karen and I noticed that she did not need to ask where, for instance, the potato-peeler was stowed.

Once the large pressure cooker was on the gas, Karen made some tea. Handing Karina a mug, she said something to the German girl, who nodded and, taking a look at Margit – now also fast asleep – began stowing her own gear away and sorting out the heavy clothing of her companions. She was obviously a helpful person – not surprising really, for she was the expedition's medic, a trained and demonstrably capable nurse. I only learned this later, of course, but her practicality was immediately obvious.

Karen came out into the cockpit with two mugs of tea and handed one to me. She sat down and caught my eye.

'What an afternoon,' she said, brushing a

curtain of hair back from her face. Beads of perspiration stood out on her forehead.

'Is it afternoon?' I responded, thanking her for the tea. 'I really have no idea.' I had lost all sense of time.

'Nor have I, to be honest,' remarked Karen with a short, humourless laugh. In fact it was about ten at night, but this only seemed to add to the unreal sense of dislocation that had transformed *Rolissa* in the last hours.

'They've had a pretty terrible time, by all accounts,' Karen said after sipping her tea. 'What state was their boat in?'

I told her, bringing *Rolissa* round to starboard.

'God, they're lucky we came along when we did.' A hummocked raft of mixed ice drew past, dotted with the black bodies of roosting auks. Our eyes met. 'It's weird, don't you think?'

I nodded. 'Bloody weird.'

'Bloody providential...'

'Whatever...' I hauled the tiller over again and slowed the engine as we negotiated another lead. We were approaching a sizeable berg, surrounded by broken and rafted floes of rotten ice.

Straightening up from the control lever, I dropped my voice and shot a glance below. I could see Karina's rump as she reached across the forward starboard saloon berth and stowed something away in the side locker. 'Karina, the one who helped you ... she was Guy's...'

'Yes, I know,' Karen said, rescuing me from the necessity of finding a noun suitable, in the circumstances, to describe the young woman. 'She knows the boat...'

'That's hardly surprising.'

'And she knows who you are.' I increased speed as we reached a patch of clear water.

'What?' Karen's voice was sharp and I looked at her. She looked very pale and I was suddenly alarmed. I said, 'You got too hot below and now you are cooling down; for God's sake don't chill down too much.'

'I'm all right,' she snapped again. Clearly, I thought, the presence of Karina aboard *Rolissa* and all that it meant to Karen had unsettled her, even though Karina's presence on board, fortuitous or not, was the successful culmination of our supposed 'quest'. I was going to change the subject, when Karen said in a low and slightly tremulous voice, evidence of her emotional state, 'I wonder how she knows me?'

'Guy must have talked about you.'

'D'you think so?'

'Of course. She's no fool; she'd have asked him about himself. Besides, didn't he have a photograph of you? Rather a nice mugshot, if I remember...'

'He'd have hidden that the instant she hove in sight, bonny lad,' Karen said, recovering herself.

'They're bound to have talked about you,' I said reassuringly, staring out at a barrier of ice.

'The similarity between our names is odd too,' she said, half to herself.

'Bizarre,' I responded, looking up at the wind vane and wondering if I should hoist the main.

'May I come up?' And the subject of our debate joined us in *Rolissa*'s cockpit and looked about her as she must have done when sitting beside Guy. I felt Karen bristle, sensing her reaction to the almost proprietorial air Karina seemed to adopt. It was more paranoia, of course.

We sat in silence for a while, awkward, all of us staring ahead; then Karina broke the brittle silence: 'The ice is bad.'

'Yes,' I replied as once more *Rolissa* entered the pack. I began again to heave this way and that on the tiller as the ketch dodged bergs and floes until the pressure cooker began to whistle and Karen suggested we stopped in the ice and all ate together. I considered her notion, for I could see her reasoning, but I began to argue the risk of being beset. At this point Karina rose and said, 'While you decide what to do, I'll get the food ready and wake Greta and Margit.'

'All right,' I finally agreed. 'Half an hour.' I looked below where Karina was busy. 'There's something else: the watch system,' I said rapidly. 'We need to sort something out quickly; we can tell them at dinner.'

'OK.'

'Karina in my watch with Margit; you have Greta in yours.'

'That's a bit unfair,' Karen said.

'I want to keep Greta separate from Margit. There's bad blood between them.'

'You're telling me,' Karen said with another short laugh.

'All right, you take the two younger girls if you want to and I'll have Greta.'

'No, I don't want Karina on watch with me.'

'That's what I thought,' I said with a hint of exasperation. 'And I didn't think you'd want just the two of us together, so I lumped Margit in as well.'

'OK,' she agreed, 'let's do it that way.' Karen lowered her voice and established the fact that Karina was busy before she leaned towards me. 'Don't go asking any damn-fool questions, Nick. I want ... I mean we've got to get the little minx on her own. I don't know how, but whatever you do,' Karen said with a sudden, insistent intensity, 'don't ask anything...'

I thought of the provocative remark I had already made to Karina following which she had learned Guy was dead. 'She's bound to ask me about Guy.'

'Tell her that he's dead.'

'I already have...'

I thought she might be annoyed at this, but she just said, 'You don't know much about it. He left you the boat; you were old friends; it was a tragedy. Say absolutely nothing about suicide.' She broke off as, below, Greta and Margit moved about and Karina poked her

253

head out of the doghouse.

'The dinner is ready.' She seemed withdrawn, yet strangely intent on being obliging, as if trying to be friendly. Or to indicate that she was already somehow involved with us personally. Did she know that Karen knew she and Guy had been lovers? I had no idea, nor how a younger woman confronts her lover's older partner, especially in the Arctic, after her life has just been saved. She bobbed below, where Greta was calling her.

'Say nothing about suicide, Nick,' Karen repeated, her hand on my arm. 'D'you understand?'

'All right, all right,' I replied, exasperated; 'you don't need to keep on about it. I'll do just as you ask.'

'You haven't mentioned it already, have you?'

'No, of course not. I only told her that Guy was dead. Reason unspecified.'

'All right.'

I slowed *Rolissa* and, as she ran her way off, let her ease into a flat, soft-edged floe. Then I followed Karen down into the warm saloon for our first meal together.

Rolissa's familiar saloon seemed suddenly alien to me. It had been taken over, requisitioned in the name of humanity. Not only did it look different, with the bright-coloured sweaters of our guests and the signs of personal effects stuffed hurriedly in the little nets and lockers which provided the only private stowage spaces, but it smelt strange,

254

full of the odour of women. I felt damnably out of place as I squeezed on to the settee, next to Karen. The bowls of stew were already steaming on the table and they were waiting for me. Margit seemed preoccupied, but Greta regarded me with what I can only describe as suspicion. I was certain that was what she felt, though I had not the slightest idea why. Was it that hint of man-hating lesbianism? No, not at all, but her emanation reminded me of something I had to do.

'Welcome aboard,' I began; 'I'm sorry it has had to happen like this...'

Greta said something to Karina, asking what I was saying, but Karina was already translating my words. As she did so, Margit looked up and stared at me.

'I'm also sorry that I have to ask you to do something I think you may find rather unpleasant.' They were all watching me now and I felt Karen's thigh tense against mine. She seemed to be warning me, but I ploughed on; this was something outside even the worldly Karen's experience. 'Look, I've been a captain in the British mercantile marine...' It was a white lie, but less complicated than the truth. Karina was stumbling a little.

'I don't understand mercantile mar...'

'Oh,' I said, 'sorry. Er ... the ... er ... *Handelsmarine*...' I have no idea where I learned the noun; I must have picked it up somewhere on my travels. Karina expressed her thanks, caught up with me and waited for me to go on.

'When somebody dies on a yacht or a ship,' I continued, 'and also when that yacht or ship is lost, it is necessary to make out a report. You can either make out individual reports...' I waited for Margit to insist on this, but she remained quiet and I resumed my little homily, '...or you can make one report and all sign it, one as principal – you, I suggest, Greta, with Margit and Karina signing as witnesses...'

Margit began to speak now, but I held up my hand. 'Please allow me to finish what I am bound to say to you.'

Karina did not translate, but snapped at Margit, who relapsed into sullen silence.

'Karina has explained to me what happened and it seems to have been a terrible tragedy. Such a thing could have happened to anyone out here in this wilderness. It is best that you simply say what took place, giving the date and the time, if you can remember. I will write what I found when I arrived at the wreck. There should be no trouble as a consequence.' I paused, then asked, 'I am assuming it was a dreadful accident. Is that so?'

I waited until Karina had finished. For a moment not one of them moved, then Karina said, 'Yes, it was an accident.'

'Greta?' I prompted.

'Yes. Very bad...'

'I understand. Margit?'

Margit was staring at the saloon table

256

before her. She did not look up but nodded, then brushed her hands across her eyes. *'Ja...'* 'Very well. We have both heard and understood what you said.' I thought this would allay any fears Greta might have entertained at our witnessing the obviously hostile and accusatory attitude of Margit towards her. I smiled with what I hoped was reassurance. 'We will inform the German vice-consul when we arrive at Hammerfest or Tromsø.

When Karina finished her translation Greta asked her something. 'Greta wishes to know your name, please.'

'Of course, I'm sorry; I should have introduced myself. My name is Nicholas, Nicholas Allen. Please call me Nick. And this is...' I paused and turned to Karen, but Karina was already translating and ignored Karen. She and I exchanged glances.

When Karina had finished, Greta leaned forward and said, 'Meester Allen – Nick – we are very please that you come to help us. It was very good. Thank...' She faltered.

'You,' Karina prompted; 'thank you.'

'Thank you,' Greta said, and I forgave her her suspicion and held out my hand. She took it; I saw tears in her eyes and noticed they were an unusually dark blue. She said something to Karina and Karina said, 'Greta would like us to share a little glass of schnapps.'

A bottle was produced and Karen produced some glasses. As this was going on, Margit came out of her shell sufficiently to hold out

257

her hand and, somewhat diffidently, said, 'Thank you.'

I smiled as reassuringly as I could. 'We have a long way to go and we must all work as a team.' Then I explained how Karen and I wanted the watch system to work. By invoking Karen's name I hoped to defuse any argument. It seemed to work. Greta appeared relieved, but whether this was because she was not on watch with Margit, or not on watch with me, I could not decide. I was about to go back on deck and get *Rolissa* under way again, when Greta said something to Karina.

'Greta wishes to know if you two are married?'

Karen gave a low laugh and shook her head. 'No, but we are very good friends.'

There was a moment's silence and then a ripple of polite laughter. I was not quite sure what they made of this revelation, but I did not really care. Perhaps, after all, Greta was a Sapphic and was content to be on watch with Karen. I was past caring. I was far more worried about how the hell I was going to get us all home.

About an hour later a clear patch of water opened to the westwards and, with a steady breeze from the north-east, I hoisted the main, unrolled the jib and shut off the engine. We needed to conserve fuel. Down below the meal had been cleared away and Karen's watch were turning in. I averted my eyes from the medley of thighs and set *Rolissa*'s helm up

258

to the self-steering. Karina and Margit joined me in the cockpit.

'I know you have been up here before,' I said to Karina, 'and I assume Margit can sail a boat.'

Karina nodded. She was guarded, but attentive. 'Yes, this is my third trip to the Arctic. It is Margit's first. She had not been on a boat before she joined *Adler* this summer.'

'But she is OK about keeping a lookout?'

'Oh, yes. Leni was good about training us.'

'OK, then why don't you take her round the deck and show her where everything is? – halliards, reefing lines, that sort of thing. You understand that, don't you? I'm sorry, my German is non-existent.' She looked at me, seeking, I think, some ulterior motive.

'You knew *Handelsmarine...*' she said, with a hint of accusation, as though I might be concealing a knowledge of her language.

'A fluke, I assure you,' I said with absolute candour, to which I simply added the comment, 'You've sailed aboard *Rolissa* before; can you remember where things are?'

'Yes. Of course.'

I left them to it and ducked below for a good look at the chart. Putting a fix down, I found that our present course would take us back towards the coast of North-East Land somewhere south and east of Cape Laura. To the south of the cape the Worsleybreen – the Worsley glacier – overspilled the actual coastline. The chart marked this limit with a

259

dotted line marked *Ice-cliff limit (1986)*, beneath which it said in brackets, *see caution No 1*. This in turn told me what I already knew: that the edge of the ice cliffs was *subject to frequent change*. At the time I took Worsley's familiar name as a good omen and traced the approximate glacial littoral as it ran away to the south-west, mile after mile of it, some seventy miles of ice cliff, until it reached its southernmost point at Cape Torrell. Even then it did not end, but trended first west and then to the north, giving way to rock faces and slopes too precipitous for ice or snow, but crowned inland by the permanent ice cap. This formed the east coast of the Hinlopen Strait between North-East Land and West Spitsbergen.

About thirty-five miles to the south-east of Cape Torrell lay a handful of islands, and between them ran the Erik Eriksen Strait.

I pondered what to do; should I go on and try to force our way south, hoping that the ice would keep moving to the south-west and that, somehow, we would get through? or should I go back, north-about, the way we had come? Conditions had been bad, but not impassable, and I thought that the sea had been free of ice well north of the Svalbard Archipelago. On the other hand, the wind had been easterly for some time now, pressing the pack south-westwards out of the Arctic wilderness, helped by the circumpolar current. The situation might be entirely different.

260

What finally persuaded me to go south was pride. It is never a good motive, still less as an impulse to a decision of such moment; but in truth, for all my boasting about my maritime experience, it was woefully inadequate then and there. What else was there, though to tip the balance one way or the other? What would *you* have done in the circumstances? You do not know now, any more than I did in that lonely moment. Perhaps, had it just been Karen and I that occupied the boat, I would not have felt so acutely the burden of command, but now with a boat-load of survivors – and female survivors at that – my bluff had been called. I thought I heard Guy chuckling at my elbow. 'Chivalry, Nick,' he seemed to whisper. 'Hold fast to the old ways, Nick. Show them they can't do without a *man*. Go down with your bloody colours flying.'

I shivered and I looked up. The sun had gone in and a grey opacity seemed to have veiled the sky. Forward, by the mainmast, Karina was pulling on the main halliard and indicating to Margit how it ran round the mast winch and belayed upon the cleat below. To port and starboard the jagged limits of the pack lay white and grey upon the dark lane of sea down which *Rolissa*, heeling a little with her booms guyed out to port, ran at six and a half knots. Somewhere ahead of us rose the ice cliff named after Worsley, marking the coast of Nifelheim, the land of mists, home of the ice-giants and perverse but insistent ghosts. Had I done what Guy had only dreamed of and saved a yacht full of women? Had it been in his raw eagerness that Guy had hurt his hand? I should have to ask Karina, when the moment was right. Then I recalled Karen's extorted moratorium on questions. Karina and Margit were right forward now. Karina was pointing out the anchor windlass to Margit; then they were coming aft and I was brought back to the present with a jerk.

Damn it, I thought in that moment of decision. I had wanted this challenge – this pseudo-captaincy – and in honour I could not shirk it.

If we were lucky, I thought, we should all take home the triumph of a circumnavigation of Svalbard. In the light of two deaths and a wrecked boat it was a small enough consolation for the Germans. As for Karen and me, well it might ... But that remained to be seen.

An hour after I handed over to Karen she called me.

'I'm sorry, Nick, but the wind's changing and it's getting foggy.'

Wearily I drew on my Polartec fleece and went on deck. It was noticeably colder. I looked at the anemometer and the wind-indicator. It read four or five knots, its direction fluky but generally from a westerly direction. The condensate accumulated round the entrance to the doghouse, formed by the heat from the Refleks heater and the breath of my enlarged crew, had frozen solid, and the air was filled with a pearly mist. I saw raw anxiety in Karen's eyes.

'I've just put a position on the chart,' she said and I stared at the sheet, trying to focus tired eyes and cudgel my brain into logical thought. The scale was lousy: 1 to 823,000 at latitude 77° 36' North. We lay in 79° 53' and on Mercator's projection the east–west distortion was formidable. Moreover, just off Worsley's glacier lay some tiny islands, the Frostøyane, and a cluster of dangerous reefs. I looked at the echo-sounder. It was set on fathoms, for Admiralty Chart 2751 still used the old measurement. We had 47 fathoms under the keel. I bent, started the engine and nodded to Karen, who put it in gear.

'Roll the jib and haul the main and mizen amidships.' She did as she was bid, Greta helping her. A rattle of tiny ice crystals fell from the surface of the sails as they flapped. I switched on the radar, thanking God that Guy had been a rich man, that dear old Jack had possessed a touch of genius and *Rolissa* was properly equipped. I waited impatiently for it to warm up.

I tried not to run it unless there was power directly available from the engine. Batteries, as far as I knew, were not keen on cold weather. Besides, I put little trust in the radar to spot low pack ice. It came in as sea-clutter, giving a similar response to sharp waves, though bergs and hummocks were visible. Once in the pack, because of the specular nature of the electronic response, I had not found the radar particularly helpful for negotiating ice, but now I was looking for something more solid, the Frostøyane and the ice cliffs of Worsley's glacier. Even if their present limit was different from that dotted edge of 1986 they ought to show up.

And there they were! Seven miles away the line of them ran obliquely across our heading indicator, swinging slightly, for our radar display was not stabilized. I looked into the cockpit. Greta had the helm and was steering a compass course.

'Auto-helm, Karen,' I said, hoping Greta would not take offence, but in these conditions the electronic gismo would steer much better than any human. It had no imagination and never let its micro-chip memory wander from the task in hand. The distant ice cliffs stopped wandering and I was about to congratulate myself, go below and put on more clothing when *Rolissa* ran full-tilt into what turned out to be a growler.

The whole ketch shuddered, the bow rode up and she heeled to starboard, making a horrible scrunching noise. Screams came from below as Margit and Karina were woken up, their previous experience adding to their shock. Mercifully the engine was only ticking over and we can have been doing no more than three or four knots, but it was enough to have shaken *Rolissa* badly.

Karen had already stopped the engine. 'Astern?' she queried. She must have remembered the parable I had told her about ships in collision, and how, when one drove her bow into the other, it had often saved the worst-wounded ship from foundering, if the other kept her offending bow plugging the hole. It took a cool head to think of that at such a moment, but Karen possessed such self-control, fearful that our withdrawal would result in our sinking.

'No!' I barked, grabbing the heavy-duty torch that we kept in the cockpit for just such emergencies. 'Shut the engine down.'

I turned and went below as silence fell upon the yacht. As I rushed forward I disregarded Margit and Karina, who peered from their bunks, Karina to port held from falling out by her lee cloth, Margit peering up at me from the low side, her face a mask of terror. I was in little better condition myself, for my heart was pounding with apprehension and a rising fear. Up in the forepeak I lifted the sole above the seacocks to the heads, lay down in the foetal position and peered below, poking the beam of the torch about. I expected to hear the rush of water and could hardly believe our luck when I could hear nothing.

Behind me, in the saloon, Margit's voice suddenly rose.

'Be quiet!' I roared, my voice edged with hypertension. I stared into *Rolissa*'s dark recesses, looking for the reflection on the bright run of water. I could see little beyond a pair of frames, a floor, and the nut and turned shank of the forward keel bolt. There was damp there, and perhaps a tiny trickle of water, but nothing untoward.

I lowered my head and shut my eyes for a moment, trying to still my heart and revive the saliva in my dry mouth. The sense of relief was immense and I felt the tension flow out of me. Possessed of the true superstition of the deep-water man, I reached down and patted the nearest floor. I think I also whispered something like 'Good girl'. Then I gathered myself, stood up and went back through the saloon.

'It's all right,' I reassured the two faces awaiting my return from the forepeak. 'We're not taking water. *Rolissa*'s fine.'

They both fell back, heads on to pillows.

Bracing herself against the list, Greta was in the galley putting tea into the pot. She looked up at me and I smiled. *'Danke,'* I said, nodding at the teapot.

'Ah...' She responded with a diffident half-smile.

I clambered out into the cockpit. Karen stood expectantly at the tiller, having disengaged the auto-helm. 'Thank God for her builders.'

'Something's happening,' she said, preoccupied.

I hauled myself on deck against the list and became immediately aware that the list was easing, slowly at first but then faster. I threw a look aloft, half-expecting that we could not have got away with so bad a collision without suffering *some* damage. The image of the

Adler, her mast and rigging lying over her side, rose unbidden in my mind, but *Rolissa*'s twin masts still stood, though they seemed to be describing a slow arc against the nacreous vapour about them.

'Nick!' I did not need to see where Karen was pointing, for the growler was rolling over, a mass of pale blue-grey ice emerging from the water and rearing up alongside us.

'Start the engine!' I bawled and struggled to get the boathook free of its lashing on the coach roof. Quite what I could achieve with it, I was not quite sure. When the engine roared into life and the clutch bit as Karen thrust the control lever to the astern position, I did manage an ineffectual poke at the smooth and glassy ice at shoulder height alongside me.

Rolissa came clear, swung upright, rolled the other way and steadied. Looking aft I saw more ice and shouted a warning to Karen, but she had already seen it and had the tiller over and the engine in neutral. I went forward and peered over the stainless-steel pulpit. We were not yet out of trouble. *Rolissa* had sternway but I knew that, once relieved of her weight, the growler, an almost totally submerged and eroded old berg which the ketch's mass had been rolling slowly over, would resume its previous equilibrium. As it did so, it could easily rise up again and strike us from below.

'Don't go ahead yet!' I shouted.

'I've got ice astern!'

'Don't go ahead!'

'For Christ's sake, Nick...!'

And then I think she realized what was happening, for the shoulder of the growler at which I had poked with my boathook subsided again. The rush of displaced water filled the air, sending a wave upon which *Rolissa* rose, and seemed to stay suspended as the portion of the berg immediately beneath the bow came up to its former position just under the surface. As it did so it scooped up the sea, which in turn poured off it, and I think it was this that carried *Rolissa* clear, for though there was a bump, it was not bad and, as the growler rocked and rolled, sending a circle of slapping waves outwards after the initial large displacement, it was clear we had floated free. It was also clear that we could hardly be blamed for not having seen the thing. It was very old ice, worn almost smooth over a succession of warm summers, and broke the surface only at one point, some yards off the port bow.

Nevertheless, we would have to keep a better lookout.

I straightened up and looked aft. 'Hard astarboard and slow ahead.'

Rolissa trembled, then the dark water began to chuckle under her bow as she gained headway. I looked ahead. There was a lead, of sorts, and I waved an indication to Karen at the tiller.

'I can see it,' she said.

I lingered for a moment, staring into the

mist. It was not yet dense enough to be fog, thank heavens. We had had a fortunate escape and I felt suddenly cold. I thought at first it was just reaction, the sensation of relief. Then I recalled the glacier edge of North-East Land. Of course! It was the proximity of the cold mass of ice that was producing this mist.

I hurried aft, swung into the doghouse and was about to stare at the radar when Greta held out a mug of steaming tea. 'Schnapps in,' she said, smiling.

I loathed spiked tea, but I expressed my thanks at her thoughtfulness.

In following the most open water, we drew closer and closer to the ice cliff. I had no real idea why the mass of the pack should lie a little offshore, if one can allude to a mass of ice as a 'shore', but it seemed to be the case. Instead of the flattish floes of the pack, generated in the open Arctic Ocean, the navigable channel seemed littered with irregular bergs of varying shapes. When I mentioned this to Karen, she said, 'They are calves from the glacier.'

'Yes, of course, I should have realized.'

'You've had other things on your mind.' She smiled and I could have kissed her. Instead I just smiled back.

'You ought to go below and turn in.'

I nodded, but although my eyes felt gritty from lack of rest, I was in no mood for sleep. The unseen presence of the ice cliff troubled me. On the radar it was only three miles away now. Back on autopilot I pointed it out to Karen, then I hunkered down in the cockpit, just in the warm airstream rising from the saloon heater. I must have dozed, for it seemed only a moment before Karen was shaking me.

'Nick darling, I hate to do this, but it's your watch.'

'Christ, I feel like shit,' I said.

'You smell a bit like it too,' she said, grinning down at me.

'Thank you,' I said, then Greta was handing me another cup of tea and Margit and Karina were emerging into the cockpit, doing up the heavy zippers of their oilskins to their chins and taking the steaming mugs Greta handed them. A moment later the three of us were left in the cockpit and the muffled sounds of laughter came from below, where Greta and Karen were stripping off prior to turning in.

Sipping the tea I found my eyes closing again. Untroubled by the sight of mist and ice, it occurred to me that I was in some kind of fantasist's paradise. Then Karina brought me back to reality.

'What happened?' she asked.

I made an effort to re-establish contact with the real world and explained, pausing while Karina translated for Margit's benefit. There was a brief exchange, then Karina said, 'Margit says we were very lucky.'

I stirred myself properly. 'Yes, and that's why we must keep a proper lookout for low ice, half-sunk in the water – ice we cannot see properly, that the radar cannot pick up and that may lie just below the surface.'

'You want someone up in the bow?'

'I think so. For twenty minutes at a time. I'll go first.'

There was method in my madness. One should always lead by example, of course, but I was roused now and I could stay awake, especially up in the bow with the ship's wind and the westerly breeze to invigorate me, for twenty minutes. After that – well, a quick nap back in the cockpit would set me to rights.

'Keep an eye on me. If I shout and wave my arm to starboard, put the auto-helm over and go that way. If I wave to port...'

'Turn to port.'

'Exactly. Tell Margit all that; explain how she works the auto-helm...'

'I already have.'

'Excellent ... and send her to relieve me in twenty minutes.'

Karina nodded. 'It is very cold,' she said as I left the cockpit. She was absolutely right. It was bloody cold.

With three in my watch, one of us could catnap and I was indulging in my second of the watch when I felt the warmth of the sun. It stirred me back towards full consciousness. It was almost noon and the sun, bearing south, had attained sufficient altitude to burn off the mist. The change was swift; the atmosphere cleared and I was brought back to full cognition by the cry from Margit forward. It was not a cry of alarm, rather a cry of astonishment, for there, all along our starboard side and stretching as far to the north-east and the south-west as the eye could see, rose the ice cliffs of North-East Land. And with this revelation came the sound of meltwater, formerly inaudible above the sound of the engine. I now realized that it had been haunting the back of my consciousness as I had stood my last stint as lookout. Had my perception not been dulled by lack of sleep, I might have realized what it was earlier. Now I realized not only what it was, but what it did, for it cascaded at intervals over the edge of the ice in torrents. Each of these waterfalls cut its way downwards through the ice in a V-shape. Some of them were young, scarcely biting the lip of the glacier; others had cut their way down to the water. It appeared like a speeded-up version of a demonstration of evolving geology, the ice standing for rock strata and eons of time being compressed into the brief interval of the Arctic summer.

It was this constant flow of meltwater running off the glacier all along its terminal cliff that washed the pack away from its foot, just allowing us room to slip along, close to the coast. I recalled having to make constant small alterations of course on the auto-steering. I had thought I was just conforming to the clear water. Actually I had been correcting the constant offshore set of this surface current without knowing it.

We regarded the remarkable spectacle with

272

undisguised curiosity. For the most part the ice cliff was more or less vertical. It had a more permanent look than the glaciers of West Spitsbergen, the leading edges of which have the crumbling appearance of imminent collapse. Here the warm influence of the Gulf Stream is absent and the calving process is much slower. But it was clear that calving took place, for we had already encountered the lumps of ice that had broken away. From time to time the cliffs threw up odd shapes – pinnacles and chimneys – and twice we passed great caves, deep arches into which we could have driven *Rolissa*, masts and all, had we been so inclined.

I should have liked to sail, but the wind now headed us directly and, as the day drew on, gradually strengthened, cutting up a choppy little sea into which *Rolissa* butted cheerfully. Offshore, I noticed, the pack rose and fell and ground together, and when we slewed past bergs, they were rocking sloppily, occasionally sending up into the air a dark cloud of little auks and guillemots. We passed close to another group of bull walruses, sunning themselves to a pink glow. The smell of them and their obvious excretions wafted over us and I – wittily, I thought – coined the collective noun 'fart' for them. I should have liked to share the joke with Karen, but held my peace as Karina and Margit pulled faces and laughed. We also saw some seals and a gaggle of glaucous gulls were tearing at the remains of another, left on a berg by a polar bear.

I had knocked off the forward lookout as soon as the visibility picked up, and the atmosphere in the cockpit was quite cheerful as we ploughed along. The ketch was making six knots and I was now glad the wind was heading us, forcing us to use the engine. The quicker we passed along this coast, the quicker we would be clear of the ice and, once clear of the Erik Eriksen Strait, could turn south for Norway.

Our cheerfulness made us drop our guard. Margit had just come up from putting the kettle on in the galley and we were about to call Karen and Greta when we heard the noise. It was a rumble, which rose quickly to a roar, and Karina, with her previous Arctic experience, knew exactly what it was. I was staring about me in alarm as she shouted something in German. I could not understand, but I looked at her for explanation. She was standing up, knees bent and bobbing up and down, staring from left to right, her face wearing an expression of absolute terror, waving both arms up and down, quite unable to translate until she managed the one word: 'Danger!'

So ominous was the noise that I already knew that, but from where it came I had no idea. Then Margit screeched, her arm outstretched, and I followed her pointing finger just as Karina also extended her arm and shouted, 'Look!'

At a point about forty-five degrees off the starboard bow a chunk of the ice cliff was breaking away. I was uncertain of its distance from us, but it seemed huge, an enormous undercut overhang. In the bright sunshine it was shot through with dark-green and blue shadows, and smaller pieces burst away from it, sparkling with reflected light, as it fractured from the parental glacier.

I do not think I perceived it in slow motion, though I might have done, because the smaller pieces, the detritus of the process of parturition, seemed to fall into the sea under the influence of gravitational pull; but the main piece – the so-called 'calf' – fell off with a ponderous slowness, the rending of it from its mother a matter of some seconds.

I had already slowed *Rolissa* and I now watched the fall of the great mass of ice, anticipating what would follow.

'A big wave will come, Nick,' Karina said to me, her voice shrill with the arsis of terror. I nodded comprehension.

'Hold on,' I commanded, just as Karen's voice from the cabin called up: 'What's the matter?'

I caught sight of her, half out of her sleeping bag. Greta was also astir. 'For Christ's sake, just stay there and hold on!'

Then we waited. It seemed like an age, but it gave me time to knock up the auto-steering gear, grab the tiller and swing *Rolissa*'s head round towards the berg in anticipation.

'Close the hatch!' I bawled and Karina pulled the hatch over the doghouse entrance while I recalled reading something about the dangers of being close to glaciers calving bergs. Worsley had said something about them generating waves up to sixty feet in height...

The ice hit the water. The splash was prodigious – a coruscation of water, ice chunks and specular sunlight; another roar, accompanied by the scream of wheeling gulls. Margit was crouched down in the bottom of the cockpit, her eyes closed, her hands clinging on to her lifeline, which she had clipped into one of the cockpit strongpoints. She must have fully understood the implications of Karina's warning, for she was muttering to herself as if in prayer. Karina had hooked her lifeline on but was kneeling on the starboard seat, clinging on to the guardrail, unable to take her eyes off the spectacular event. I was crouched at the tiller, ready to gun the engine but trying, at that moment, to clip my own lifeline on to the after strongpoint. I heard the carbine hook click just as I perceived the advancing crest of the wave generated by the falling mass of ice. Though the laws of physics told me it was an advancing circle of energy, stirred outwards from the point of impact, it seemed to me like a wall of water. I had no idea then, and I have no idea now, how high it was. It was, I am pretty sure, higher than *Rolissa*'s length. All I truly recall was that I held the tiller steady, at right angles to the thing, and increased speed just enough to prevent *Rolissa*'s head from falling off. When it struck, however, I think my eyes must have been closed – certainly my head was down – for the water that came aboard and poured after over the coach roof went straight down my back and felt like a sword cut. I was pierced with cold and roared my shock, as Karina and Margit screamed beside me. I have a vague memory of seeing *Rolissa*'s bow flung up, but that might be an impression, garnered afterwards from what Karina said she had seen and transplanted into my own memory. I have, too, a notion that the sunlight shone brilliantly through the crest of the wave that reared over us a nano-second before it smashed down upon us; but thinking about it afterwards, the sun was on our port quarter, and it makes no sense. I do not know for sure and these things are over so quickly that one can never be certain.

The cold was real, though, the icy wet slash down my back, and the three of us in the well of the cockpit, kneeling in ice-cold water, which poured over the sea-step into the cabin and then, as we gasped with the chill of it and shook the wet hair from our eyes, gurgled out through the cockpit drains. I noticed it ran red with blood.

Karen told me afterwards that they had been flung about down below, but by staying in bed had received only bruises, whereas we three watch-keepers were cut, though quite how and on what, again, I really have no idea. Margit said she saw lumps of sharp ice and perhaps the cut on her hand was attributable to that cause, but if the cut on my leg had been caused by ice, then surely my oilskins would have been severed.

What we realized was, of course, that apart from a soaking and some cuts, there were no broken bones, and *Rolissa* had ridden over the top of the disturbance and now lay pitching in the sequence of lesser, subsequent waves. I looked aloft, acutely aware of the vicious movement to which the mastheads must have been subjected. They seemed all right. We began to laugh with relief, the cold holding back the pain of our cuts, the shuddering of our shocked and chilled bodies yet to strike. I had just raised my head to see where, in relation to ourselves, the new berg lay, when the second wave hit us.

This time we were unprepared and it came from almost abeam, slamming into *Rolissa* and rolling her over to port, bearing her bodily and perceptibly in that direction. Not much water came aboard, but the heavy roll tumbled everything loose from its stowage down below and caught both Karen and Greta as they were getting out of their sleeping bags. In the cockpit I fell heavily upon Margit, who struck her head on the adjacent strongpoint and passed out, while Karina fell on top of me, followed by more water.

It could have been far worse, but the sense of chaos, of having been exposed to the overwhelming and primeval forces of nature, upset us. As *Rolissa* recovered and the succession of rolls gradually diminished, Karina pulled herself clear of me, as though contaminated by the contact. I rose shuddering with shock, cold and blue funk. My hands were shaking as I recovered the tiller. Karina had retreated into the forward starboard corner of the cockpit, where she huddled in a foetal ball. Below, Greta was crying and Karen, a trembling mass, stared at me white-faced and open-mouthed. Margit groaned at my feet, her legs briefly kicking.

'The ship comes first,' I heard myself saying, though perhaps it was only inside my head that the words came.

I could see the berg ahead of us. It was still finding its own equilibrium in its new milieu and it looked insignificant enough now. Oddly, the water surrounding it, although still undulating under a succession of annular waves emanating from the rocking berg, was otherwise smooth. The wind had not yet had time to ruffle it. I hauled the tiller over and took *Rolissa* in a wide circle to seaward of the new berg. At the same time it dawned upon me where the second wave had come from: it was the first, bounced off the ice cliff abeam of us, and sent out to sea again, colliding as it came with the succession of lesser waves following the first major crest. The hydrodynamics were complicated, yet the flawless elegance of the phenomenon struck me and I think I must have given a rueful smile, for Karen, her voice edged with hysteria, shouted, 'What the fuck is there to laugh about?'

I looked at her, uncomprehending for a moment. As far as I was concerned, as the

279

elevated and responsible party – the commander, if you like, of this rag-taggle, so-called 'expedition' – I was suffused with a sense of relief. We were alive when we might very well have been drowned; twice in one day the ship had saved us. Sure, we were cold and battered, but we were alive. I completely forgot that I had the short memory of the seaman. The danger was past. I was shaken and cold and had been frightened, but I was not going to rail against a Providence that had saved us.

For Karen and the others the experience was wholly subjective. For Karen and Greta, torn from slumber, it was particularly so. I heard Guy whispering, 'They're bloody women, Nick, what d'you expect?' But I knew that some men, caught like that, and not having the prime responsibility against which to measure the incident, would have reacted in a similar vein. The thought of Guy reminded me of Karina. My eyes flicked to her. Karen's bellow had roused her; she met my brief scrutiny with a steady gaze. No, they were not all alike either. The paradox struck me, along with a silly pun: Guy might guy women, but I saw more of what attracted him to the resourceful Karina. Paradoxically it also probably repelled him: he was uneasy acknowledging any equality with her gender.

Not that this should be taken as some sort of evidence at any inadequacy on Karen's part. In fact, she was already shaking her head as I shifted swiftly back to her.

'I'm sorry, Nick...'

'Forget it,' I said. 'I didn't know I was smiling and if I was it was from relief.'

'Once was enough ... Twice was intolerable...'

'We're all right, though.'

Karen looked about her. 'You might be up there, but look at the mess down here...'

This banter drew a reaction from Karina. Leaping as though galvanized from her refuge, she was at my feet, bent over Margit. She raised her head and almost snarled at Karen.

'We are cold, wet and ... and wounded! Nick is bleeding and Margit is unconscious! There is nothing the matter with you!'

Karen was, as I learned later, badly bruised, but she had the sense to bite her lip and was already coming up to help Karina get Margit below. The girl was already coming round and, just as they got her head into the doghouse, vomited, adding to the mess.

'Sod's bloody law,' I heard Karen mumble, and knew she had not taken offence at Karina's outburst. Greta too was eager to help and, although dropping with fatigue and having to resort to all sorts of silly devices to keep my eyes open, I made no reference to the change of watch until they had all turned to and cleaned up down below.

No one seemed to notice this rigid and politically improper and thoroughly dubious division of the chores except the ghost of Guy. Standing at the tiller in the brilliant sunshine, I heard him chuckling maliciously at my elbow. 'Leave the women's work to the women, Nick, my lad.'

I turned and looked astern to conceal my frank grin. I did not think Karen would understand it this time.

Merging with the distance, the calved berg looked as if it had been bobbing there for years; already a crowd of auks had roosted upon it. I watched it for some time, shaking with cold until my body heat, confined within the layers of thermal clothing, began to overcome the chill.

The Thirteenth Part

They lifted Margit on to the settee. While Karen and Greta set to to mop up the water, blood and vomit, Karina felt carefully all over her cranium and pronounced it fracture-free. She then dressed Margit's cuts, Karen set up the lee cloths and we left Margit alone for a while. Once the saloon was squared off, soup and rusks were served before Karen and Greta climbed into their gear and came up to relieve me. I went below and began to peel off my oilskins. Karina was swabbing her own cuts, the worst of which was a gash on the forehead from contact with the jib sheet winch. It had bled for a while until the cold did its work, arresting the haemorrhage. She was stripped off to pants and brassière and took no notice of me as I peeled off my own clothes. I changed my wet silk T-shirt for a dry cotton one and spread the silk one out on the cabin handrails to dry while I slept. Then I bent to tug off my long johns. I gave an involuntary moan as I tugged at a mass of coagulating blood. I had no idea that I had cut myself, the wound having subsided to the dull, throbbing thud of what I had assumed to be a bad bruise. Now my precipitate action in the warmth of the saloon had precipitated a revival of the bleeding.

Karina turned and saw my grimace. 'What's the matter? Oh...'

The gash ran down my shin and my half-removed long johns exposed only part of it. 'Sit down and wait. I must get some more hot water.'

I backed up and sat on the steps up to the doghouse. If I was going to bleed again, it was the best place to wreck the ladies' house-keeping. After putting on a kettle Karina tugged a T-shirt over her head.

'That should stop you bleeding quite so quickly,' Karen called down from the cockpit, where she and Greta had seen what was going on below. The laughter made Margit raise a pallid face from her pillow and Greta said something to Karina, who looked at me, then at her, and laughed.

'What did she say?' I asked, aware that I was the butt of the joke. Karina, laughing, shook her head.

'I cannot tell you,' she said.

'You had better tell *me*,' said Karen from the cockpit behind me, though I suspect she understood; her German was pretty good and I had heard her in conversation with Greta.

Karina laughed again and, reaching for the kettle, said, 'Greta said that she hoped the cold was still keeping Nick's penis in its proper place: in his pants.'

'I shouldn't worry,' I said, thankful that I wore a pair of jockeys under my thermal long johns. 'Though now you come to mention it...'

'Nick...' Karen's tone was cautionary, but by now Karina was dabbing my lower right leg with warm water and easing the long johns down it. It was a nasty gash, long and jagged. Swabbing it clean and dry, Karina delved about in the medicine locker and produced four butterfly closures. She was briskly competent and I tried not to notice the bulge of her breasts, or the warm pink of her thighs as she knelt at my feet, but it was rather difficult. I felt the old familiar stirring and hurriedly grasped at a straw. In the cockpit Greta and Karen were chattering.

'Did you do this for Guy?' I asked, as her hand smoothed over the third closure. She hesitated. 'On his hand,' I prompted.

She looked up and nodded. Then she shook her head and looked down at my leg, though she was not seeing it. 'Well, I tried to. He was a difficult patient.'

'What happened to his hand?' I asked, risking – or perhaps defying – Karen's ire.

'He was towing us clear of the ice. Something happened to the rope; it got round the propeller and he tried to cut it. He was on his own and the knife slipped. His hands were cold...'

'You were in trouble?'

Karina looked up at me, then went on with her work. 'Yes. Leni nearly got stuck in the ice last year. This boat pulled her clear, but not until after Guy had cut himself. After we had

285

been pulled out when Guy tried again, we could see he was hurt. He pretended there was nothing wrong with him. Leni ran the *Adler* alongside and told me to help him, but he swore at us and, you know...' She made a gesture with her hand.

'Sheered you ... no, fended you off...'

She nodded. 'Leni suggested the boats kept company in the ice, which was a good idea. At first Guy waved his bandaged hand at us. He seemed OK, but then he knocked it and we heard him, still swearing. In the end he didn't stop me going and having a look at it. It would have been OK if he'd let me dress it at first, but by the time I got to it, it was, er...'

'Septic...? Infected...?'

'Yes. Maybe the knife was dirty...'

I remembered the old knife Guy used to keep handy in the cockpit for gutting the fish he liked to catch with a spinner over the stern. It was certainly never spotless, though he had a huge, ugly diving knife tucked in the doghouse for more seamanlike tasks. In the heat of the moment, manoeuvring alone in the ice with a tow rope trailing over *Rolissa*'s counter stern, I could quite understand him grabbing the nearer of the two. And now I came to think of it, I had tossed the thing, redundant, into the rubbish skip at the Halls' yard weeks earlier.

She smoothed the last butterfly closure over my shin and, patting my knee, stood up. 'He was a – how do you say it? – a stubborn man. Very proud.'

Then she turned away, into the heads, to empty the basin of dilute disinfectant, and the moment was over. When she came back into the saloon, she climbed into her sleeping bag.

'The hand was still bad when he got home,' I said, making for my own berth, suddenly aware of the downdraught from the cockpit cold on my back.

'Yes,' she said.

As I drifted off to sleep, I knew that I had guessed correctly about the sequence of events in respect of those few cryptic words and the timing of his injury.

We ran into dense pack again about twenty-three miles south of Cape Torrell, where the ice cliffs fell away to the north at the opening of the Hinlopen Strait. Karen and Greta were on watch and, rather than call me, there being no immediate danger, they left me in bed, slowing the engine and allowing *Rolissa* to come to a stop. After she had lost way, surrounded by ice, Karen cut the engine. I think I must have stirred at this point because I have a vague recollection of Margit getting out of bed and later, when the watches changed, she was already in the cockpit, feeling much better. She had had a good break and, happily, seemed none the worse for her tumble.

When Karina and I joined her, Karen handed over the watch with a crestfallen air. I noticed Greta passing over one of the guns to Karina.

'I don't see how I could have avoided it, Nick,' she said, staring round at the encircling ice. 'Greta's worried about bears and – well, it's not a comfortable thought.'

'I'll have some flares up here handy. They should frighten Bruin off,' I said with an air of forced cheerfulness. Actually the thought of a prowling and hungry bear was nothing short of terrifying.

'I'm really worried about being beset and nipped. We've been squeezed a couple of times, but the ice seems to be moving.'

I was suffering identical apprehensions in a higher mental gear than mere worry. Why is it the English think there is a virtue in understatement?

'God help us,' I muttered, then asked, 'Where are we?'

'I put a fix down when we stopped.'

'OK.' And she and Greta went below.

I will not bore you with the details of the hours that followed, for they were, in their way, the worst part of our voyage, an ordeal marked by their very tedium and uncertainty. I discovered that, when the ice seemed ready to trap us, I could work *Rolissa* back and forth under low power, increasing speed once I was up against a floe, and by this means, keep her surrounded by what amounted to a mere gutter-width of sea; but it proved enough to keep her from being nipped.

We were helped by one or two other things. The first was the weather. The wind stayed in the west or south-west, a relatively warm maritime airstream that was actually melting the ice, although this was impossible for us to detect and any real melting was not from the air but from the ambient temperature of the seawater. Second was the slow south-westerly drift, augmented by the current coming out of the Hinlopen Strait. I detected this soon after Karen had gone below on the morning – at least I think it was morning – when Margit resumed watch-keeping. Anyway, I put my own fix on the chart, out of habit rather than as running a check on Karen; it was a routine matter, a formal check that the vessel was where the last watch-keeper had said she was. Quite fortuitously this revealed that we were subject to drift and I offered up a prayer of thanks to the Global Positioning System and dear old Jack who had harnessed it. I would not have felt confident with the small shift in position had I determined it by astro-navigation, but one felt happy that such a difference, detected by GPS, represented real distance. It was not much, but over time the increments built up and it lent encouragement to us.

Then there was the warmth inherent in our hull. The Refleks stove belted out a terrific heat at full blast, so that it was almost stifling below. But *Rolissa*'s hull, though a lousy conductor in absolute terms, radiated just sufficient heat to help. The cumulative effect of all this saved us, I think.

Not that we did not have a number of

moments of anxiety. Old sea floes, the flat pancakes of decaying ice, having reached what the polar experts call a 'rotten' stage, were not particularly dangerous. But the movement of polar ice is like the hands of a clock, possessing an inexorable but almost invisible movement. Watch it, and one can see no shift; reappear after going below to make a cup of tea, and a berg looms up where no berg existed before. Watching the compass, too, we observed the ketch rotate as she drifted – this way, then that – as floes and bergs came together, rasped at each other, each absorbing its neighbour's energy in action and reaction. Mostly we were sur-rounded by flattish floes, though several of these were rafted, shards and slabs of impacted ice, formed over years, driven one over the other in fantastic angular shapes. There were bergs too, and some of these were more than indistinct growlers, or awkward lumps of glaciers, but strangely magical, castellated things, possessing something of the ethereal landscapes one may observe in clouds, except that they were solid, very solid, the result of long-term erosion by ice-laden wind and sea, sunlight and the recrudescence of the cyclical freezing and thawing process.

Karina told me more about the turning of bergs which, as they melt, alter their shape and suffer a change of their centre of gravity. Sometimes, if they are jammed against other ice, this happens suddenly as they break free, and can be almost as dramatic as calving from glaciers. Nor, I relearned from her – though I had read of it first in Worsley's pages – was this always as simple as the birth we had ourselves witnessed.

'Sometimes,' she explained, 'bergs break from the top of the glacier and then the glacier melts at sea level and is washed away. This can leave a...' She was lost for the word and stuck her tongue out and pointed at it.

'A tongue?' I offered.

'Yes, a tongue of ice, below the water. It is more ... What do you say, not floating...'

'Buoyant?'

'Yes, it is more buoyant than the sea and it breaks off and rises...' Her voice trailed off as I imagined this: a Kraken of glittering ice welling up with a roar from below the surface of the sea.

'It could lift a whole ship up,' I said, with unfeigned wonderment. Up there, sitting it out in the pack, it all seemed quite possible.

There was a splendid grandeur to it, a sense of being caught up in something massive – no, beyond imagination and eternal. Alongside this numinous perception lurked the knowledge that being set fast meant a slow death. Our location was far beyond assistance. We were remote: small and petty gods on the limits of existence, hovering on the edge of Nifelheim at the very gates of the Norse hereafter, the *hel* of the Viking imagination.

Several times I had to get down upon the ice and bash at it with the boathook, an exercise I had to give up when the thing broke. Three times thereafter I shot a heavy slug into the ice, in an attempt to crack it. It never worked, but I felt the kick of a powerful recoil for the first time in my life.

And then we did have an encounter with a bear – several, in fact, though only one was serious. I suppose it was inevitable, though at the time I felt a strange, unpleasantly liquid sensation in my gut. Indoctrinated with the gloomy scenario of the end of all life forms under the polluting mess of civilization, I was surprised at how many there were.

The first was an old male, a huge animal who loped across our bow, head lifted towards us. You could see the eyes and the coal-black snout and the vague yellow mantle of his coat against the ice. Margit saw him and the first I knew was her hand, gripping my arm. I had not thought she had the power in her, until I saw her eyes and followed her line of gaze.

The animal paused. He was upwind of us, but I was sure he could smell us and he stared at us for some time. Perhaps he was not hungry – seals must have been plentiful and available among that loose ice – or experience had made him cautious. Anyway, he did not trouble us further, but disappeared behind a hummock.

Our second encounter was more frightening. We had opened a small lead and had been running down it for about half an hour under sail. I had been reluctant to start the engine and wake the watch-below, so we ghosted along until the light wind dropped and we lay becalmed. The ice was closing in again and we were surrounded by a damp mist. I was standing up, trying to judge our drift and which particular chunk of ice we were most likely to edge up against, when I saw the next bear.

It was swimming down the lead towards us. I do not know what it made of us, only that it came directly for us. I alerted Karina and Margit.

'Keep very quiet and still – there's a bear swimming towards us – but pass me the gun...' I did not take my eyes off that noble head. I felt a tingling excitement as Karina pressed the gun into my hand and whispered a translation to Margit. I heard the younger girl squeak. At this point *Rolissa* gave a slight lurch. A lump of ice had run in under the long overhang of her counter and the jerk made me stumble. The sudden movement must have startled the bear, for it veered away and, about fifty yards to port, hauled itself out on to a small floe. It dipped under the weight. We could see a line of black teats: it was a she-bear.

We saw another female a few days later; she had a pair of cubs in tow, but as we had recently passed a dead and disembowelled seal over which the glaucous gulls were fighting, we thought them all well fed. Certainly they did not trouble us.

The same could not be said of our climactic

encounter with a younger, predatory male, for he attacked us with unequivocal vigour. Greta saw him and shouted a warning so loudly that there was no need to translate her cry of 'Ice bear!'

Polar bear is a complete misnomer for this animal. Not only is its habitat confined to the Arctic pole, but it is upon the ice, or in the water that *Ursus maritimus* hunts; and this fellow, hungry or not, was in hunting mode. Half a ton of raw energy ran at us across the ice as our port side grazed a floe. I saw him coming as I emerged into the cockpit straight from my berth. I had a flare in my hand and the cap off it even as Greta cocked the cockpit gun. Karina was behind me with the second gun, grabbed from its slings across the forward saloon bulkhead.

I pressed the firing lever, felt the pin strike and a second later the cockpit was full of smoke as the distress rocket shot out. The thing whooshed past the bear and struck ice fifty yards behind him, spewing smoke. A second later it belched out its red parachute flare. The thing lay on the ice, sputtering in crimson brilliance.

The bear stopped, swung his head and looked for a moment at the flare. Then he turned back to us and regarded us with suspicion. We could see his nose sniffing, the stink of the powder propellant strange to him. He turned again and regarded the fizzing red light burning itself into a melt-hole. Then he resumed his advance, but more cautiously, his head lowered a little and swinging from side to side.

Watching, we remained absolutely silent, so that we could hear him breathe and the click of his terrible claws on the ice. Then Margit squealed again, unable to control herself, her squeal rapidly rising in a scream. The bear recognized fear, smelt it stronger than the rocket fuel. Margit collapsed into a ball as Greta fired.

The bear stopped dead, shook his head and rose up on his hind legs, stung by the cloud of shot and exposing his belly. Greta fired again, a heavy slug which brought Bruin thumping down on all four paws with a shock that we could feel aboard *Rolissa*. It was the way the bears broke through ice to get at seals beneath it.

Then, to our astonishment, he came on again. He was ten, eight yards away when Greta fired a third time. At almost the same instant Karina fired the second gun. One of the shots hit the bear in the skull. The smashed head went down between the two front legs as they slithered forward on the ice. The rasp of its claws was chilling. For a second or two the bear's stern remained upright; then it slowly fell over to one side.

There was a long moment of collective paralysis among us then, as Margit's scream subsided and she looked up. Then, still holding the gun, Greta was peering over the side. She turned and poured a stream of instructions to Karina. Twice Karina interrupted her and looked at me, but clearly Greta was brushing any objection aside. Even before she had finished speaking, Greta was on the ice.

'Greta...' Karen and I began to protest. 'There may be other bears about...' Our words fell on deaf ears, for Greta had galvanized even Margit into obedience, and while Karina hesitated, the student did as she had been bidden. Ducking below, Margit reappeared an instant later with a sharp knife from the galley.

Karina threw me a despairing look and held out her gun. 'Please,' she pleaded, 'you guard her...' Then she disappeared below, emerging with two large glass jars with screw tops.

'What the hell...? They're specimen jars,' Karen said.

'The fucking woman's gone bloody mad.' I raised my voice: 'Greta!'

But she had reached the bear and was bending over it, still calling out instructions over her shoulder. Karina held out the glass jars to Margit, but Margit was damned if she was going on to the ice. Karina swore at her and jumped down herself. She walked hurriedly over to Greta, staring about her, and I was forced to take note not of the evisceration now under way but of the surroundings. Almost at the instant the welter of red spilled from the bear's opened flank the glaucous gulls arrived, shrieking the glad news of death and food out over the barren ice.

'Oh, Christ...' Karen said, her hand up to her mouth.

I shot a glance at Greta. She was down on her knees, her hands inside the steaming innards, her face averted. I caught the whiff and then Karen stumbled below. I scanned the ice again, my eyes unable to avoid returning to the grim spot. I saw Karina bend, holding one of the jars, as Greta placed a brown-red slithering liver into it. It reminded me, with a painfully poignant pang, of Adam's afterbirth. More specimens followed, then Karina was coming back to the boat holding the two jars, Greta still bent over the mutilated corpse. A moment later she too was on her way back, her bare arms red with blood, one bear's paw in her left hand. In her right she held the bloody knife.

She said something to Margit, who rose, fumbled in a locker and drew out a bucket. Filling it with seawater, she placed it on the deck by the rail. Before coming aboard Greta dropped the paw on to the deck over the counter, then rinsed her hands and the knife. As she came over the rail, she smiled at me – triumphantly, I thought – said 'Danke,' and kissed me on the cheek.

The three Germans went below. Greta got out five of my glasses and her bottle of schnapps. It was a particularly repulsive brew, I thought. She handed me a glass. 'Drink!' she commanded. When she turned away, I ditched the stuff overboard. Then I looked at the bear. The gulls were already tearing at the carcass; soon the stink of it would draw other bears, I felt sure. I looked round, seeking a way out. Was that a lead to the north-west? I would have gone back the way we had come to get away from the ignoble scene. I fired up the engine, screwed *Rolissa* off the ice and began to work clear. I should never have treated the ketch the way I did in the next few hours, but I managed to put about seven miles between us and the position of the dead bear.

On the counter a thin stream of blood leached out of the huge paw and trickled away over the yacht's side. I leaned over to throw the thing overboard but Margit was suddenly there. *'Nein!'* she cried shrilly, adding a few words of amplification that I could not understand in detail, though their intent was clear enough.

I am afraid at that moment I was filled with a historically tribal contempt for Germans.

Later that evening we all sat down to dinner except Margit. I had insisted upon her remaining on watch for bears and she ate her meal in the cockpit. As I came below, Karen was dishing up and Greta was putting a row of what I thought were pickle jars on the table. They were smaller than the large specimen jars she had filled earlier and whose present whereabouts I had no knowledge of. It was a moment or two before I realized that they were, nonetheless, smaller versions of the same thing.

'Where the hell did they come from?' I asked. Karen looked round.

'You carried them from the *Adler*,' explained Karina.

'In the bag of food?'

'Yes.'

'Well, what on earth are they? On my dining table too,' Karen protested. I did not argue the point of ownership. I was dreading the reply and stared closer. They seemed full of cloudy water, though I could see small, shrimp-like things in one and, in another, what seemed like snails, only dark snails with undulating wings, some sort of membrane with which they propelled themselves. Only a few still seemed capable of this, however; most lay dead on the bottom of the jar.

I looked up at Greta. She was staring proprietorially at the jars, smiling at them. She looked from Karen to me and then began to speak. Karen translated. I cannot reproduce exactly what she said, but it was something to the effect that she, Greta Leimküller had originally specialized in helminthology, the study of parasitic worms such as nematodes, flukes and tapeworms. However, her interest had been drawn increasingly towards the study of pollution and she had come north on this, her first expedition into the Arctic. She had conceived the idea after seeing an advertisement in the academic press in which Helga Leni Reisenburg annually offered to convey minor scientific expeditions to Svalbard – for a fee, of course. In this way Reisenburg underwrote her own obsession with sailing in high latitudes, employing

Karina, a cousin of hers and a trained nurse, as the expedition's essential medical expert. Seizing her opportunity, Greta Leimküller had realized this might be a way of carrying out a feasibility, or preliminary, study into the best way to determine something in which she had become increasingly interested.

She needed these specimens – at this point I do recall she patted each of the jars upon its screw-top lid – and those of the bear's liver and portions of intestine (now pickled, I later gathered, in vinegar requisitioned from the galley), in order to do preliminary work to persuade her principals back in Germany that her ideas were important. Ultimately she hoped to fund a major expedition.

Her ideas, since this time fully vindicated and currently undergoing proper evaluation both by the German university for which she worked and also by the Norwegian Polar Institute, I understand, were as follows. Far from being the pure and wild place that romantics thought it to be, the Arctic, Greta contended, was becoming the repository of all the industrial world's pollutants. All airborne horrors, she claimed, ultimately fell into the sea. And because it was largely uninhabited, but possessed a closely linked food chain, the Arctic provided an ideal place for investigating the potential long-term effects of these substances. Chief among these were polychlorinated biphenyl products (popularly known as PCBs) which, although banned in Europe since 1978, remained in the thin wafer of the atmosphere, along with DDT, or dichlorodiphenyltrichloroethane, which was still used as an antimalarial insecticide in the Third World.

These chemicals were insoluble, Greta maintained, and were taken up by the lipid-rich plankton and krill. These in turn were eaten by birds and fish. Further up the food chain, setting aside the baleen whales that consumed tons of the stuff, seals ingested these contaminants with their food. Consequently, and especially at the time of breeding and feeding their young, high levels of poison were taken up by their young in their mothers' milk. At the bitter end of this complex food chain were the ice bears. Mammals like bears and seals relied upon fatty blubber to survive in the cold of the high Arctic, and the contaminant substances congregated in fat, overloading these species in particular, so that the effects were most marked among these predators – most notably the ice bears.

There were already suspicions generated by Norwegian biologists that the bears in the European and Siberian Arctic lived significantly shorter lives than their Canadian cousins. Although she admitted there was as yet insufficient evidence to corroborate it, Greta also insisted there was a vigorous rumour of the existence of pseudo-hermaphrodite bears, animals genetically compromised by this pollution.

Preliminary work had been carried out in

Norway and the Faeroe Isles investigating the eggs of seabirds, which were consumed in large quantities by the Norwegians and Faeroese. The findings were worrying. Now Greta wanted to establish the facts 'for the benefit of humanity'. Karina concluded her translation. Then she added as a droll supplement, 'And for her own reputation.'

We sat for a moment ingesting this information; then Karen asked if there had been anything wrong with that bear's genitalia.

Karina translated, then shook her head. 'No, it was a normal male.'

Greta looked at me and said something else, which Karina translated with a downward look. 'She is rude, Nick; I'm sorry, but she says it is the fault of men and that industrialization is to blame – that you will be punished and already your sperm count is falling.'

I took it in good part. 'Ask her what car she drives,' I riposted. The barb went home and I had the satisfaction of seeing Greta colour a little. 'The truth is, we are all to blame,' I said, 'and will go on being to blame until it all ends in a rather unhappy whimper...'

Karina frowned over the word whimper, but I let it go. Greta and I agreed on one thing: that the long-term prospects for humanity and the planet were not marvellous.

And quite unexpectedly I felt the brush of Karen's hand across my own.

The Fourteenth Part

I should like to say that we broke out of the ice on the thirteenth day, but it would be more accurate to say that the ice relinquished us. It was a gradual process, for at first we made a little progress, then a little more, until eventually we were in open pack and able to make headway. In the last days the weather became warmer, the westerly wind picking up again and carrying a low, insulating layer of overcast across the sky. It was rather depressing, even though we hoped it was helping us edge ever southwards. I had spent the last five days worrying about the passing of time and our consumption rate of diesel oil. We had been consuming the stuff at an alarming rate, both in the engine and in the heater. I was therefore supremely grateful when I was able to shut off the former and let *Rolissa* gather way under her sails alone. We were heading south-south-west, our course line passing close to the east of Bear Island. Setting aside the effect of the grey cloud cover, one could not have ordered a better, nor a more timely, breeze. It was just as well. August was far advanced; already the Arctic autumn was upon us. Only afterwards did I really appreciate our good fortune.

I pondered this. Was it just luck? Or was it providential? Had it somehow been engineered by that cosmic intelligence whose existence I could not deny. And why us, when Helga Leni Reisenburg and Kirsten Lenzmann – I had learned their names from the statements Greta and the others had prepared and that I had had poor Karina translate into English so that I could demonstrate my understanding to any suspicious bureaucracy – lay dead on the ice far, far behind us. I became intermittently tormented by the notion that I should have buried them, that to leave them to be picked clean by the glaucous gulls was somehow uncivilized, but how could we have buried them, out there on the ice? Even the land is under permafrost, and I had read that the graves of those long-dead Dutch whalers, killed in the seventeenth century and lying in droves at Smeerenburg, had all been pushed to the surface and lay about in their split coffins where the curious traveller could stare at their exposed bones.

Was luck so capricious? It certainly seemed so.

As we drew south away from the ice, the sky cleared. *Rolissa* seemed to sense the lightening of our mood. She raced along, reeling off the knots and spinning the thin and insubstantial thread of her wake behind her across the grey waters of the Barents Sea. One evening, as we changed the watch with the peaks of Bear Island rising dark and forbidding about six miles to the west of us, we were treated to our final manifestation of the high Arctic. I am not quite sure what caught Margit's eye, unless undergraduate biologists have some sixth sense for such things, but we all crowded into the cockpit, staring upwards at the plummeting dot. We watched spellbound, as a heavily built gyrfalcon stooped out of the cloudless sky, and fell upon a small flock of dark scoters as they lifted off the surface of the sea and climbed, wheeling round towards the grim fastness of the island. The flock scattered as the compact falcon struck and the hapless victim, broken-backed in a cloud of feathers, fell towards the sea. But the predator passed its quarry, spread its wings and twisted with talons extended, catching the descending duck. In a soar of triumph the gyrfalcon bore its food upwards, riding the air with a cool majesty before heading off for the island.

'*Natur naturans*,' said Karen, lowering the glasses.

'My Latin is non-existent,' I confessed.

'Nature naturing – red in tooth and claw and all that sort of stuff.'

When it was over, we all went back to our previous occupations. Karen and I completed the transfer of the watch while below Karina was finishing the washing-up, Margit was drying and Greta was writing up some notes. She had been working on these ever since we broke out of the ice and the watch routine became less stressful. It was an obvious attempt to redeem what she could of her

Arctic experience.

Seeing the Germans busy, Karen asked, 'How are we going to speak with Karina?' Her voice was low and she was peering through the binoculars at the peaked island to the west. 'We'll be in Hammerfest in a day or two...'

'I'm not going to Hammerfest. I'm going to Tromsø. It gives us a little longer, but we're just going to have to challenge her.' I thought for a moment and then I added, 'There is one way.'

'Oh?'

'Now we're in clear water, I've been standing one of the girls down. Margit has far less stamina than Karina and usually falls fast asleep in her oilies on the doghouse steps.'

'She seems to favour the foetal position,' Karen observed dryly.

'You could get up and join Karina and me in the cockpit. I could shake you when I came below for a pee.'

Karen considered the proposal for a moment. 'All right. But I'll make certain we isolate Karina.'

'What d'you mean?'

'Never mind. Just leave it to me.'

I stared at Karen. 'Don't worry, Nick; I'm not really the bitch you think I am.'

'I never thought you were a bitch, Karen,' I protested, but she just smiled and gave me a shove.

'Go and get your chauvinistic pig-head down. You need the kip.'

306

Passing through the saloon I ignored the two younger women as, chatting, they completed their chore. I went forward, cleaned my teeth and emptied my bladder. Then I went aft and prepared to turn into the starboard quarter-berth. Greta watched me and I felt oddly uncomfortable under her scrutiny. We had all seen each other climbing into or out of our clothes, peeling off the layers. I always stripped to jockeys and T-shirt, having a high tog-factor sleeping bag and a natural aversion to being too hot in bed. I ignored Greta's obvious importunity, tucking myself in with the wry thought that perhaps she was not lesbian after all, that I had misjudged her and that she fancied me like mad. Preposterous though the notion was, it amused me for a moment. My silly mood actually had nothing whatsoever to do with Greta. It was a measure of my sense of triumph: we had accomplished a circumnavigation of Svalbard. I could indulge myself with a little self-congratulation. Hugging the smug knowledge, I rolled over and, forgetting my conceit over Greta, fell fast asleep.

I was woken from the depths of a slumber as deep as the Barents Sea. I had no idea where I was, nor what was expected of me. Then I remembered and stretched luxuriously, recalling my earlier mood. Forward, Margit and Karina were stirring and I lay for a moment before getting up. In the good old days when Britain had a sizeable merchant fleet and most of my friends were at sea, we used to have a name for the feeling of euphoria liable to attack people nearing the end of the voyage. It was called 'The Channels', a mild and pleasant disorder, compounded of anticipation of a warm and welcoming homecoming, days of idleness on leave, and the satisfaction of a voyage over and a job done. It usually evaporated within an hour of docking and encountering the unkindly zealous face of Her Majesty's Customs Officers, who inevitably made the innocent feel like criminals and would rob an impoverished cadet of half his miserable payoff if he tried to take home an extra packet of cigarettes for his girlfriend, his mum, or his dad. But during their onset, The Channels forced the voyage's acquaintances to pretend that they were friends, and the true friends to pledge long-term amity.

Lying there, feeling a mild symptom of this malady, I chid myself for being a complete fool. We had hundreds of miles to go yet before we even crossed the Arctic Circle, never mind raised the English coast. What was more, we had to deal with Karina. I got up.

As I did so, I realized the wind had increased and that *Rolissa* was heeled at a sharp angle. Feeling her motion, I knew the wind remained on the starboard quarter, though it might have shifted nearer the beam, for the ketch was scending along, with an urgent tremor running through her fabric. I guessed the speed at eight knots and was astonished when I passed through the doghouse, zipping up my heavy-weather jacket, to see that the log showed nine point eight.

'My God, you're doing brilliantly,' I said, turning to Karen.

'I thought we ought to be thinking about a reef,' she said and I stared about me, at the full main with its elegant curve rising in a graceful twist to the mainmasthead. I put one hand on the mainsheet. It was taut as a steel rod. *Rolissa* rolled to leeward and the end of the boom skimmed just above the surface of the retreating wave.

'I'll give it half an hour.'

'All right. I'll turn in.'

'OK.'

She stood next to me for a moment. 'Any time you like,' she whispered in my ear as she passed and went below. Taking the reef gave me an excellent opportunity to tire Margit. I left things as they were for about three-quarters of an hour and then I nodded to Karina. She had been wearing an anxious expression since she had come on deck. 'Take the helm,' I said, and she disconnected the self-steering as I shook Margit, as she sat, knees drawn up and head down, on the lee seat.

'OK, Margit, let's go forward and haul a reef down.' Margit knew what I meant, looked up and pulled a face. 'Let's have a luff then, Karina.'

Karina put the helm down and hauled in the mizen sheet. I hauled in the main and Margit stood up, clutching at a handhold and yawning. As *Rolissa* came up into the wind and lost way, she began to swoop up and down, her sails flogging. I let fly the jib sheet and rolled it, then, tapping Margit on the shoulder, led the way forward. I glanced behind me once to see that Margit had clipped her harness safety line to the jackstay.

Heading into the wind we felt the strength of it on that wildly moving deck. As I belayed the topping lift and nodded for Margit to lower the main halliard, I reached for the second reefing pendant. I judged there was going to be more wind and it was better to haul two reefs down now and have done with it. Margit pulled the clew earing down, could not hold it and let it go. I took over, finished the job and worked round to her side of the mast to help her set up the halliard again. With the ketch plunging up and down, motion far more pronounced up forward by the mast than in the cockpit, Margit was having difficulty keeping her feet, hanging on and accomplishing her task. I did not blame her: she was neither experienced nor particularly interested in the sailing element of her Arctic adventure, nor did she have Karina's strength; but it was difficult not to feel a slight irritation that she seemed to want to put so little into the corporate effort. I jerked my head in the direction of the cockpit. 'OK, *danke!*' I called above the noise of the wind and the slap of the ropes on the mast.

She began to work her way aft as I returned

310

round the mast and slackened the topping lift again. Then I followed, waving to Karina, who already had the helm over to resume our course and was resetting the jib. Margit was about to climb into the cockpit when *Rolissa* breasted a high comber and her bow dropped into the succeeding trough. The stern kicked up and Margit slipped. There was no risk of her falling overboard, but she landed heavily, was badly winded and severely bruised herself. The net effect of all this was to prevent any collusion between Karen and myself and we thus failed to confront Karina on that occasion.

We might have done it a few hours later, but by that time the wind had risen to gale force and we were far too preoccupied. It was the first time our guests had been aboard *Rolissa* in heavy weather and, with the exception of Karina, it was clear they did not enjoy it. Greta found sleeping difficult and though she was not actually sick, she was obviously not well. Full-blown seasickness struck Margit, who was, ironically enough, now out of the running and *hors de combat* in her bunk. Pallid as a street urchin, she had Greta fussing over her, all trace of their former animosity now vanished.

'She has been OK up to now,' Karina explained; 'we had a good passage north with not very much strong wind. This' – she waved a hand at the welter of spume-streaked seas now heaping up on the starboard beam – 'is the worst she will ever have seen.'

'But not the worst you have seen, eh?' I asked with a grin, sensing that she, like me, was rather enjoying the crazy ride.

'No,' she said. Her face became serious, so that I was reminded of a cloud passing over the sun, and I thought she was going to say more and remained looking at her. I was witness to a struggle, and formed the impression that Karina too sensed the end of the voyage and what that meant – that she too wanted a confrontation, if that is not too loaded a word. It was an odd, inadequate moment. We were both poised to jump, but neither could. Frankness was constrained by suspicion, or perhaps by reticence, that old and insidious obstruction to so much that might be simply sorted out.

Had *Rolissa*'s exposed weather bilge not received a solid thump as a wave drove into it, causing her to lurch in response to leeward, we might have cleared the air. As it was, we both slid over to leeward and clung on. When we and the boat had recovered our equilibrium, the moment had gone. Karina bent to coil up the snarl of sheets that the lurch had flung into the wet bottom of the cockpit, and I remembered my already compromised promise not to ask anything without Karen. I peered below. Greta was back in her bunk but wide awake, while Karen was fast asleep.

This was not, I decided, the time for revelations.

We berthed at Tromsø one evening a few days

later. We had endured the gale until it had backed into the south-west and given us a hard time, gradually dying away to an oily calm, so that it was under motor that we approached the Norwegian coast and the wild archipelago that studs the northern shoulder of the Scandinavian peninsula. On those last days Margit had complained of feeling unwell and Greta had insisted there was something wrong with her. Karina expressed doubt, though she conceded that, without proper tests, it was impossible to say. These preoccupations set any thought of unravelling the mystery of Guy's last passage aside; the quiet opportunity simply did not present itself. I was frustrated at the steady loss of opportunities, but Karen took a more mature view. I suppose this was because she had long been tamping down her natural dislike for Karina as the usurper of her lover's affections, or because Karen was a woman who sought to get her own way and if it failed by one means, she sought out another. In any case, we had Karina's address and Karen whispered her intention of 'catching up with her later'. Seeing my dull, masculine in-comprehension, she added, 'In Germany, if necessary,' making her point until the *pfennig* dropped.

I was privately of the opinion that Karina and Guy had had a blazing row and fallen out, that Guy had not mentioned her because of this and that this disagreement and the presence of the German women in the Arctic had depressed him. The theory, preposterous at first with a man of Guy's character, seemed increasingly to fit. I could only guess at the true state of Guy's mental health, but I now had experience of conducting a small yacht through the Arctic Ocean. Guy had done it – or much of it – alone. And he had gone up there in the first place because of some inner motive. Initially we had assumed this to be a kind of affirmation of his manhood, perhaps attached to a failing of it in the purely sexual sense, a self-justification that had grown out of his being the age he was, a manifestation of the male menopause – a hateful expression, but it communicates our analysis of Guy's condition. But suppose his mental disintegration had started long before; suppose that the decision to go up there had in itself been part of the process – a process begun a long time before, in Northern Ireland perhaps? Then the impact of finding his convalescent, man-hood-affirming voyage trumped by a bunch of German women had hit his psychological condition, already affected by weeks of solitary sailing, with an unimaginable impact. He had tailed them, *followed* them, because he had foolishly fallen for one of them; then fate had given him the opportunity to help – no, to *rescue* them. The silly, foolish girlies had got their boat stuck in the ice! What else could you expect? But Guy had been there on hand, ready to help them in true knightly mode.

In the middle of this flamboyant demonstration of superior British seamanship and

314

manly endeavour, he had fucked up and gashed himself. A moment later he had been in trouble and had had himself to solicit help. Under these circumstances, on their way back to England, where Karina – and knowing her now I could quite imagine the power of her persuasion – had insisted on coming with him, reality would have impinged: Karen and the hall, the normality of his comfortable existence, the spectre of having to explain his failure to accomplish his solo voyage, the compromising effect this would have had on his projected book. To this fairly logical, if speculative, stream of reasoning one could add a little colour. Perhaps he had failed to make it in the sack with Karina; or she herself, realizing or intending that the affair should be a brief one, with her own life re-establishing its gravitational pull, had withdrawn her favours. Perhaps she had never vouchsafed them – now there was a thought!

In all these circumstances, cooped up aboard *Rolissa*, a row seemed unavoidable. As far as I was concerned, the *mystery* surrounding Guy's voyage had really been solved once we knew he had not completed it alone. That we had actually *met* his siren made the yarn a little improbable – though improbable things happened in the Arctic – but was little more than a corroboration underlining the truth.

It struck me as quite understandable that, sad as it was, all these things had played upon Guy's mind and, in due course, brought him to his moment of culmination. Guy was not a man who could submit easily to the notion of doing nothing. He came from a background – I ought to say class, except that the point is lost in its hackneyed use – that made the running. It distinguished him from me. I was bred not to 'do' but to put up or shut up; I might be allowed to clean the blackboard, but I could never write on it; I was of the breed who, when the officer led over the top, turned to the lads and told them to follow. Whether they ultimately followed me or the officer was irrelevant; it was I who followed the Guys of this world.

It was only when I finished my private rehearsal of the causal chain leading to Guy's taking of his own life, only when I set it in relation to myself with this rather melodramatic metaphor, that I felt the first sensation of real disquiet. Up to then I had been trying to see it either as a seamlessly logical flow, one thing leading to another, or as it had affected, or been influenced by, Karen.

But now it occurred to me that Guy's death did have a point – even a message; and that message was that Guy had given up: he had shot himself to relinquish the leadership. And there was an odd coincidence to my analogy in that the agent of his destruction was German. It was a coincidence, of course, but its aptness brought home to me the crux of the matter: if, in leading his soldiers out of the trench with or without good old 'Sergeant' Nick in support, the German

316

enemy had shot him, Guy would have died a hero.

If heroism was denied to him, as in the self-perceived failure of his voyage, he could not accept defeat at the hands of a young woman or her colleagues. That she and they were German was fortuitous, but might have been an ironic twist of the screw. Indeed Guy, whatever his state of mind, might not have seen their nationality as fortuitous at all; he might have seen it as providential.

He did not like the Germans – a prejudice of his generation – and he had often used to ask, rhetorically I have to admit, why it was that they produced not only some of the world's foremost thinkers, but also 'men who composed the world's most sublime noises'!

Somewhere in the North Sea Karina's gender and nationality must have foamed up like an overwhelming sea, like the wave that had washed me the length of *Rolissa*'s deck years before and brought me to his feet as he jeered at my predicament. But now the boot was on the other foot: Guy was the reduced and humiliated one. The only heroic thing to do, the only dynamic action he could take was, quite simply, to end his own existence. It was a final act of rebellion at a world he spurned.

Knowing Guy as I did, and having some insight into his voyage, there seemed to me no other possible explanation.

It was uncanny how nearly right I was. And yet how much I had yet to discover.

317

The Fifteenth Part

It was Margit and her illness who provided
the catalyst and resolved the tragedy. At
Tromsø, instead of flying straight home, as
she had originally intended, Greta insisted
that Margit went into hospital, where colitis
was diagnosed. It had been caused by stress
and 'dietary indiscretion', Karina informed
us when she returned to *Rolissa* from the
hospital. They were keeping Margit in for a
few days' observation, as she had the severe
ulcerative condition of the disease. Karina,
who did not much like Margit, was remorse-
ful. She should have known; the symptoms
were there: weakness, abdominal cramps
causing Margit to favour the foetal position,
the pallor of anaemia, frequent bowel
movements. It was a disease to which women,
from the age of twenty or so, were susceptible, I learned.

'She didn't complain,' Karina said, biting
her lip. 'She should have said something ...
She must have been in a lot of pain. It is a
horrible thing.'

I thought how I had made Margit go
forward with me to take those two reefs in.
The reason, justifiable at the time, now

318

seemed malicious and cruel. No wonder her performance had been lacklustre.

'Don't blame yourself, Karina,' I said, sympathizing with her; 'we have all had much on our minds. At least she is in hospital now. She will be properly looked after.'

Karina nodded. 'Yes, you are right.' She pulled herself together, drawing in her breath, and nodded.

Karen agreed brusquely. 'There's no harm done.' It was clear she had other priorities. 'So much for your theory that yachtsmen never get the diseases they deserve,' she remarked dryly to me. Turning back to Karina, she asked, 'So what do you want to do?'

'Greta is going to stay near the hospital. She has found a place, a guest house. I am going to take her things up there now.'

'Is she in love with Margit?' Karen asked callously, as if the question were devoid of implication.

Apparently it was. Stepping aboard, Karina replied, 'Yes, I think so. But I think Greta falls in love with most of her pretty students. Margit's illness makes her vulnerable and therefore more attractive.'

As Karina passed below, I asked, out of sheer curiosity, 'And Margit?' There seemed to be more to Margit than I had supposed and I was wondering how she responded to Greta's advances. Karen gave me a sharp look, as if reproving my prurience as an objectionable manifestation of my maleness.

But Karina, scooping Greta's things into a small bag and looking up at us in the cockpit from the cabin, only laughed. 'Oh, Margit loves only herself. She will love Greta as much as is necessary. She will get a first-class degree and have a wonderful career. If she marries, she will make her husband unhappy, and if she has children, she will expect others to bring them up. Greta will die in her shadow claiming that, but for herself, Margit would have amounted to nothing, and had she not saved her life in the Arctic...' She zipped up the bag and climbed out into the cockpit. 'The story will probably mutate so that in due course Greta will have saved Margit from an ice bear...'

'Where did you learn to speak such good English?' Karen asked abruptly.

'I grew up in Bielefeld. I was very friendly with some British children from your army. I often stayed in their house. It was unusual, but that is how.'

'And you – what about you yourself? Are you going to stay with them in this guest house?'

Karina tossed her head. 'With Greta? No.' Then she looked at us both, one at a time. In that instant the atmosphere was recharged; the focus shifted away from Greta and Margit. There were now just the three of us. 'I think I must come back and we must talk. That is what you want and that is what I want. It will not be easy, but it must be done. We must break the ice masks we are all wearing.'

'The ice masks,' I said, intrigued; 'what do you mean?'

'Leni said that when a person sails in the Arctic they become changed. An ice mask forms upon them.'

Then she was gone, climbing ashore, Greta's bag on her shoulder. We watched her go in silence, pondering this weird image. Then I remembered something I should have thought about earlier. 'Oh shit,' I swore.

'What's the matter?' Karen asked.

'I must leave those depositions with the German vice-consul. And I suppose I'd better return that gun and notify the Norwegian authorities about the polar bears we shot.' I cast a glance in the direction of the bucket lashed to the push-pit which contained seawater and the bear's paw.

'You go ashore and see to all that while I square up the boat,' Karen offered.

'OK.'

Then, seeing my attention drawn aft, she added, 'If Greta does not claim that thing, it is going overboard.'

'Good. You'll not start anything with Karina until I come back?'

'No, Nick...'

'Promise?' I said, aware of our reversal of roles.

'Don't you trust me?' She was half-serious, or serious enough to cause me to proceed with caution.

'Of course.' I stepped below to collect the

paperwork, which I had stuffed in a plastic bag and shoved in the chart stowage under the table. I pulled on an anorak and, gathering the plastic bag up, was about to climb ashore past Karen when she caught me.

'I'm sorry, Nick.'

'Whatever for?' Her breath was warm on my face.

'Left alone we might have made love up there, in the Arctic.' The remark surprised me; then I realized that we had not been alone on the boat since that fateful afternoon we had seen the red flare from the *Adler*.

'We have a long way to go yet,' I said. 'Somewhere down this coast there is a perfect anchorage, remember? Why don't you ask Karina where it is?' My heart was beating and I bent and kissed her, but she drew away after the most perfunctory contact.

'I couldn't do that,' she said, as though I had asked her to commit some disgusting act.

I was cross. I had no idea why she had mentioned *us* in that context at that moment. 'Suit yourself,' I said with unnecessary brutality, and went ashore.

It took me some time to find what I was looking for. The harbour master's office was closed – I had forgotten exactly what the time was in the infernal and endless daylight – but that did not matter, and I shoved my note through his letter box. I discovered the arms of the Bundesrepublik above those of The Netherlands and Sweden next to the door of some small offices, but this was also, and

322

unsurprisingly, shut. There was a phone number and in a small café not far away they let me use their telephone. I did not want any later accusations of delay to be levelled at me, and thought it best that I delivered my reports as soon after *Rolissa*'s arrival as possible. The vice-consul, a Norwegian businessman, was obliging and asked me to bring them to his house. Obtaining directions, I called on him and his wife a few minutes later. I outlined the circumstances, told him about Greta, Margit and Karina and left the papers with him. He thanked me, said he would read them after his dinner and that he would be in touch with me the next morning.

'Please,' he added as we shook hands, 'you must not leave until I have been in touch with you.'

'Of course,' I replied, 'I quite understand.'

I had abandoned my anger by the time I returned to the ketch. Karina was already back on board and these two women, each beautiful in their way, with names so similar as to be confusing, were sitting surrounded by a pregnant silence in the saloon. An uncorked and untouched bottle of wine stood on the table between them, along with three glasses. The silence was palpable as I clumped down below. Taking off my anorak, I squeezed in and sat down next to Karen.

Karina shook her gold-blonde hair. 'This is too like an interrogation,' she said, standing up.

It was my fault, of course, so I stood up myself. 'Do sit down, Karina. I'm sorry, I was not thinking, forgive me.' I poured the wine as a distraction. 'Of course it is not an interrogation. We simply want...' I began, but Karen cut in, leaving me to move aft and, bunching my anorak beneath me, sit on the step up to the doghouse.

'We want to know what happened aboard here last summer. We know Guy picked you up, and we know you became lovers...'

'Do you mind that?' Karina said sharply. 'Do you blame me?'

I watched Karen falter and soften. 'Yes, Karina, I mind it very much. Guy and I had made a life together ... But I don't blame you. Well, not entirely.'

'So we are not to be enemies?'

Karen shrugged. 'You were my enemy; perhaps you still are. At least until I understand Guy's death.'

Karina lowered her head. 'If I tell you the truth,' she began, looking first at Karen and then at me, 'what will you do?'

'Do?' I said. 'Why, what will there be to do...?'

'Go on, Karina,' Karen said, her voice very level and controlled, and it suddenly struck me that something odd was happening. I could not put my finger on it at the time, but it was the first intimation that Karen might know something she had not told me before. It was just a whiff of suspicion, nothing more, something contained in the tone of her voice

324

and the way she added, 'Tell us all about it, from the time you first met.'

It had all begun very prosaically, if an encounter between two yachts in such a remote place as Ny Ålesund can be ordinary. *Rolissa* had arrived and secured alongside *Adler*, much as we had done alongside the Colin Archer type ourselves. There had been the usual exchange of pleasantries. They had become gallantries once Guy, eager for a friendly face let alone a beautiful one, realized what he had come across. Drinks had been passed across, just as they might be between yachties anywhere in Norwegian territory, given the fabulous prices charged ashore. Karina recalled Guy's dawning realization that this bevy of women had no male or males in their company. Karina had not been the only English speaker aboard the *Adler*. Leni spoke it well, and another of the crew had a good command of the language, so the evening had been quite jolly. Towards the end of their session, Guy, a little the worse for wear, had made one or two tactless remarks. None of the Germans had taken offence, writing Guy off as a reactionary English gentleman. Afterwards Leni had admitted that she found him attractive, at which point Karina had agreed.

'I had better tell you,' she said at this point, 'that I lost my virginity to an older man, an Englishman. He was the father of my child-hood friends. I met him quite unexpectedly when I was on a visit to Berlin. He was there without his wife, doing something for NATO. He was very kind and sweet, even if he was cheating on his wife. He was the first man to make me feel grown-up and, of course, he made sure there was no risk of my becoming pregnant.' She looked at me. 'I seem to like older men. Back home I am living with a surgeon from the hospital where I work. He arranged for me to have time off to come north, otherwise it would be impossible. He thinks Greta's work is important...'

Assimilating this serial infidelity, I felt awkward under Karina's scrutiny. Her candour was also a little unnerving, though Karen did not seem to think so. I was not used to listening to the confessions of women and wondered if this was how they spoke among themselves. It would explain why women always had something to talk about to each other, but it was foreign to men, who would never admit to anything other than an unspecified run of success as sexual conquerors.

'So you are not married,' Karen said.

'No, I have never married. Nor were you married to Guy...'

I felt like a tennis umpire, sitting between the two of them as they confronted each other across the saloon table, my head turning from one to another. But I was damned if I was keeping a tally of the score, or was going to shout 'Fault'. Not yet, anyway, though I drew in my breath at the precision of the barb.

'That was my decision,' Karen said. 'I had a career to protect.'

'And that was why you stopped making love with him?'

'Is that what he told you?'

'Yes.'

'Tell me, my darling,' said Karen icily, topping up her glass, 'did he always manage to get it up for you?'

'Of course,' Karina said triumphantly, 'there are ways...'

'Oh sure, there are ways, but grovelling round the floor on my hands and knees...'

'I didn't do anything like that!' Karina snapped. 'There was no grovelling...' Her voice softened, became almost caressingly reminiscent as she attenuated the last word: 'We made *love*.'

'Of course you did,' riposted Karen, her voice like shot silk. 'I'm sorry if I thought you might just have enjoyed a fuck.'

'But all this happened later,' I put in, half-donning my umpire's hat.

Karina looked at me, then away again, as if surprised to see me still there. 'Yes...' And she went on to say how Guy had followed them after they had left Ny Ålesund. They had been amused at first, but they had serious work to do and he became something of a nuisance. In the end Leni gave him the slip among the ice east of Moffen, where it was quite bad.

'She didn't want to fuck him then, despite being attracted to him,' Karen interrupted.

'Oh, she might have done if she had had the opportunity,' Karina said. 'But she was far too involved with the expedition.'

'Then you had problems in the ice,' I prompted, eager to get on with the narrative.

'Yes, we got beset. It is so easy...'

She recounted the reappearance of Guy, the fouled towline, the gashed hand and the eventual transfer of herself aboard *Rolissa*.

'Leni felt guilty, I think, because Guy hurt himself helping us. "You like him," she said to me. "Go and look after him." '

'You did not mind being put aboard alone with Guy?' I asked.

She shrugged. 'No. I *did* like him. He was so confident. I like that, and he had sailed all alone. I admired that. And, of course, Leni wanted me to get rid of him. I think she was embarrassed to have become set in the ice and more embarrassed for it to be Guy who pulled the *Adler* clear. She would not have believed the same thing could happen twice...'

'Except that it didn't,' I said. 'Not in the same way.'

'No.' There was a pause.

'So you sailed south with Guy, and then what happened? You didn't take *him* to hospital,' Karen needled.

'No, I should have done; I should have insisted, but he wouldn't. He refused. Absolutely. I don't know why. Was his hand still bad?' Karina directed the question at Karen.

'Oh yes, you know that...'

'Go on.'

I missed the significance of this little exchange, except that I experienced again that shadowy suspicion that Karen was playing a game independent of me. At the time the conversation – or at least Karina's account – rushed on and I lost such perceptions, as my imagination busied itself constructing its own version of Guy's southward passage from Spitsbergen.

'Once we left Svalbard,' Karina was saying, 'Guy wanted to get straight home. He seemed disappointed. No, he told me he *was* disappointed and that the trip had been a failure. He said that, when I came aboard, it was finished.'

I remembered that line, written carefully down the spine of the log book: *I am all there is and it is ~~completed~~ finished.* In his deletion of the word *completed* I had missed his emphasis upon the personal pronoun. That sentence was pregnant with other things, I now realized, but Karina demanded my attention. 'Much as we have done with you,' she was saying, 'we ate together once every twenty-four hours. *That* was when I got to know him properly.'

I looked at Karen, waiting for her to scoff at the younger woman's claim that she had got to know Guy on so short and intermittent a basis. But she was resting her chin on her hand, paying intent attention to her rival.

'We talked a lot about his trip. He said that

329

he did not want me on board. He wanted to complete his voyage alone. He had given in, taking me on board in a moment of pain and weakness. He was a little in shock by the wound. He despised himself for that. As a soldier.'

'He would,' Karen remarked in a low voice.

Karina took no notice. 'I asked him why he wanted to make the voyage by himself and he said, "Every man must do something utterly alone," that it was the "only way a man proves to himself that he is an autonomous being". I asked him why a man felt like that and he said if I was a man I wouldn't ask the question. Most men avoided the challenge, he said. Men like him found it impossible – not irresistible, like a temptation, just impossible to avoid. I said that was a false argument and he laughed. I liked him when he laughed.'

Without raising her chin from her hand Karen said, 'We all liked him when he laughed,' and I knew she too was making a parallel voyage in her mind's eye.

'He agreed, then said that men bound themselves too closely to women and that it had proved their downfall...' She ceased speaking and looked at Karen across the table.

'Go on, I've done all my crying.'

'He told me that he had loved a woman...' Again Karina faltered.

'Go on.' Karen's voice had an edge I knew to be dangerous, but it was clear she was not going to lose her self-control.

330

'Of course,' said Karina, 'I knew nothing about you personally, only that you were not married and had no children.'

I saw the flicker of muscle along Karen's jaw and the bob of her swallowing. She asked, her voice suddenly husky with the power of her inward emotions, 'Did that bother him?'

Karina shrugged. 'I think so. Does it not worry every man if he has no children?' She looked at me, but I merely shrugged; I was at least the biological father of Adam. Further enquiry would prove too painful. Seeing my apparent indifference, Karina went on. 'He could not admit it. Instead he said he had come north because the climate was extreme, that he had sought a place of – I had to ask him to write the word down because I had never heard it before – a place of...' Her forehead creased as she recalled the word. '...excoriation. He said he wanted a wilderness, a place like the desert where he could exist on the edge.'

'How it must have hurt him to find it populated by you and your colleagues,' Karen said wryly.

'Of course,' Karina agreed. 'To find *women* sailing the Arctic like himself was difficult for him. It made him angry, very angry...'

'Did he admit this to you?' I asked.

'Oh yes. He said it deprived him of something important to his existence, that he was demeaned by it.'

'Ah, Guy the perfect chauvinist,' Karen said

331

wistfully. She sipped her wine. 'But he meant it.'

'He said it was because technology – the Polartec fleece, Goretex clothing, the strength of modern boats, everything like that – had made it easy for unexceptional people to do things that would have been unthinkable only fifty years ago. Things like coming north, or going south. He meant women, of course...'

'Or ordinary men, like me,' I said, coming inexplicably to Guy's defence, for we had had some such discussion as this years earlier, and I knew Guy hated the notion of Everyman being able to toddle up Everest, let alone Everywoman.

'He said that the world was nearing its end,' Karina went on. 'I thought him crazy at first, until, of course, I realized that he was not a religious madman but saw the very pollution our expeditions were beginning to discover was evidence of not being able to...' She faltered, having difficulty with her English.

'Of not being able to stop the rot, of irreversible decline...' I tried to help.

'Nick...' Karen said, meaning that I was being pompous and sententious. But Karina grasped the metaphorical lifebelt I had flung her. Germans, perhaps, are not so sensitive to pomposity as my fellow countrywomen.

'And what did you say to all this heavy philosophy?'

'It is not philosophy, Karen,' Karina said, almost proving my extemporized theory, brushing aside Karen's irony. 'It is already established scientific fact. Guy thought it was already too late.'

'Do *you* think it is too late?'

'I hope not, but I am not sure...'

'You are young, you are certainly too young to have tasted despair.' I was surprised to see the two of them turn and look at me. It took a moment for me to realize that I had articulated my own thoughts. For a moment I was abashed, then I added, 'You are young and beautiful; it would be perverse of you to feel despair.'

'Why?' Karina said. 'I am German, you know. It has not been easy to grow up as a German, knowing why my English friends lived in my country.'

'Then can we do anything about it – the pollution, I mean,' I asked, 'or do we have to wait until the very rich, the fat cats at the top of our human food chain are gasping for breath before we take the pollution of the planet seriously?'

'That would be far too late,' she replied. 'Anyway, I don't think we will reverse it, no, but we might delay things. I am a nurse, I have to believe that. I have never been nursing in the middle of a famine in Somalia, but you do not see those people who do walking away saying, "The death of all these wretched starving people is inevitable, so let us shorten their agony by letting them die quickly." '

'Perhaps we should,' Karen said, topping up her glass, then leaning over and refilling

333

Karina's. I held out my own. The bottle was empty.

'But supposing we delayed things long enough for other developments to occur, other advances to be made, things that replace pollutants; d'you understand what I am trying to say?'

'D'you think that human greed will give you sufficient time?'

She thought a moment and said, 'Guy once said that he thought the only chance was that if enough people realized in time, that if they would make the collective self-sacrifices necessary to arrest the process, there was an outside chance. He said that ideas had to connect, *could* connect, if the atmosphere was right, but he didn't think that this would ever happen.' She frowned and looked at Karen. 'He said he knew that from Northern Ireland. I did not quite understand what he meant...'

'We do,' Karen said shortly. She drew herself up and added, 'Yes, Guy had a theory about ideas. Every idea, he claimed, was an imperfect groping towards perfection. It might exist as the product of a discrete process of thought, but it was beset by thousands of influences and therefore linked indirectly with every other idea. If a coincidence of influences was achieved, as for instance by a universal concern for a massive issue, then this would produce a coincidence of ideas and the gear of human thinking might be changed. *Might*, mark you. Marx and Lenin managed to set a spark to such tinder, but they only had a success rate of about ten per cent, and look what they achieved. It didn't last, of course, because the constructed solution failed to fit the problem, but, in its way, it was a noble experiment...'

'Guy said *that*?' I asked, bewildered.

Karen nodded. 'Yes. He wasn't quite the Tory bigot you thought him. Inter alia, Northern Ireland had a profound effect upon him.'

'Well...' I faltered. I had nothing to say really. 'He often quoted Donne: "No man is an island, entire of itself ..." '

'Yet he went north to be alone,' Karen said, then came back from this reflective excursion and faced Karina again. 'But he came back with you.'

'Yes. How did you know? I mean, how did you find out I had been with him?'

Karen shrugged. 'Nick will tell you.'

I explained the long chain of discovery. When I had finished, Karina said, throwing her head up with an oddly incongruous air of defiance, 'Then you had already guessed we made love. You knew before we met.'

'Yes.' Karen's acknowledgement was a sibilant and, it seemed, sinister hiss. 'Of course we had. Did you enjoy it?'

'He was a good, considerate lover.'

'He made you come...'

'Oh yes...'

Once again I felt embarrassed, utterly and completely embarrassed. This frank and open discussion of Guy's amorous skills might have been perfectly acceptable in the women's lavatory, but I found it wincingly excruciating.

'Then why did you kill him?'

Karen dropped the question into my distracted mind like a pebble, falling into a well shaft. It took an age to reach the water, but I can still hear the splash.

The Sixteenth Part

Karina and I both protested at once – I to contest Karen's silly, jealous accusation and Karina to challenge it. She made no wild physical movement and, to me, her self-possession seemed proof of her innocence. At least that was my immediate, instinctive impression, though logic tells one that a murderer must possess qualities absent from the majority of us.

'Is that what you think I did?' she said. 'Is that why you have made it your business to follow me all this way, to accuse me of killing a man whose child I nearly had...'

'*What?*' Karen's astonishment was unfeigned.

'Oh,' said Karina almost ruefully; then, adding the venom of sarcasm: 'He was not quite impotent, *darling*, nor was he infertile.' Leaving Karen to master her shock, she turned to me, 'And do tell me, please, how you had time to come all the way to Svalbard to find me. I come every year and yet I have to beg for the time free of work...'

'We both lost our jobs,' I said, hand outstretched and moving towards Karen. I impulsively forgave her her long deception, her concealment of all this, in an emotional lurch, sensing the last bond with Guy might at that moment be parting. She had made a mistake, her accusation of Karina an appalling error, the result of a long-festering wound in her soul. I felt moved by pity. And self-interest. I touched her shoulder, but she shrugged me off.

'Don't condescend, damn you!'

'Karen! For God's sake, you know I'm not condescending...'

But Karen was not listening. She turned back to Karina. 'Why did you do it?' Her face was contorted with rage and pain.

'I didn't.'

'But you were there! In his study! I saw you!' Karen was relentless, her verbal pursuit across the table caused Karina to shrink back against the settee squab behind her.

'But I *didn't* do it.' Karina had lost her aplomb. She began to take alarm at the vitriolic attack and turned to me. 'Nick, for God's sake believe me! I had no hand in Guy's death!'

Karen was on her feet now, leaning on her hands, straining across the table. 'Now that *is* a lie. You were there! *I saw you!*' Spittle flew from Karen's mouth, her face savage, imbued with the spirit of wrathful accuracy.

'Nick ... Please, Nick...' Karina turned from one of us to the other. Her arms waved in supplication towards me and then across her face in a gesture of defence. I leapt to my feet and called out:

'Stop this! For God's sake stop it!'

In the silence I could hear the breath rasping in Karen's throat. Slowly, very slowly, never taking her eyes off Karina, she sat down. Tears were bright in Karina's eyes.

'Karina,' I said gently. I was confused, fascinated, and only slowly aware of the enormity of Karen's concealment. It rose palpably between us, something seen properly for the first time. I had divined it, but not defined it. In my masculine conceit I had thought it another legacy of Guy's, the remnant of the intimacy between him and Karen – evidence of my status as a Johnny-come-lately, a loser.

Along with this non-specific sense of betrayal, was a simultaneous attempt to make sense out of what Karen had actually said. One thing seemed incontrovertible. If it was true. 'Karina,' I repeated, 'Karen says she *saw* you. In Guy's study. Were you there when Guy died?'

And to my astonishment she nodded.

We had, not a few moments before, been discussing the end of the world. It might happen, but it was to be a remote event affecting an amorphous humanity, in the future, at a time which would not directly affect us, even though we predicted it and it concerned us. Yet the end of Guy was real and had impacted upon us. It had suddenly become an event as cataclysmic for us as the prospect of the end of the world – a life-changing event. What I am trying to say is that the effect of these revelations struck me with almost as much violence as a physical blow. I felt winded by it, diminished, reduced to something less than I had been ten minutes earlier.

'You *were* there?' I was incredulous, despite Karen's own eyewitness evidence. I looked at Karen. She had asked me earlier if I believed her. I had said that of course I did. Now I thought ... No, it does not matter what I thought; it becomes too complicated. I was looking at Karen. There was no triumph on her face, which was turned towards me, though she looked at Karina. Karina wiped the tears from her eyes, sniffed and sat up. She recovered her self-possession and I wondered if it was a spin-off from her characteristic practical competence. I simply did not – could not – see her as a murderer. And yet I recalled her lack of surprise when, on realizing she was aboard *Rolissa* and had enquired about Guy, I had told her he was dead.

'Yes, I was there ... until *she* must have come in.' Here she nodded at Karen. 'Then I left.'

'You arrived at almost the same moment,' Karen said to me. 'I could never understand why you did not bump into each other.'

'Me?' I frowned. How was I involved? Then I remembered the car with which I had almost collided on the bend. 'The Fiesta. You were driving a Ford Fiesta,' I said to Karina.

'A hire car. It was a small Ford, yes.'

But something was wrong. Karen had called me some time earlier. I had had time to drive over to the hall. With Karen's words ringing in my ears I had driven fast, almost recklessly, but it had taken me at least twenty minutes, certainly more than fifteen. I shifted my thinking to a much later date; besides, I had been certain that when Karina had first come aboard *Rolissa* in the ice and she had seen Karen, she was doing so for the first time. Was that flash of intuition so completely wrong?

'Did you see Karen?' I asked Karina.

She shook her head. 'But I knew she was there. Guy had told me we were alone. Then we saw the car headlights, heard the door slam as she came into the house.'

I heard Karen draw in her breath. Quickly I said in as reasonable a tone of voice as I could muster, 'Karina, please tell us exactly what happened.'

'I came on the ferry from Hamburg to Harwich. I had trouble hiring a car and finding the hall, but I waited until it was getting dark and drove in through the gates. I parked the car in some small trees, then I walked up to the house. Even in the twilight I could see it was beautiful, a beautiful English house...' She paused, as if recalling some sweet anticipation. I forbore from pointing out the untypicality of the hall. 'Very carefully I walked right round. Some lights were on. I opened the garden gate and found Guy's study, with the glass doors open. I had seen

341

no one else, but I saw him inside at his desk. His desk lamp was on and the desk was covered with papers.'

I could visualize the scene. Guy's study opened on to a walled garden at the side of the house. The French windows would have been on his right. He liked having them open. When I had last seen him, Guy had been wearing an open-necked check shirt, a cravat, corduroy trousers and a body-warmer. I threw off the horror of the image and tried to recreate him sitting there, in the quiet solitude of his study, wrestling with his book, the book he couldn't write. Unless he was actually working on it, his computer and keyboard were pushed to the left. His desk light, perched on the right-hand corner, would have thrown the light away from the window and on to him. He could not have seen anyone in the doorway without some inconvenience from the desk lamp.

'He was staring at some papers in front of him,' Karina said. 'I thought he was reading. Very quietly I approached the open doors and stood outside them. I could hear him breathing. I did not need to open the doors and I moved forward a little at a time. I was right inside the room before he looked up. The light was on him and I don't quite know what made him look up, for I'd been there for what seemed like some time...'

'He would have smelt you,' Karen said.

Karina nodded. 'Perhaps, yes...'

'Was he surprised?' Karen asked.

'Yes. Very. He ... Oh, what do you say?' She started back in mock fright.

'He jerked,' I suggested.

'OK ... Yes, I frightened him, but you know Guy. He was Mister Cool. "Good God!" he said, turning the desk light round so that it shone in my face, "where did you spring from?" I knew he would be surprised. He had never expected to see me again.'

'You had had an argument before you parted?' Karen asked.

'Oh yes. A big argument...' There was a wry look on Karina's face, as though the recollections amused her. 'Just how big you cannot imagine, Karen.'

'I think I can, I knew Guy...'

'No, you didn't...'

'Go on,' I broke in, seeing the two of them baring their claws. 'What happened next?'

'I let him hold the light on me. I was no longer pregnant, but I wanted him to get a good look at me. We talked for a little. It got bad. He began shouting, I shouted ... Then the car arrived.' Karina looked at Karen. 'Neither of us knew what to do for a moment and then Guy sat down. Very quietly he sat down and looked up at me. "Now what are you going to do? Tell Karen everything?"

'Seeing him so cool, I said yes, why not? "Because I shall stop you," he said, and pushing aside some sheets of paper he exposed the gun. It must have been on his desk all the time. Before I came in.

' "Don't worry," he said, picking it up in a

343

movement so quick that he scattered the papers on to the floor and, before I had recovered from the shock of seeing it, he had put it to his mouth...'

Karina was trembling now, so powerful was the memory of that terrible moment. The sound of the shot and the mess that erupted from Guy's head had galvanized her, she said. She had fled in terror, blundering back out through the French windows.

'My eyesight had been affected by the lamplight. Near the gate I tripped and fell against the garden wall. I hit my head and it knocked me silly for a few moments. I was semiconscious, and when I came round properly and stood up, I felt sick. I remember standing beside the wall. I could see the glass doors and the light. Someone – you I guess,' she said, looking at Karen – 'had shut the doors. I had to get away. I had difficulty finding my way back to my car. I couldn't find it in the trees. I found it in the end, but I couldn't drive it away. I was shaking too much. I just sat. It sounds stupid, but I wasn't running away from a murder...'

She looked from one to the other of us. It seemed incontrovertible proof of her innocence.

'It was only when I realized that I might become involved with the police and that the person who had shut the doors would have called the police by then that I drove away. I had trouble getting the car going ... the tyres spun in the ground. I thought that someone

... the person ... was coming; there was a light ... I left on the first ferry from Harwich. It took me to the Hoek van Holland. It was a long journey home...'

Karina's voice trailed off and a profound silence lay between us in *Rolissa*'s saloon. I looked at Karen. 'When you rang me, you seemed quite certain that it was suicide. You said as much – words to the effect that Guy had blown his ... Sorry, had committed suicide.'

Karen nodded. I saw her swallow. Somehow she seemed chastened. 'Yes, that's what I thought when I rang...'

'So tell us exactly what happened to you as you came home,' I prompted.

Karen sighed. 'Me? I was late back from London. Late meeting and a late train. Things weren't going too well and I was preoccupied. Very preoccupied. As I drove up the drive, I thought I saw something unusual – something white, or a flash, I don't know. I didn't think anything of it at the time. I'm not even sure I gave it a thought beyond perhaps guessing that I had seen a barn owl. We had had them around and the headlights might have caught one. As I say, I was thinking about other things.'

'Things about Guy as well as things about work?'

She nodded. 'I had just opened the front door when I heard the shot. I knew what it was. Guy has had a gun – I mean an automatic pistol rather than a shotgun – ever since

345

he left the army ... ever since he was in Ulster. I'd seen it, but he knew I didn't like the thing and usually he kept it tucked away, though sometimes he wore it in a holster and I would feel it under his clothes. He had had it conspicuously on his desk several times during the previous weeks. I thought he was being silly, that it was some perverse kind of macho plea for attention. You know...' She looked at me and I understood this to be an allusion to his impotence. '...we had been having some problems.' She paused, then went on: 'I think this was how I knew what he had done the moment I opened the study door, before I had even seen him. In fact, I knew so positively that I could not bring myself to look, though I could smell...'

She put her hand up to her mouth, then lowered it and shook her head, as if clearing it.

'I went straight across to the French windows and shut them. A delaying tactic, of course, a grab at our old world together. I was always cross with him for leaving them open after dark. Twice he had come up to bed and we had discovered them still open next morning. Of course, as I closed the windows and turned round, I found the light pointing at me. I didn't ask myself at that moment why this should be so. I was simply rather grateful that, instead of seeing Guy under its light, I had at first only an impression, a dark and horrible mess that spread ... you know ... you both saw it. Half-closing my eyes, I stumbled

346

out of the study and phoned you, Nick.

'I sat for a few minutes on the stairs and then I knew that I had to go back in there, to be the first to look at him, to say goodbye, to be angry with him, to curse his soul. And I remembered that I shouldn't have shut the windows, that the soul must have time to escape, and not be confined. Had it already gone, or was it still in there? I felt death like a cold hand round my throat and felt sick in the pit of my stomach. Getting up I hurried back. Then I stopped. Should I phone the police? I was alone in the hall with Guy's body...

'The sense of vacillation was terrible. When you are alone like that you desperately need to communicate with someone else. I had called to you for help, Nick, but you hadn't arrived. I needed to do something else, to talk to somebody else. I was about to go back to the phone when I made myself look at Guy. I don't know whether I should be ashamed of the way my mind worked, but I seemed to be two different people: one cold, almost mathematical, the person who had decided to go back and look at Guy before doing anything else; the other a shuddering jelly of terror, anger, love and pity. I thought I ought to cry and thought I ought to deal with the matter sensibly...

'Somehow the latter triumphed, at least for the moment. I found that I couldn't see him properly. I walked across to the desk lamp and, very slowly, my heart thumping, I turned it on to him. As the heat of the lamp burnt my

347

hand, it occurred to me that it was odd the light was swung round, not over the desk and Guy's papers.

'I suddenly recalled the flash of white, or whatever it was I had seen. I looked down. I saw damp footprints on the rug by the French windows. And the rug was twisted. Guy was an army man. He might leave the French windows open, but he would tweak anything out of place like that. I now know it was Karina, turning to flee, that caused that twist in the rug.

'I went back through the house. We kept a big torch beside the front door. I picked it up and ran out across the gravel to the drive. Immediately, I saw the lights in the rhodo-dendron bushes and heard the revving of the car. I began to run towards it. Then I realized I had no means of stopping it and that I myself might be in danger. I stopped running ... I actually stopped running. The car swung out of the bushes and away down the drive. A sudden fear now turned me to jelly; I reverted to a frightened person. I forgot all about getting the car's registration number. I almost forgot to use the torch, and all I got for my pains was a fleeting glimpse of a young woman's face in profile...' She turned from Karina and stared at me. 'I was a mess by the time I got back to the hall. Then you arrived, then the police.'

'Why did you not tell the police about me?' Karina asked, her voice low, as if to speak normally would bring down upon her some latent wrath.

Karen shrugged her shoulders. 'Why did I shut the French windows? Why did I turn that light...? Why did I go back into that room and straighten the rug? I don't know. I only knew that I didn't want Guy to have been murdered...'

'Surely to have him kill himself was worse,' Karina said. 'For you, in particular.'

Karen nodded. 'Yes, perhaps it was. But the police looked no further. They found no evidence of foul play.' She spoke the last two words with some irony. 'Not that they could have done.'

'What about the tyre marks on the drive?' I asked. 'I mean, the marks where Karina had stuck her car.'

Karen shrugged. 'They didn't look. Besides, there were several sets of tyre marks next morning when a detective constable arrived to run through things again. There was no reason for them to look further, Nick. They're busy ... other things, other priorities, other targets ... Besides, he had committed suicide. Karina has told us.'

I sensed relief flow out of Karina like a long-held breath.

'They suspected me, I think, for a while,' Karen went on, 'but I had complained about the lateness of the train and the man in the ticket office remembered me rather well.' Her tone was ironic again. 'I always said it paid to complain.' She shrugged. 'You know the rest. More or less.'

'More or less?'

She sighed. 'Later I had a visit from Special Branch. I knew then that I had done the right thing by Guy, if not quite by myself.'

'I'm sorry, I don't understand...'

'The Ulster connection. A publicized murder would have been useful. For factional propaganda. The elimination of a British undercover officer ... it could have been useful to one side or the other. A so-called victory in their God-damned war.'

'Couldn't suicide have been shown in a similar light? An attack of remorse on Guy's part.'

'Perhaps,' she admitted, 'but better by far than a spurious claim of success. You don't come away cleanly from the sort of thing Guy was mixed up in, Nick. That's why he was only happy at sea, in control, with only God and His elements to worry about. He could wander about the wilderness in comparative safety.'

'So you pursued the murderer as a personal vendetta?' I asked her, looking at Karina.

'Yes.' Karen looked at Karina too. 'Had you come to kill him?'

Karina's eyes dropped from our scrutiny as she shook her head. 'No, not really...'

'Not *really*?' Karen flared up, full of scorn. 'Not *really*? What were you going to do? Ask him to pay for the abortion?'

'Karen...' I began.

'Shut up, Nick!' She swung back to Karina. 'You came into my house and after you had

350

gone my lover of many years blew his brains out! Did you think that the matter ended in some sweetly compassionate understanding of your predicament?'

'I'm sorry, Karen, but I came to surprise him.'

'What in God's name is *that* supposed to mean?'

'I did not expect anything like...' Karina broke off. 'He had made me pregnant, yes, but that was not really what I came to see him about...'

'There's that damned weasel-word *really* again.'

'Shut up yourself!' Karina said, suddenly seizing the initiative and leaning forward in Karen's face, 'and you be quiet,' she snarled at me, 'and I'll tell you about your precious fucking Guy!'

She sat back with a thump. 'OK, the thought of killing him *had* crossed my mind, as you say. I'll admit it. But I had not thought seriously about doing such a thing. He deserved to die and it would have been good if I *had* killed him...'

'What the hell d'you mean?' Karen exclaimed.

'Because he had tried to kill me.'

The Seventeenth Part

We sat in silence. I was stunned, though I cannot answer for Karen.

'I came to England,' Karina said, seeing our astonishment, 'to surprise Guy because he thought I was dead. I wanted to show him I wasn't dead and that he had failed to kill me.'

'Why did he want to kill you?' Karen asked. 'He couldn't have known you were pregnant. Or did he?'

'He could have done, if I had told him. I wasn't sure in Norway, but I was already late. No, it had nothing to do with any baby.'

'What happened to the baby?'

'Oh, you needn't worry. There is no little Anglo-German Guy running round Hamburg.'

'You had an abortion?'

'Of course I had it aborted!'

'And this allegation against Guy,' I broke in, 'about him trying to kill you. That happened aboard here did it?'

Karina stared about her, as if seeing the inside of *Rolissa* for the first time since. She nodded. 'Yes. Right here. A stupid argument, over dinner.'

'Don't you think you had better tell us?' I prompted.

352

Karina sighed and nodded. 'We were making good progress down the North Sea. Guy was on watch and cooked the dinner. He called me. It was cloudy with a strong wind and there was nothing in sight. *Rolissa* was on self-steering and running like a fast horse. It was a good day, but a little cold; not like the Arctic, but ... well, Guy suggested we ate below. He got out a bottle of wine too. Perhaps that was the problem.

'I don't remember exactly how the argument started. We had been often talking about the difference between men and women and the way things had changed. He had lived longer than me, so he could represent the old ideas. I spoke for the new point of view. You both understand these arguments. You are not a chauvinist, Nick, even if she says you are. You are a nice man. You should be married. But Guy would not be moved. As we argued, we became more polarized, farther and farther apart. In the end it came down to one simple thing: that men were physically and mentally tougher than women. Perhaps that is not simple, but it seemed to be at the time. I argued that women were as tough as men *and* they bore children.

'I don't know why that remark changed him, but it did. I had heard it said many times before, in my student days. Perhaps Guy hadn't heard it.' She paused a moment. 'I should like to say he went mad, that he acted without rationality, but he didn't. In fact, at

353

first I didn't think anything had gone wrong. It was already dark and from time to time he got up and had a look round the horizon.

'When he went out on this occasion, I thought he had seen a ship, or seen something that needed adjusting, for he left the cockpit and I heard him on deck. I thought he had abandoned the argument and would come below, hand over the watch and go into his bed. I began to clear away, to put the plates into the sink. I didn't hear anything that Guy was doing on deck, and then he came below. He seemed quite normal: his voice was level, his eyes were not dilated. He was puffing a bit, but then I knew he had been doing something active on deck. I had begun to wash up when he spoke.

' "Karina," he said, "I want to make one thing clear to you." I asked what he meant by this and he said, "This is your chance to prove you can stand by what you say. I have had enough of your sort speaking out with no experience of anything and a brain full of theories. I have had enough of it. It is up to you. You are in defiance of all that I have learned in life, all I believe in, all that I stand for..."

'I hadn't got a clue what he was talking about. Like once before I had thought for a moment that he was in some religious frenzy – is that what you say? Yes, a frenzy; but then he motioned me out of the way and I saw he was carrying a five-litre water container. He began to fill it at the sink, then went back out

354

into the cockpit. I watched him and then, thinking he was just cross with me, I got on again with the washing-up.

'The next thing I knew, *Rolissa* was coming round into the wind. I thought he was going to turn back, to land me or something. Then I knew she was stopped, hove to. I looked into the cockpit, but Guy wasn't there; he was back on the coach roof. I had begun to dry up when he shouted down below:

' "Come on. Leave that. You're on watch. Get your bloody gear on and look sharp about it." I still thought he was just fed-up and angry. I put my heavy-weather gear on and went out into the cockpit. It was then that I saw what he had been doing. But I still didn't understand...'

'What had he done?' Karen asked, her concentration fixed on Karina. I too was riveted by an anticipation so strong that my heart beat painfully.

'He'd inflated the life raft. It was lashed alongside. "Get in," he commanded. I said no and he said, "Don't think that I'm going to lay a finger on you, but you are going to get into this even if we sit here all night."

'I told him he was frightening me. He said that was impossible since I was, apparently, his equal. I asked him what he was going to do and he said, "Give you the ride of your life." I thought he was going to tow me astern – a joke, a humiliation. I was frightened, but not terrified. I tried to make a joke, to appeal to our loving when he had been kind to me ...

355

At Kalvenholm on the Norwegian coast ...
"But you have already given me the ride of
my life," I said. I tried to flatter him, but it did
not work. It did not make him angry and I
wished it had. He was so cold...'

'You got into the life raft, didn't you?'

Karina nodded at Karen. 'Yes ... He let the
lashings go. "There is a knife to cut the
painter just inside," he said. My hand was
already on it. I knew it was there. They are
special knives, sharp-bladed but with no
point, so that you cannot puncture the
buoyancy as you cut yourself free of the yacht
if it is sinking. But I was too late. I was
already trailing astern. He was beyond my
reach. Anyway I could not have cut him, not
after ... not with his baby ... I was confused...'

Karen bit her lip. Then she pulled herself
together.

'He let the backed jib fly, sheeted it in on
the lee side and *Rolissa* picked up her speed.
A second or two later I could just see the glow
of the lights in the doghouse, and the
reflections of the stern light on the black sea.
Still I was not really terrified. But I was angry.
I had got into the life raft myself, as he knew
I would. He was challenging me, making me
eat my words, or prove that I was tough, as
tough as him.

'As the rope paid out it came straight and
jerked me. I fell back into the raft and in a
few moments was sick, horribly sick. The
movement was terrible ... It went on and on.
After a bit I tried shouting at him. Then I

realized that even shouting betrayed my weakness. I was supposed to endure, be stoical, like one of his soldiers under training. It went on for hours...'

Karina fell silent as we came to terms with this appalling scene. Then something of the truth began to dawn on me.

'Did you cut the painter, or did he?' I asked. I was remembering a short length of braided line, cut off short on *Rolissa*'s deck, which I had casually dropped on the concrete of Halls' boatyard. I remembered too the 'ditched' life raft that Karen had had to replace. During almost every cruise something broke, or got lost; it had not seemed significant at the time. We had had other things to think of. I waited expectantly for Karina to answer my question.

Karina remained silent for a long time. Then, in a small voice, she said, 'I did.'

For a moment or two I could not understand why she had done it. I knew Guy would not have left her to drown, that this was his hard, uncompromising way to make his point. I do not think he believed in the innate superiority of men, merely that they had their own part to play in creation and that if women elbowed them out of it, they would find something worse to get up to. No animal likes to be squeezed out of its habitat. The natural thing to do was to fight back. That meant taking on women as enemies, ousting them from those areas the beleaguered male valued as his own preserve. Rape was an

357

almost unknown crime when Guy, Karen and I were children. It seems no coincidence that it is no longer unusual. The same could be said of street crime. Drugs played their part, of course, but that did not mean they were the only cause. Much of the drug culture might be blamed upon the dispossession of the young male. Besides, in contemporary society, who is going to take any notice of such a notion? It is politically incorrect and therefore cannot even be exposed to honest debate. Freedom of speech is gone. I knew Guy and I agreed on that!

But none of this explained why it had been Karina who cut the painter. 'I don't understand...'

'I do,' said Karen.

I should have remembered her explanation of how she had reconciled herself to the notion of Guy's suicide, even when at the time she thought he had been murdered. I looked at her anew. All the time that I had been making my own plodding sense of Guy's last voyage and indulging myself in pseudo-psychoanalysis of Guy's mental condition, she had been in possession of hard facts. From the moment she had decided to coerce me into a voyage north I had been an admittedly willing victim, though a victim nonetheless, of her deceit. I felt again that strange shrivelling, even as she elucidated.

'He would never have cut you adrift himself, so you decided to place him eternally in the wrong. He had goaded you, told you where the knife was, dared you, and you, in your own pride, took the game one step too far.'

'You may be right. I cannot describe to you what it was like, towing at seven knots...'

'But it was you who did it, Karina, and yet you accused Guy of trying to kill you. Do you really think that was true?' I asked.

'No, she doesn't,' Karen answered for her. 'That is why she had to come back and see him. As far as she was concerned, the matter was unfinished.'

'But Guy thought it was,' I said to Karen; 'hence that message, in the spine of the log book: *I am all there is and it is ... finished.*' And what of that deleted word, I thought to myself, the word *completed*? Could Guy simply have sailed away, unaffected by the outcome? I thought it quite possible, given the circumstances. Even the influence of the cut hand could be adduced to explain his mental state. But why change the words? Was he that fastidious about self-expression?

I considered the matter a moment.

He was, after all, a professional writer. He had a literary bent and he had a calculating mind. Had Guy himself cut the line, he would have *completed* the affair. He would have used that particular verb in a subjective sense. In the event it did not fit, because Karina had cut the painter. Guy had only indirectly set up the final outcome. The matter was *finished*, but by her.

I thought of explaining this to Karen, but

359

there were other counters falling into place and I wanted time to think. But Karen was then asking Karina a question the answer to which was fundamental.

'You cut yourself adrift and ⁻ yet you survived. How?'

'There were flares, of course, and smoke floats in the life raft. I saw the lights of some fishing boats. They were Danish boats; they took me to Thyborøn. I told them my yacht had sunk, that I was a lone sailor.'

'You did not want Guy to pay some price for what he had done?' Karen asked.

Karina shrugged. 'I thought he would suffer some remorse, perhaps. But I would come back, like a ghost. I did not want others involved.'

'You were at war,' I said in a low voice.

There was a silence. Then Karen reached across the table and touched Karina's hand. 'I'm sorry, my dear.'

Karina pronated her wrist and took Karen's hand. 'I do not think I loved him like you did,' she said.

For them, I think, the matter ended there. For myself that was not the case. I do not know whether they realized all the implications, but it seemed unkind and tactless to say more myself. I was, after all, a peripheral observer of all this, involved for my practical skills, important, but not a principal player. Perhaps that is why I am telling you all this, because I see it as important not to leave

Guy's reputation in quite so tattered a state. Besides, I did not understand it all at the time. Certainty came later.

Why, you ask?

Because he was my friend. Because he was complex. Because neither Karen nor Karina had quite revealed – or perhaps discovered – the truth. Not as I saw it. I do not know if the image of Guy sailing away into the night, to wake to a dawn of self-doubt, anxiety and remorse satisfied Karen and Karina. If not, they gave no indication of it. Karina was, in her own way, a fine person. She had become involved with a complex man, had almost borne him a child and their relationship had ended tragically. Star-crossed lovers, as the Bard would have had them.

I cannot tell you how Karina resolved in her own mind the effect of her sudden appearance on Guy in those last minutes. It must have played on her mind, though, and will continue to do so, inhabiting the fringes of her thoughts for her lifetime. I have never seen her since. She sent me one Christmas card before we lost touch.

Karen is more robust. We talked of the events on our final passage home, after we had landed Karina, and said goodbye to Greta and Margit. (Our departure was cleared by the harbour master, and some weeks after our return I had to attend the German embassy in London, where I swore an affidavit about the loss of the *Adler*.) But the relentless watch-and-watch dulled it all, and it was a long passage from Tromsø to Harwich.

We see each other from time to time. When I am ashore here. We lunch in London, where she lives now. She set up on her own and is now in partnership with a chap called Peter Marshall. They run a radio and television production company. We never became lovers, though she is, I think, the only woman I ever really counted as a true friend. She has been sleeping with Marshall for some time and will end up living with him.

The following year I made another voyage to Norway. I sailed *Rolissa* alone and I found that *perfect anchorage*, a circle of rocks in which one can anchor and regard the distant mountains. Even when one is alone it is a beautiful place.

I suppose an observer might call me a sad loser, and perhaps they would be right. The world is full of sad losers, few of whom, seeing me aboard *Rolissa*, would consider me among their number. If I have become anything, it is a kind of latter-day Flying Dutchman, condemned to sail about the oceans of the world, if not for eternity, at least until I fall overboard and drown. Old age or infirmity will ensure this.

Often I sit aboard *Rolissa* and think of Guy. I drank a toast to him in the perfect anchorage at Kalvenholm and tried to persuade his ghost to stay there, but I failed. Sometimes still, I hear him laugh and once, off the Azores, when I was turned in, I distinctly heard him call me. I was on deck and stripped *Rolissa* of all sail just before the white squall struck.

Now and again I catch sight of him, a grey, shadowy figure, looking astern in the dawn's light, to see the life raft no longer in tow. He bends, to cut away the trailing painter. Odd he never got rid of the evidence entirely, I used to think, before concluding that he did not want to. The only reality is the present and I think that loop of rope reminded him that he had been north, as far north as a man in a small boat can go, and that what had happened to him up there and afterwards had been extraordinary.

I think too he knew that Karina, having cut the rope herself, would never bring any charges against him if she lived. If not, I do not think her fate really troubled Guy. He had seen death before, at close quarters. Did he run any risk of some busy-bodying official, finding her body and the life raft, catching up with him? I do not think so, because I think he had already resolved to blow his brains out. He had passed beyond all the trammels of the world.

The obvious, most comprehensible explanation was that Guy was destroyed by his own failure and that this was compounded by his treatment of Karina. Having come home he brooded upon this, whereupon her sudden appearance had tipped the balance of his already disturbed mind. This seemed to me to be Karen's view, expressed during our discussions on the passage south from Tromsø.

'Everything was changed by that quixotic act of assistance in the ice,' Karen had asserted. 'He was forced, ironically by his own standards, to assume a mask of indifference and he simply could not do it. His failure ate him up.'

'An ice mask?' I had asked quizzically, recalling Karina's borrowed phrase.

'If you like,' Karen had said.

I did not accept that view – not at the time and not now. It was too pat, too simplistic. Guy would not have allowed himself to be destroyed by an act of common humanity, of a tradition of the sea. Karen's use of the word quixotic was unfair, unkind and unjustified. Guy was tough, very tough. Moreover, he could be harsh and ruthless, but he was not a villain devoid of moral sense. Nor did I think his wound, nor his placing of Karina in the life raft, would have tipped the balance of his mind. He underwent enormous strain in Ulster – perhaps trauma is the right word – but he was mentally vigorous and now I put his last weeks of apparent depression – that diminution we had thought we had seen in him – down to a withdrawal from the world about him.

Disappointing though it must have been to him in one way, I do not think the fact that he failed to complete the voyage alone upset Guy at all. After all, he left home thinking he was impotent and he enjoyed the compensation of an affair with a beautiful young woman. Karen might dismiss this liaison in any way she wished, but I did not think Guy would have regarded himself as overly hard-done-by. I rather think he relished that final fight with Karina.

Certainly, he would have been furious at the presence of women in the Arctic, but it would have been a general anger, not specific. Their being German would have annoyed him in its way, but he would have seen the irony in the fact. The row with Karina, though, when the general *became* specific, when he was actually confronted with an argument and was forced to react – that was different. Guy was a fighter, in all senses. And he was *trained* to fight; it was in his blood and his bones. It was what made him such a good seaman as, I presume, it had made him a brilliant soldier. He fought with the genius of the clever tactician, constantly outwitting his enemy. I think he considered Karina a worthy foe too. He objected mostly to Karina's self-righteousness. It was not a personal attribute, of course; she had imbibed it with her argument and projected it with the same argument. It was common to all who held views similar to her own. But that was why Guy had decided, in cold blood, to teach her a lesson and isolate her astern in the life raft.

When Karina had cut herself adrift, Guy must have realized that fate had allowed him to return home alone. He could have fooled us all – indeed he almost did – by saying nothing about Karina. But I do not think he could be that dishonourable. He deliberately let it slip his mind. Besides, he was thinking of something more significant. The loss of Karina set him adrift spiritually too; he turned his solitariness into complete solitude. He was still inhabiting the Arctic wilderness, even when he was back at the hall, wearing the mask of Karina's metaphor that he had brought back from *up there*.

He had, I think, also seen in himself the immense capacity for damage he represented both as a man and as a human being. I suspect he had come to this conclusion a long time ago. But he also thought that humanity had lost its sense of sexual balance, of sexual proportion, and that it had become a victim of self-delusion. He wanted none of that.

He would have shot himself in due course. Of that I am certain. Perhaps he was contemplating it that very evening, with Karen late home and the gun on the desk in front of him. Perhaps he often sat with the gun ready; I do not know. Perhaps had he known he had almost had a child, things might have been quite different. Fate, however, had decided otherwise – fate and science, of course. But then a catalysing event took place: Karina suddenly reappeared in his study. To Guy this represented an affront, an augmentation of her overweening righteousness. With that instant quick-wittedness he possessed, he saw how he could turn the tables on her – pull the rug from under her feet. And he saw too that

366

he could give specific meaning to his long-meditated resolution to his life. Just as she had sought to lay blame and a moral burden upon him with that slash of the knife, he could saddle her with a far heavier load.

The slug shattered more than the mask of ice he had acquired in the Arctic. Suicide is held to be a mortal sin, but I cannot see this to be the case. I think Guy thought it to be a unique right few of us have the courage to exercise. In Guy's case it was an act of defiance. But that is not all; he *took* his life as a gesture towards Karina and all she represented in his eyes. But he *gave* it in a cause in which he believed.

Guy's tragedy was that only he and I understood it to be so.